ALEXANDER McCALL SMITH

THE NO. 1 LADIES' DETECTIVE AGENCY

Alexander McCall Smith is a professor of medical law at Edinburgh University. He was born in what is now known as Zimbabwe and taught law at the University of Botswana. He is the author of over fifty books on a wide range of subjects, including specialist titles such as *Forensic Aspects of Sleep* and *The Criminal Law of Botswana*, children's books such as *The Perfect Hamburger*, and a collection of stories called *Portuguese Irregular Verbs*.

THE NO. 1 LADIES' DETECTIVE AGENCY

BY ALEXANDER McCALL SMITH

The No. 1 Ladies' Detective Agency

Tears of the Giraffe

Morality for Beautiful Girls

THE NO. 1 LADIES' DETECTIVE AGENCY

Alexander McCall Smith

Anchor Books

A Division of Random House, Inc.

New York

This book is for
Anne Gordon-Gillies
in Scotland

and for
Joe and Mimi McKnight
in Dallas, Texas

First Anchor Books Edition, August 2002

Copyright © 1998 by Alexander McCall Smith

Library of Congress Cataloging-in-Publication Data
McCall Smith, R. A.
The No. 1 Ladies' Detective Agency / Alexander McCall Smith.
p.   cm.
ISBN 1-4000-3134-6 (pbk.)
1. Women private investigators—Botswana—Fiction.   2. Botswana—Fiction.
I. Title: Number One Ladies' Detective Agency. II. Title.
PR6063.C326 N6 2002
821'.914—dc21
2002018694

www.anchorbooks.com

Printed in the United States of America
10   9   8   7   6

THE NO. 1

LADIES'

DETECTIVE AGENCY

CHAPTER ONE

THE DADDY

MMA RAMOTSWE had a detective agency in Africa, at the foot of Kgale Hill. These were its assets: a tiny white van, two desks, two chairs, a telephone, and an old typewriter. Then there was a teapot, in which Mma Ramotswe—the only lady private detective in Botswana—brewed redbush tea. And three mugs—one for herself, one for her secretary, and one for the client. What else does a detective agency really need? Detective agencies rely on human intuition and intelligence, both of which Mma Ramotswe had in abundance. No inventory would ever include those, of course.

But there was also the view, which again could appear on no inventory. How could any such list describe what one saw when one looked out from Mma Ramotswe's door? To the front, an acacia tree, the thorn tree which dots the wide edges of the Kalahari; the great white thorns, a warning; the olive-grey leaves, by contrast, so delicate. In its branches, in the late afternoon, or in the cool of the early morning, one might see a Go-Away Bird, or hear it, rather. And beyond the acacia, over the dusty road, the roofs of the town under a cover of trees and scrub bush; on the horizon, in a blue shimmer of heat, the hills, like improbable, overgrown termite mounds.

Everybody called her Mma Ramotswe, although if people had wanted to be formal, they would have addressed her as Mme Mma Ramotswe. This is the right thing for a person of stature, but which she had never used of herself. So it was always Mma Ramotswe, rather than Precious Ramotswe, a name which very few people employed.

She was a good detective, and a good woman. A good woman in a good country, one might say. She loved her country, Botswana, which is a place of peace, and she loved Africa, for all its trials. I am not ashamed to be called an African patriot, said Mma Ramotswe. I love all the people whom God made, but I especially know how to love the people who live in this place. They are my people, my brothers and sisters. It is my duty to help them to solve the mysteries in their lives. That is what I am called to do.

In idle moments, when there were no pressing matters to be dealt with, and when everybody seemed to be sleepy from the heat, she would sit under her acacia tree. It was a dusty place to sit, and the chickens would occasionally come and peck about her feet, but it was a place which seemed to encourage thought. It was here that Mma Ramotswe would contemplate some of the issues which, in everyday life, may so easily be pushed to one side.

Everything, thought Mma Ramotswe, has been something before. Here I am, the only lady private detective in the whole of Botswana, sitting in front of my detective agency. But only a few years ago there was no detective agency, and before that, before there were even any buildings here, there were just the acacia trees, and the riverbed in the distance, and the Kalahari over there, so close.

In those days there was no Botswana even, just the Bechuanaland Protectorate, and before that again there was Khama's Country, and lions with the dry wind in their manes. But look at it now: a detective agency, right here in Gaborone, with me, the fat lady detective, sitting outside and thinking these thoughts about how what is one thing today becomes quite another thing tomorrow.

Mma Ramotswe set up the No. 1 Ladies' Detective Agency with the proceeds of the sale of her father's cattle. He had owned a big herd, and had no other children; so every single beast, all one hundred and eighty of them, including the white Brahmin bulls whose grandparents he had bred himself, went to her. The cattle were moved from the cattle post, back to Mochudi where they waited, in the dust, under the eyes of the chattering herd boys, until the livestock agent came.

They fetched a good price, as there had been heavy rains that year, and the grass had been lush. Had it been the year before, when most of that southern part of Africa had been wracked by drought, it would have been a different matter. People had dithered then, wanting to hold on to their cattle, as without your cattle you were naked; others, feeling more desperate, sold, because the rains had failed year after year and they had seen the animals become thinner and thinner. Mma Ramotswe was pleased that her father's illness had prevented his making any decision, as now the price had gone up and those who had held on were well rewarded.

"I want you to have your own business," he said to her on his death bed. "You'll get a good price for the cattle now. Sell them and buy a business. A butchery maybe. A bottle store. Whatever you like."

She held her father's hand and looked into the eyes of the man she loved beyond all others, her Daddy, her wise Daddy, whose lungs had been filled with dust in those mines and who had scrimped and saved to make life good for her.

It was difficult to talk through her tears, but she managed to say: "I'm going to set up a detective agency. Down in Gaborone. It will be the best one in Botswana. The No. 1 Agency."

For a moment her father's eyes opened wide and it seemed as if he was struggling to speak.

"But . . . but . . ."

But he died before he could say anything more, and Mma Ramotswe fell on his chest and wept for all the dignity, love and suffering that died with him.

SHE HAD a sign painted in bright colours, which was then set up just off the Lobatse Road, on the edge of town, pointing to the small building she had purchased: THE NO. 1 LADIES' DETECTIVE AGENCY. FOR ALL CONFIDENTIAL MATTERS AND ENQUIRIES. SATISFACTION GUARANTEED FOR ALL PARTIES. UNDER PERSONAL MANAGEMENT.

There was considerable public interest in the setting up of her agency. There was an interview on Radio Botswana, in which she thought she was rather rudely pressed to reveal her qualifications, and a rather more satisfactory article in *The Botswana News,* which drew attention to the fact that she was the only lady private detective in the country. This article was cut out, copied, and placed prominently on a small board beside the front door of the agency.

After a slow start, she was rather surprised to find that her services were in considerable demand. She was consulted about missing husbands, about the creditworthiness of potential business partners, and about suspected fraud by employees. In almost every case, she was able to come up with at least some information for the client; when she could not, she waived her fee, which meant that virtually nobody who consulted her was dissatisfied. People in Botswana liked to talk, she discovered, and the mere mention of the fact that she was a private detective would let loose a positive outpouring of information on all sorts of subjects. It flattered people, she concluded, to be approached by a private detective, and this effectively loosened their tongues. This happened with Happy Bapetsi, one of her earlier clients. Poor Happy! To have lost your daddy and then found him, and then lost him again . . .

"I USED to have a happy life," said Happy Bapetsi. "A very happy life. Then this thing happened, and I can't say that anymore."

Mma Ramotswe watched her client as she sipped her bush tea. Everything you wanted to know about a person was written in the face, she believed. It's not that she believed that the shape of the head was what counted—even if there were many who still clung to that belief; it was more a question of taking care to scrutinise the lines and the general look. And the eyes, of course; they were very important. The eyes allowed you to see right into a person, to penetrate their very essence, and that was why people with something to hide wore sunglasses indoors. They were the ones you had to watch very carefully.

Now this Happy Bapetsi was intelligent; that was immediately apparent. She also had few worries—this was shown by the fact that there were no lines on her face, other than smile lines of course. So it was man trouble, thought Mma Ramotswe. Some man has turned up and spoilt everything, destroying her happiness with his bad behaviour.

"Let me tell you a little about myself first," said Happy Bapetsi. "I come from Maun, you see, right up on the Okavango. My mother had a small shop and I lived with her in the house at the back. We had lots of chickens and we were very happy.

"My mother told me that my Daddy had left a long time ago, when I was still a little baby. He had gone off to work in Bulawayo and he had never come back. Somebody had written to us—another Motswana living there—to say that he thought that my Daddy was dead, but he wasn't sure. He said that he had gone to see somebody at Mpilo Hospital one day and as he was walking along a corridor he saw them wheeling somebody out on a stretcher and that the dead person on the stretcher looked remarkably like my Daddy. But he couldn't be certain.

"So we decided that he was probably dead, but my mother did not mind a great deal because she had never really liked him very much. And of course I couldn't even remember him, so it did not make much difference to me.

"I went to school in Maun at a place run by some Catholic missionaries. One of them discovered that I could do arithmetic rather well and he spent a lot of time helping me. He said that he had never met a girl who could count so well.

"I suppose it was very odd. I could see a group of figures and

I would just remember it. Then I would find that I had added the figures in my head, even without thinking about it. It just came very easily—I didn't have to work at it at all.

"I did very well in my exams and at the end of the day I went off to Gaborone and learned how to be a bookkeeper. Again it was very simple for me; I could look at a whole sheet of figures and understand it immediately. Then, the next day, I could remember every figure exactly and write them all down if I needed to.

"I got a job in the bank and I was given promotion after promotion. Now I am the No. 1 subaccountant and I don't think I can go any further because all the men are worried that I'll make them look stupid. But I don't mind. I get very good pay and I can finish all my work by three in the afternoon, sometimes earlier. I go shopping after that. I have a nice house with four rooms and I am very happy. To have all that by the time you are thirty-eight is good enough, I think."

Mma Ramotswe smiled. "That is all very interesting. You're right. You've done well."

"I'm very lucky," said Happy Bapetsi. "But then this thing happened. My Daddy arrived at the house."

Mma Ramotswe drew in her breath. She had not expected this; she had thought it would be a boyfriend problem. Fathers were a different matter altogether.

"He just knocked on the door," said Happy Bapetsi. "It was a Saturday afternoon and I was taking a rest on my bed when I heard his knocking. I got up, went to the door, and there was this man, about sixty or so, standing there with his hat in his hands. He told me that he was my Daddy, and that he had been living in Bulawayo for a long time but was now back in Botswana and had come to see me.

"You can understand how shocked I was. I had to sit down, or I think I would have fainted. In the meantime, he spoke. He told me my mother's name, which was correct, and he said that he was sorry that he hadn't been in touch before. Then he asked if he could stay in one of the spare rooms, as he had nowhere else to go.

"I said that of course he could. In a way I was very excited to see my Daddy and I thought that it would be good to be able to make up for all those lost years and to have him staying with me, particularly since my poor mother died. So I made a bed for him in one of the rooms and cooked him a large meal of steak and potatoes, which he ate very quickly. Then he asked for more.

"That was about three months ago. Since then, he has been living in that room and I have been doing all the work for him. I make his breakfast, cook him some lunch, which I leave in the kitchen, and then make his supper at night. I buy him one bottle of beer a day and have also bought him some new clothes and a pair of good shoes. All he does is sit in his chair outside the front door and tell me what to do for him next."

"Many men are like that," interrupted Mma Ramotswe.

Happy Bapetsi nodded. "This one is especially like that. He has not washed a single cooking pot since he arrived and I have been getting very tired running after him. He also spends a lot of my money on vitamin pills and biltong.

"I would not resent this, you know, except for one thing. I do not think that he is my real Daddy. I have no way of proving this, but I think that this man is an impostor and that he heard about our family from my real Daddy before he died and is now just pretending. I think he is a man who has been looking for a retirement home and who is very pleased because he has found a good one."

Mma Ramotswe found herself staring in frank wonderment at Happy Bapetsi. There was no doubt but that she was telling the truth; what astonished her was the effrontery, the sheer, naked effrontery of men. How dare this person come and impose on this helpful, happy person! What a piece of chicanery, of fraud! What a piece of outright theft in fact!

"Can you help me?" asked Happy Bapetsi. "Can you find out whether this man is really my Daddy? If he is, then I will be a dutiful daughter and put up with him. If he is not, then I should prefer for him to go somewhere else."

Mma Ramotswe did not hesitate. "I'll find out," she said. "It may take me a day or two, but I'll find out!"

Of course it was easier said than done. There were blood tests these days, but she doubted very much whether this person would agree to that. No, she would have to try something more subtle, something that would show beyond any argument whether he was the Daddy or not. She stopped in her line of thought. Yes! There was something biblical about this story. What, she thought, would Solomon have done?

MMA RAMOTSWE picked up the nurse's uniform from her friend Sister Gogwe. It was a bit tight, especially round the arms, as Sister Gogwe, although generously proportioned, was slightly more slender than Mma Ramotswe. But once she was in it, and had pinned the nurse's watch to her front, she was a perfect picture of a staff sister at the Princess Marina Hospital. It was a good disguise, she thought, and she made a mental note to use it at some time in the future.

As she drove to Happy Bapetsi's house in her tiny white van, she reflected on how the African tradition of support for relatives could cripple people. She knew of one man, a sergeant of police, who was supporting an uncle, two aunts, and a second cousin. If you believed in the old Setswana morality, you couldn't turn a relative away, and there was a lot to be said for that. But it did mean that charlatans and parasites had a very much easier time of it than they did elsewhere. They were the people who ruined the system, she thought. They're the ones who are giving the old ways a bad name.

As she neared the house, she increased her speed. This was an errand of mercy, after all, and if the Daddy were sitting in his chair outside the front door he would have to see her arrive in a cloud of dust. The Daddy was there, of course, enjoying the morning sun, and he sat up straight in his chair as he saw the tiny white van sweep up to the gate. Mma Ramotswe turned off the engine and ran out of the car up to the house.

"Dumela Rra," she greeted him rapidly. "Are you Happy Bapetsi's Daddy?"

The Daddy rose to his feet. "Yes," he said proudly. "I am the Daddy."

Mma Ramotswe panted, as if trying to get her breath back.

"I'm sorry to say that there has been an accident. Happy was run over and is very sick at the hospital. Even now they are performing a big operation on her."

The Daddy let out a wail. "Aiee! My daughter! My little baby Happy!"

A good actor, thought Mma Ramotswe, unless . . . No, she preferred to trust Happy Bapetsi's instinct. A girl should know her own Daddy even if she had not seen him since she was a baby.

"Yes," she went on. "It is very sad. She is very sick, very sick.

And they need lots of blood to make up for all the blood she's lost."

The Daddy frowned. "They must give her that blood. Lots of blood. I can pay."

"It's not the money," said Mma Ramotswe. "Blood is free. We don't have the right sort. We will have to get some from her family, and you are the only one she has. We must ask you for some blood."

The Daddy sat down heavily.

"I am an old man," he said.

Mma Ramotswe sensed that it would work. Yes, this man was an impostor.

"That is why we are asking you," she said. "Because she needs so much blood, they will have to take about half your blood. And that is very dangerous for you. In fact, you might die."

The Daddy's mouth fell open.

"Die?"

"Yes," said Mma Ramotswe. "But then you are her father and we know that you would do this thing for your daughter. Now could you come quickly, or it will be too late. Doctor Moghile is waiting."

The Daddy opened his mouth, and then closed it.

"Come on," said Mma Ramotswe, reaching down and taking his wrist. "I'll help you to the van."

The Daddy rose to his feet, and then tried to sit down again. Mma Ramotswe gave him a tug,

"No," he said. "I don't want to."

"You must," said Mma Ramotswe. "Now come on."

The Daddy shook his head. "No," he said faintly. "I won't. You see, I'm not really her Daddy. There has been a mistake."

Mma Ramotswe let go of his wrist. Then, her arms folded, she stood before him and addressed him directly.

"So you are not the Daddy! I see! I see! Then what are you doing sitting in that chair and eating her food? Have you heard of the Botswana Penal Code and what it says about people like you? Have you?"

The Daddy looked down at the ground and shook his head.

"Well," said Mma Ramotswe. "You go inside that house and get your things. You have five minutes. Then I am going to take you to the bus station and you are going to get on a bus. Where do you really live?"

"Lobatse," said the Daddy. "But I don't like it down there."

"Well," said Mma Ramotswe. "Maybe if you started doing something instead of just sitting in a chair you might like it a bit more. There are lots of melons to grow down there. How about that, for a start?"

The Daddy looked miserable.

"Inside!" she ordered. "Four minutes left now!"

WHEN HAPPY Bapetsi returned home she found the Daddy gone and his room cleared out. There was a note from Mma Ramotswe on the kitchen table, which she read, and as she did so, her smile returned.

THAT WAS not your Daddy after all. I found out the best way. I got him to tell me himself. Maybe you will find the real Daddy one day. Maybe not. But in the meantime, you can be happy again.

CHAPTER TWO

ALL THOSE YEARS AGO

WE DON'T forget, thought Mma Ramotswe. Our heads may be small, but they are as full of memories as the sky may sometimes be full of swarming bees, thousands and thousands of memories, of smells, of places, of little things that happened to us and which come back, unexpectedly, to remind us who we are. And who am I? I am Precious Ramotswe, citizen of Botswana, daughter of Obed Ramotswe who died because he had been a miner and could no longer breathe. His life was unrecorded; who is there to write down the lives of ordinary people?

I AM Obed Ramotswe, and I was born near Mahalapye in 1930. Mahalapye is halfway between Gaborone and Francistown, on that road that seems to go on and on forever. It was a dirt road in those days, of course, and the railway line was much more important. The track came down from Bulawayo, crossed into Botswana at Plumtree, and then headed south down the side of the country all the way to Mafikeng, on the other side.

As a boy I used to watch the trains as they drew up at the siding. They let out great clouds of steam, and we would dare one another to run as close as we could to it. The stokers would shout at us, and the station master would blow his whistle, but they never managed to get rid of us. We hid behind plants and boxes and dashed out to ask for coins from the closed windows of the trains. We saw the white people look out of their windows, like ghosts, and sometimes they would toss us one of their Rhodesian pennies—large copper coins with a hole in the middle—or, if we were lucky, a tiny silver coin we called a tickey, which could buy us a small tin of syrup.

Mahalapye was a straggling village of huts made of brown, sun-baked mud bricks and a few tin-roofed buildings. These belonged to the Government or the Railways, and they seemed to us to represent distant, unattainable luxury. There was a school run by an old Anglican priest and a white woman whose face had been half-destroyed by the sun. They both spoke Setswana, which was unusual, but they taught us in English, insisting, on the pain of a thrashing, that we left our own language outside in the playground.

On the other side of the road was the beginning of the plain that stretched out into the Kalahari. It was featureless land, cluttered with low thorn trees, on the branches of which there perched the hornbills and the fluttering molopes, with their long, trailing tail feathers. It was a world that seemed to have no end, and that, I think, is what made Africa in those days so different. There was no end to it. A man could walk, or ride, forever, and he would never get anywhere.

I am sixty now, and I do not think God wants me to live much longer. Perhaps there will be a few years more, but I doubt it; I saw Dr Moffat at the Dutch Reformed Hospital in Mochudi who listened to my chest. He could tell that I had been a miner, just by listening, and he shook his head and said that the mines have many different ways of hurting a man. As he spoke, I remembered a song which the Sotho miners used to sing. They sang: "The mines eat men. Even when you have left them, the mines may still be eating you." We all knew this was true. You could be killed by falling rock or you could be killed years later, when going underground was just a memory, or even a bad dream that visited you at night. The mines would come back for their payment, just as they were coming back for me now. So I was not surprised by what Dr Moffat said.

Some people cannot bear news like that. They think they must live forever, and they cry and wail when they realise that their time is coming. I do not feel that, and I did not weep at that news which the doctor gave me. The only thing that makes me sad is that I shall be leaving Africa when I die. I love Africa, which is my mother and my father. When I am dead, I shall miss the smell of Africa, because they say that where you go, wherever that may be, there is no smell and no taste.

I'm not saying that I'm a brave man—I'm not—but I really don't seem to mind this news I have been given. I can look back over my sixty years and think of everything that I have seen and of how I started with nothing and ended up with almost two hundred cattle. And I have a good daughter, a loyal daughter, who looks after me well and makes me tea while I sit here in the sun and look out to the hills in the distance. When you see these hills from a distance, they are blue; as all the distances in this country are. We are far from the sea here, with Angola and Namibia between us and the coast, and yet we have this great empty ocean of blue above us and around us. No sailor could be lonelier than a man standing in the middle of our land, with the miles and miles of blue about him.

I have never seen the sea, although a man I worked with in the mines once invited me to his place down in Zululand. He told me that it had green hills that reached down to the Indian Ocean and that he could look out of his doorway and see ships in the distance. He said that the women in his village brewed the best beer in the country and that a man could sit in the sun there for many years and never do anything except make children and drink maize beer. He said that if I went with him, he might be able to get me a wife and that they might overlook the fact that I was not a Zulu—if I was prepared to pay the father enough money for the girl.

But why should I want to go to Zululand? Why should I ever want anything but to live in Botswana, and to marry a Tswana girl? I said to him that Zululand sounded fine, but that every man has a map in his heart of his own country and that the heart will never allow you to forget this map. I told him that in Botswana we did not have the green hills that he had in his place, nor the sea, but we had the Kalahari and land that stretched farther than one could imagine. I told him that if a man is born in a dry place, then although he may dream of rain, he does not want too much, and that he will not mind the sun that beats down and down. So I never went with him to Zululand and I never saw the sea, ever. But that has not made me unhappy, not once.

So I sit here now, quite near the end, and think of everything that has happened to me. Not a day passes, though, that my mind does not go to God and to thoughts of what it will be like to die. I am not frightened of this, because I do not mind pain, and the pain that I feel is really quite bearable. They gave me pills—large white ones—and they told me to take these if the pain in my chest became too great. But these pills make me sleepy, and I prefer to be awake. So I think of God and wonder what he will say to me when I stand before him.

Some people think of God as a white man, which is an idea which the missionaries brought with them all those years ago and which seems to have stuck in people's mind. I do not think this is so, because there is no difference between white men and black men; we are all the same; we are just people. And God was here anyway, before the missionaries came. We called him by a different name, then, and he did not live over at the Jews' place; he lived here in Africa, in the rocks, in the sky, in places where we knew he liked to be. When you died, you went somewhere else, and God would have been there too, but you would not be able to get specially close to him. Why should he want that?

We have a story in Botswana about two children, a brother and sister, who are taken up to heaven by a whirlwind and find that heaven is full of beautiful white cattle. That is how I like to think of it, and I hope that it is true. I hope that when I die I find myself in a place where there are cattle like that, who have sweet breath, and who are all about me. If that is what awaits me, then I am happy to go tomorrow, or even now, right at this moment. I should like to say goodbye to Precious, though, and to hold my daughter's hand as I went. That would be a happy way to go.

*   *   *

I LOVE our country, and I am proud to be a Motswana. There's no other country in Africa that can hold its head up as we can. We have no political prisoners, and never have had any. We have democracy. We have been careful. The Bank of Botswana is full of money, from our diamonds. We owe nothing.

But things were bad in the past. Before we built our country we had to go off to South Africa to work. We went to the mines, just as people did from Lesotho and Mozambique and Malawi and all those countries. The mines sucked our men in and left the old men and the children at home. We dug for gold and diamonds and made those white men rich. They built their big houses, with their walls and their cars. And we dug down below them and brought out the rock on which they built it all.

I went to the mines when I was eighteen. We were the Bechuanaland Protectorate then, and the British ran our country, to protect us from the Boers (or that is what they said). There was a Commissioner down in Mafikeng, over the border into South Africa, and he would come up the road and speak to the chiefs. He would say: "You do this thing; you do that thing." And the chiefs all obeyed him because they knew that if they did not he would have them deposed. But some of them were clever, and while the British said "You do this," they would say "Yes, yes, sir, I will do that" and all the time, behind their backs, they did the other thing or they just pretended to do something. So for many years, nothing at all happened. It was a good system of government, because most people want nothing to happen. That is the problem with governments these days. They want to do things all the time; they are always very busy thinking of what things they can do next. That is not what people want. People want to be left alone to look after their cattle.

We had left Mahalapye by then, and gone to live in Mochudi, where my mother's people lived. I liked Mochudi, and would have been happy to stay there, but my father said I should go to the mines, as his lands were not good enough to support me and a wife. We did not have many cattle, and we grew just enough crops to keep us through the year. So when the recruiting truck came from over the border I went to them and they put me on a scale and listened to my chest and made me run up and down a ladder for ten minutes. Then a man said that I would be a good miner and they made me write my name on a piece of paper. They asked me the name of my chief and asked me whether I had ever been in any trouble with the police. That was all.

I went off on the truck the next day. I had one trunk, which my father had bought for me at the Indian Store. I only had one pair of shoes, but I had a spare shirt and some spare trousers. These were all the things I had, apart from some biltong which my mother had made for me. I loaded my trunk on top of the truck and then all the families who had come to say goodbye started to sing. The women cried and we waved goodbye. Young men always try not to cry or look sad, but I knew that within us all our hearts were cold.

It took twelve hours to reach Johannesburg, as the roads were rough in those days and if the truck went too fast it could break an axle. We travelled through the Western Transvaal, through the heat, cooped up in the truck like cattle. Every hour, the driver would stop and come round to the back and pass out canteens of water which they filled at each town we went through. You were allowed the canteen for a few seconds only, and in that time you had to take as much water as you could. Men who were on their second or third contract knew all about this, and they had bottles of water which they would share if you were desperate. We were all Batswana together, and a man would not see a fellow Motswana suffer.

The older men were about the younger ones. They told them that now that they had signed on for the mines, they were no longer boys. They told us that we would see things in Johannesburg which we could never have imagined existing, and that if we were weak, or stupid, or if we did not work hard enough, our life from now on would be nothing but suffering. They told us that we would see cruelty and wickedness, but that if we stuck with other Batswana and did what we were told by the older men, we would survive. I thought that perhaps they were exaggerating. I remembered the older boys telling us about the initiation school that we all had to go to and warning us of what lay ahead of us. They said all this to frighten us, and the reality was quite different. But these men spoke the absolute truth. What lay ahead of us was exactly what they had predicted, and even worse.

In Johannesburg they spent two weeks training us. We were all quite fit and strong, but nobody could be sent down the mines until he had been made even stronger. So they took us to a building which they had heated with steam and they made us jump up and down onto benches for four hours each day. This was too much for some men, who collapsed, and had to be hauled back to their feet, but somehow I survived it and passed on to the next part of our training. They told us how we would be taken down into the mines and about the work we would be expected to do. They talked to us about safety, and how the rock could fall and crush us if we were careless. They carried in a man with no legs and put him down on a table and made us listen to him as he told us what had happened to him.

They taught us Funagalo, which is the language used for giving orders underground. It is a strange language. The Zulus laugh when they hear it, because there are so many Zulu words in it but it is not Zulu. It is a language which is good for telling people what to do. There are many words for push, take, shove, carry, load, and no words for love, or happiness, or the sounds which birds make in the morning.

Then we went down to the shafts and were shown what to do. They put us in cages, beneath great wheels, and these cages shot down as fast as hawks falling upon their prey. They had trains down there—small trains—and they put us on these and took us to the end of long, dark tunnels, which were filled with green rock and dust. My job was to load rock after it had been blasted, and I did this for seven hours a day. I grew strong, but all the time there was dust, dust, dust.

Some of the mines were more dangerous than others, and we all knew which these were. In a safe mine you hardly ever see the stretchers underground. In a dangerous one, though, the stretchers are often out, and you see men being carried up in the cages, crying with pain, or, worse still, silent under the heavy red blankets. We all knew that the only way to survive was to get into a crew where the men had what everybody called rock sense. This was something which every good miner had. He had to be able to see what the rock was doing—what it was feeling—and to know when new supports were needed. If one or two men in a crew did not know this, then it did not matter how good the others were. The rock would come down and it fell on good miners and bad.

There was another thing which affected your chances of

survival, and this was the sort of white miner you had. The white miners were put in charge of the teams, but many of them had very little to do. If a team was good, then the boss boy knew exactly what to do and how to do it. The white miner would pretend to give the orders, but he knew that it would be the boss boy who really got the work done. But a stupid white miner—and there were plenty of those—would drive his team too hard. He would shout and hit the men if he thought they were not working quickly enough and this could be very dangerous. Yet when the rock came down, the white miner would never be there; he would be back down the tunnel with the other white miners, waiting for us to report that the work had been finished.

It was not unusual for a white miner to beat his men if he got into a temper. They were not meant to, but the shift bosses always turned a blind eye and let them get on with it. Yet we were never allowed to hit back, no matter how undeserved the blows. If you hit a white miner, you were finished. The mine police would be waiting for you at the top of the shaft and you could spend a year or two in prison.

They kept us apart, because that is how they worked, these white men. The Swazis were all in one gang, and the Zulus in another, and the Malawians in another. And so on. Everybody was with his people, and had to obey the boss boy. If you didn't, and the boss boy said that a man was making trouble, they would send him home or arrange for the police to beat him until he started to be reasonable again.

We were all afraid of the Zulus, although I had that friend who was a kind Zulu. The Zulus thought they were better than any of us and sometimes they called us women. If there was a fight, it was almost always the Zulus or the Basotho, but never the Batswana. We did not like fighting. Once a drunk Motswana wandered into a Zulu hostel by mistake on a Saturday night. They beat him with sjamboks and left him lying on the road to be run over. Fortunately a police van saw him and rescued him, or he would have been killed. All for wandering into the wrong hostel.

I worked for years in those mines, and I saved all my money. Other men spent it on town women, and drink, and on fancy clothes. I bought nothing, not even a gramophone. I sent the money home to the Standard Bank and then I bought cattle with it. Each year I bought a few cows, and gave them to my cousin to look after. They had calves, and slowly my herd got bigger.

I would have stayed in the mines, I suppose, had I not witnessed a terrible thing. It happened after I had been there for fifteen years. I had then been given a much better job, as an assistant to a blaster. They would not give us blasting tickets, as that was a job that the white men kept for themselves, but I was given the job of carrying explosives for a blaster and helping him with the fuses. This was a good job, and I liked the man I worked for.

He had left something in a tunnel once—his tin can in which he carried his sandwiches—and he had asked me to fetch it. So I went off down the tunnel where he had been working and looked for this can. The tunnel was lit by bulbs which were attached to the roof all the way along, so it was quite safe to walk along it. But you still had to be careful, because here and there were great galleries which had been blasted out of the rock. These could be two hundred feet deep, and they opened out from the sides of the tunnel to drop down to another working level, like underground quarries. Men fell into these galleries from time to time, and it was always their fault. They were not looking where they were walking, or were walking along an unlit tunnel when the batteries in their helmet lights were weak. Sometimes a man just walked over the edge for no reason at all, or because he was unhappy and did not want to live anymore. You could never tell; there are many sadnesses in the hearts of men who are far away from their countries.

I turned a corner in this tunnel and found myself in a round chamber. There was a gallery at the end of this, and there was a warning sign. Four men were standing at the edge of this, and they were holding another man by his arms and legs. As I came round the corner, they lifted him and threw him forwards, over the edge and into the dark. The man screamed, in Xhosa, and I heard what he said. He said something about a child, but I did not catch it all as I am not very good at Xhosa. Then he was gone.

I stood where I was. The men had not seen me yet, but one turned round and shouted out in Zulu. Then they began to run towards me. I turned round and ran back along the tunnel. I knew that if they caught me I would follow their victim into the gallery. It was not a race I could let myself lose.

Although I got away, I knew that those men had seen me and that I would be killed. I had seen their murder and could be a witness, and so I knew that I could not stay in the mines.

I spoke to the blaster. He was a good man and he listened to me carefully when I told him that I would have to go. There was no other white man I could have spoken to like that, but he understood.

Still, he tried to persuade me to go to the police.

"Tell them what you saw," he said in Afrikaans. "Tell them. They can catch these Zulus and hang them."

"I don't know who these men are. They'll catch me first. I am going home to my place."

He looked at me and nodded. Then he took my hand and shook it, which is the first time a white man had done that to me. So I called him my brother, which is the first time I had done that to a white man.

"You go back home to your wife," he said. "If a man leaves his wife too long, she starts to make trouble for him. Believe me. Go back and give her more children."

So I left the mines, secretly, like a thief, and came back to Botswana in 1960. I cannot tell you how full my heart was when I crossed the border back into Botswana and left South Africa behind me forever. In that place I had felt every day that I might die. Danger and sorrow hung over Johannesburg like a cloud, and I could never be happy there. In Botswana it was different. There were no policemen with dogs; there were no *totsis* with knives, waiting to rob you; you did not wake up every morning to a wailing siren calling you down into the hot earth. There were not the same great crowds of men, all from some distant place, all sickening for home, all wanting to be somewhere else. I had left a prison—a great, groaning prison, under the sunlight.

When I came home that time, and got off the bus at Mochudi, and saw the *kopje* and the chief's place and the goats, I just stood and cried. A man came up to me—a man I did not know—and he put his hand on my shoulder and asked me whether I was just back from the mines. I told him that I was, and he just nodded and left his hand there until I had stopped weeping.

Then he smiled and walked away. He had seen my wife coming for me, and he did not want to interfere with the homecoming of a husband.

I had taken this wife three years earlier, although we had seen very little of one another since the marriage. I came back from Johannesburg once a year, for one month, and this was all the life we had had together. After my last trip she had become pregnant, and my little girl had been born while I was still away. Now I was to see her, and my wife had brought her to meet me off the bus. She stood there, with the child in her arms, the child who was more valuable to me than all the gold taken out of those mines in Johannesburg. This was my firstborn, and my only child, my girl, my Precious Ramotswe.

Precious was like her mother, who was a good fat woman. She played in the yard outside the house and laughed when I picked her up. I had a cow that gave good milk, and I kept this nearby for Precious. We gave her plenty of syrup too, and eggs every day. My wife put Vaseline on her skin, and polished it, so that she shone. They said she was the most beautiful child in Bechuanaland and women would come from miles away to look at her and hold her.

Then my wife, the mother of Precious, died. We were living just outside Mochudi then, and she used to go from our place to visit an aunt of hers who lived over the railway line near the Francistown Road. She carried food there, as that aunt was too old to look after herself and she only had one son there, who was sick with sufuba and could not walk very far.

I don't know how it happened. Some people said that it was because there was a storm brewing up and there was lightning that she may have run without looking where she was going.

But she was on the railway line when the train from Bulawayo came down and hit her. The engine driver was very sorry, but he had not seen her at all, which was probably true.

My cousin came to look after Precious. She made her clothes, took her to school and cooked our meals. I was a sad man, and I thought: Now there is nothing left for you in this life but Precious and your cattle. In my sorrow, I went out to the cattle post to see how my cattle were, and to pay the herd boys. I had more cattle now, and I had even thought of buying a store. But I decided to wait, and to let Precious buy a store once I was dead. Besides, the dust from the mines had ruined my chest, and I could not walk fast or lift things.

One day I was on my way back from the cattle post and I had reached the main road that led from Francistown to Gaborone. It was a hot day, and I was sitting under a tree by the roadside, waiting for the bus that would go that way later on. I fell asleep from the heat, and was woken by the sound of a car drawing up.

It was a large car, an American car, I think, and there was a man sitting in the back. The driver came up to me and spoke to me in Setswana, although the number plate of the car was from South Africa. The driver said that there was a leak in the radiator and did I know where they might find some water. As it happened, there was a cattle-watering tank along the track to my cattle post, and so I went with the driver and we filled a can with water.

When we came back to put the water in the radiator, the man who had been sitting in the back had got out and was standing looking at me. He smiled, to show that he was grateful for my help, and I smiled back. Then I realised that I knew who this man was, and that it was the man who managed all those mines in Johannesburg—one of Mr Oppenheimer's men.

I went over to this man and told him who I was. I told him that I was Ramotswe, who had worked in his mines, and I was sorry that I had had to leave early, but that it had been because of circumstances beyond my control.

He laughed, and said that it was good of me to have worked in the mines for so many years. He said I could ride back in his car and that he would take me to Mochudi.

So I arrived back in Mochudi in that car and this important man came into my house. He saw Precious and told me that she was a very fine child. Then, after he had drunk some tea, he looked at his watch.

"I must go back now," he said. "I have to get back to Johannesburg."

I said that his wife would be angry if he was not back in time for the food she had cooked him. He said this would probably be so.

We walked outside. Mr Oppenheimer's man reached into his pocket and took out a wallet. I turned away while he opened it; I did not want money from him, but he insisted. He said I had been one of Mr Oppenheimer's people and Mr Oppenheimer liked to look after his people. He then gave me two hundred rands, and I said that I would use it to buy a bull, since I had just lost one.

He was pleased with this. I told him to go in peace and he said that I should stay in peace. So we left one another and I never saw my friend again, although he is always there, in my heart.

_____

CHAPTER THREE

LESSONS ABOUT BOYS AND GOATS

OBED RAMOTSWE installed his cousin in a room at the back of the small house he had built for himself at the edge of the village when he had returned from the mines. He had originally planned this as a storeroom, in which to keep his tin trunks and spare blankets and the supplies of paraffin he used for cooking, but there was room for these elsewhere. With the addition of a bed and a small cupboard, and with a coat of whitewash applied to the walls, the room was soon fit for occupation. From the point of view of the cousin, it was luxury almost beyond imagination; after the departure of her husband, six years previously, she had returned to live with her mother and her grandmother and had been required to sleep in a room which had only three walls, one of which did not quite reach the roof. They had treated her with quiet contempt, being old-fashioned people, who believed that a woman who was left by her husband would almost always have deserved her fate. They had to take her in, of course, but it was duty, rather than affection, which opened their door to her.

Her husband had left her because she was barren, a fate which was almost inevitable for the childless woman. She had spent what little money she had on consultations with traditional healers, one of whom had promised her that she would conceive within months of his attentions. He had administered a variety of herbs and powdered barks and, when these did not work, he had turned to charms. Several of the potions had made her ill, and one had almost killed her, which was not surprising, given its contents, but the barrenness remained and she knew that her husband was losing patience. Shortly after he left, he wrote to her from Lobatse and told her—proudly—that his new wife was pregnant. Then, a year and a half later, there came a short letter with a photograph of his child. No money was sent, and that was the last time she heard from him.

Now, holding Precious in her arms, standing in her own room with its four stout, whitewashed walls, her happiness was complete. She allowed Precious, now four, to sleep with her in her bed, lying awake at night for long hours to listen to the child's breathing. She stroked her skin, held the tiny hand between her fingers, and marvelled at the completeness of the child's body. When Precious slept during the afternoon, in the heat, she would sit beside her, knitting and sewing tiny jackets and socks in bright reds and blues, and brush flies away from the sleeping child.

Obed, too, was content. He gave his cousin money each week to buy food for the household and a little extra each month for herself. She husbanded resources well, and there was always money left over, which she spent on something for Precious. He never had occasion to reprove her, or to find fault in her upbringing of his daughter. Everything was perfect.

The cousin wanted Precious to be clever. She had had little education herself, but had struggled at reading, and persisted, and now she sensed the possibilities for change. There was a political party, now, which women could join, although some men grumbled about this and said it was asking for trouble. Women were beginning to speak amongst themselves about their lot. Nobody challenged men openly, of course, but when women spoke now amongst themselves, there were whispers, and looks exchanged. She thought of her own life; of the early marriage to a man she had barely met, and of the shame of her inability to bear children. She remembered the years of living in the room with three walls, and the tasks which had been imposed upon her, unpaid. One day, women would be able to sound their own voice, perhaps, and would point out what was wrong. But they would need to be able to read to do that.

She started by teaching Precious to count. They counted goats and cattle. They counted boys playing in the dust. They counted trees, giving each tree a name: crooked one; one with no leaves; one where mopani worms like to hide; one where no bird will go. Then she said: "If we chop down the tree which looks like an old man, then how many trees are there left?" She made Precious remember lists of things—the names of members of the family, the names of cattle her grandfather had owned, the names of the chiefs. Sometimes they sat outside the store nearby, the Small Upright General Dealer, and waited for a car or a truck to bump its way past on the pothole-pitted road. The cousin would call out the number on the registration plate and Precious would have to remember it the next day when she was asked, and perhaps even the day after that. They also played a variety of Kim's Game, in which the cousin would load a basket-work tray with familiar objects and a blanket would then be draped over it and one object removed.

"What has been taken from the tray?"

"An old marula pip, all gnarled and chewed up."

"And what else?"

"Nothing."

She was never wrong, this child who watched everybody and everything with her wide, solemn eyes. And slowly, without anybody ever having intended this, the qualities of curiosity and awareness were nurtured in the child's mind.

By the time Precious went to school at the age of six, she knew her alphabet, her numbers up to two hundred, and she could recite the entire first chapter of the Book of Genesis in the Setswana translation. She had also learnt a few words of English, and could declaim all four verses of an English poem about ships and the sea. The teacher was impressed and complimented the cousin on what she had done. This was virtually the first praise that she had ever received for any task she had performed; Obed had thanked her, and done so often, and generously, but it had not occurred to him to praise her, because in his view she was just doing her duty as a woman and there was nothing special about that.

"We are the ones who first ploughed the earth when Modise (God) made it," ran an old Setswana poem. "We were the ones who made the food. We are the ones who look after the men when they are little boys, when they are young men, and when they are old and about to die. We are always there. But we are just women, and nobody sees us."

Lessons About Boys

Mma Ramotswe thought: God put us on this earth. We were all Africans then, in the beginning, because man started in Kenya, as Dr Leakey and his Daddy have proved. So, if one thinks carefully about it, we are all brothers and sisters, and yet everywhere you look, what do you see? Fighting, fighting, fighting. Rich people killing poor people; poor people killing rich people. Everywhere, except Botswana. That's thanks to Sir Seretse Khama, who was a good man, who invented Botswana and made it a good place. She still cried for him sometimes, when she thought of him in his last illness and all those clever doctors in London saying to the Government: "We're sorry but we cannot cure your President."

The problem, of course, was that people did not seem to understand the difference between right and wrong. They needed to be reminded about this, because if you left it to them to work out for themselves, they would never bother. They would just find out what was best for them, and then they would call that the right thing. That's how most people thought.

Precious Ramotswe had learned about good and evil at Sunday School. The cousin had taken her there when she was six, and she had gone there every Sunday without fail until she was eleven. That was enough time for her to learn all about right and wrong, although she had been puzzled—and remained so—when it came to certain other aspects of religion. She could not believe that the Lord had walked on water—you just couldn't do that—nor had she believed the story about the feeding of the five thousand, which was equally impossible. These were lies, she was sure of it, and the biggest lie of all was that the Lord had no Daddy on this earth. That was untrue because even children knew that you needed a father to make a child, and that rule applied to cattle and chickens and people, all the same. But right and wrong—that was another matter, and she had experienced no difficulty in understanding that it was wrong to lie, and steal, and kill other people.

If people needed clear guidelines, there was nobody better to do this than Mma Mothibi, who had run the Sunday School at Mochudi for over twelve years. She was a short lady, almost entirely round, who spoke with an exceptionally deep voice. She taught the children hymns, in both Setswana and English, and because they learned their singing from her the children's choir all sang an octave below everybody else, as if they were frogs.

The children, dressed in their best clothes, sat in rows at the back of the church when the service had finished and were taught by Mma Mothibi. She read the Bible to them, and made them recite the Ten Commandments over and over again, and told them religious stories from a small blue book which she said came from London and was not available anywhere else in the country.

"These are the rules for being good," she intoned. "A boy must always rise early and say his prayers. Then he must clean his shoes and help his mother to prepare the family's breakfast, if they have breakfast. Some people have no breakfast because they are poor. Then he must go to school and do everything that his teacher tells him. In that way he will learn to be a clever Christian boy who will go to Heaven later on, when the Lord calls him home. For girls, the rules are the same, but they must also be careful about boys and must be ready to tell boys that they are Christians. Some boys will not understand this . . ."

Yes, thought Precious Ramotswe. Some boys do not understand this, and even there, in that Sunday School there was such a boy, that Josiah, who was a wicked boy, although he was only nine. He insisted on sitting next to Precious in Sunday School, even when she tried to avoid him. He was always looking at her and smiling encouragingly, although she was two years older than he was. He tried also to make sure that his leg touched hers, which angered her, and made her shift in her seat, away from him.

But worst of all, he would undo the buttons of his trousers and point to that thing that boys have, and expect her to look. She did not like this, as it was not something that should happen in a Sunday School. What was so special about that, anyway? All boys had that thing.

At last she told Mma Mothibi about it, and the teacher listened gravely.

"Boys, men," she said. "They're all the same. They think that this thing is something special and they're all so proud of it. They do not know how ridiculous it is."

She told Precious to tell her next time it happened. She just had to raise her hand a little, and Mma Mothibi would see her. That would be the signal.

It happened the next week. While Mma Mothibi was at the back of the class, looking at the Sunday School books which the children had laid out before them, Josiah undid a button and whispered to Precious that she should look down. She kept her eyes on her book and raised her left hand slightly. He could not see this, of course, but Mma Mothibi did. She crept up behind the boy and raised her Bible into the air. Then she brought it down on his head, with a resounding thud that made the children start.

Josiah buckled under the blow. Mma Mothibi now came round to his front and pointed at his open fly. Then she raised the Bible and struck him on the top of the head again, even harder than before.

That was the last time that Josiah bothered Precious Ramotswe, or any other girl for that matter. For her part, Precious learned an important lesson about how to deal with men, and this lesson stayed with her for many years, and was to prove very useful later on, as were all the lessons of Sunday School.

The Cousin's Departure

The cousin looked after Precious for the first eight years of her life. She might have stayed indefinitely—which would have suited Obed—as the cousin kept house for him and never complained or asked him for money. But he recognised, when the time came, that there might be issues of pride and that the cousin might wish to marry again, in spite of what had happened last time. So he readily gave his blessing when the cousin announced that she had been seeing a man, that he had proposed, and that she had accepted.

"I could take Precious with me," she said. "I feel that she is my daughter now. But then, there is you . . ."

"Yes," said Obed. "There is me. Would you take me too?"

The cousin laughed. "My new husband is a rich man, but I think that he wants to marry only one person."

Obed made arrangements for the wedding, as he was the cousin's nearest relative and it fell to him to do this. He did it readily, though, because of all she had done for him. He arranged for the slaughter of two cattle and for the brewing of enough beer for two hundred people. Then, with the cousin on his arm, he entered the church and saw the new husband and his people, and other distant cousins, and their friends, and people from the village, invited and uninvited, waiting and watching.

After the wedding ceremony, they went back to the house, where canvas tarpaulins had been hooked up between thorn trees and borrowed chairs set out. The old people sat down while the young moved about and talked to one another, and sniffed the air at the great quantities of meat that were sizzling on the open fires. Then they ate, and Obed made a speech of thanks to the cousin and the new husband, and the new husband replied that he was grateful to Obed for looking after this woman so well.

The new husband owned two buses, which made him wealthy. One of these, the Molepolole Special Express, had been pressed into service for the wedding, and was decked for the occasion with bright blue cloth. In the other, they drove off after the party, with the husband at the wheel and the new bride sitting in the seat immediately behind him. There were cries of excitement, and ululation from the women, and the bus drove off into happiness.

They set up home ten miles south of Gaborone, in an adobe-plastered house which the new husband's brother had built for him. It had a red roof and white walls, and a compound, in the traditional style, with a walled yard to the front.

At the back, there was a small shack for a servant to live in, and a lean-to latrine made out of galvanised tin. The cousin had a kitchen with a shining new set of pans and two cookers. She had a large new South African paraffin-powered fridge, which purred quietly all day, and kept everything icy cold within. Every evening, her husband came home with the day's takings from his buses, and she helped him to count the money. She proved to be an excellent bookkeeper, and was soon running that part of the business with conspicuous success.

She made her new husband happy in other ways. As a boy he had been bitten by a jackal, and had scars across his face where a junior doctor at the Scottish Missionary Hospital at Molepolole had ineptly sewn the wounds. No woman had told him that he was handsome before, and he had never dreamed that any would, being more used to the wince of sympathy. The cousin, though, said that he was the most good-looking man she had ever met, and the most virile too. This was not mere flattery—she was telling the truth, as she saw it, and his heart was filled with the warmth that flows from the well-directed compliment.

"I know you are missing me," the cousin wrote to Precious. "But I know that you want me to be happy. I am very happy now. I have a very kind husband who has bought me wonderful clothes and makes me very happy every day. One day, you will come and stay with us, and we can count the trees again and sing hymns together, as we always used to. Now you must look after your father, as you are old enough to do that, and he is a good man too. I want you to be happy, and that is what I pray for, every night. God look after Precious Ramotswe. God watch her tonight and forever. Amen."

Goats

As a girl, Precious Ramotswe liked to draw, an activity which the cousin had encouraged from an early age. She had been given a sketching pad and a set of coloured pencils for her tenth birthday, and her talent had soon become apparent. Obed Ramotswe was proud of her ability to fill the virgin pages of her sketchbook with scenes of everyday Mochudi life. Here was a sketch which showed the pond in front of the hospital—it was all quite recognisable—and here was a picture of the hospital matron looking at a donkey. And on this page was a picture of the shop, of the Small Upright General Dealer, with things in front of it which could be sacks of mealies or perhaps people sitting down—one could not tell—but they were excellent sketches and he had already pinned several up on the walls of the living room of their house, high up, near the ceiling, where the flies sat.

Her teachers knew of this ability, and told her that she might one day be a great artist, with her pictures on the cover of the Botswana Calendar. This encouraged her, and sketch followed sketch. Goats, cattle, hills, pumpkins, houses; there was so much for the artist's eye around Mochudi that there was no danger that she would run out of subjects.

The school got to hear of an art competition for children. The Museum in Gaborone had asked every school in the country to submit a picture by one of its pupils, on the theme "Life in Botswana of Today." Of course there was no doubt about whose work would be submitted. Precious was asked to draw a special picture—to take her time doing it—and then this would be sent down to Gaborone as the entry from Mochudi.

She drew her picture on a Saturday, going out early with her sketchbook and returning some hours later to fill in the details inside the house. It was a very good drawing, she thought, and her teacher was enthusiastic when she showed it to her the following Monday.

"This will win the prize for Mochudi," she said. "Everybody will be proud."

The drawing was placed carefully between two sheets of corrugated cardboard and sent off, registered post, to the Museum. Then there was a silence for five weeks, during which time everybody forgot about the competition. Only when the letter came to the Principal, and he, beaming, read it out to Precious, were they reminded.

"You have won first prize," he said. "You are to go to Gaborone, with your teacher and myself, and your father, to get the prize from the Minister of Education at a special ceremony."

It was too much for her, and she wept, but soon stopped, and was allowed to leave school early to run back to give the news to her Daddy.

They travelled down with the Principal in his truck, arriving far too early for the ceremony, and spent several hours sitting in the Museum yard, waiting for the doors to open. But at last they did, and others came, teachers, people from the newspapers, members of the Legislature. Then the Minister arrived in a black car and people put down their glasses of orange juice and swallowed the last of their sandwiches.

She saw her painting hanging in a special place, on a room divider, and there was a small card pinned underneath it. She went with her teacher to look at it, and she saw, with leaping heart, her name neatly typed out underneath the picture: PRE-

CIOUS RAMOTSWE (10) (MOCHUDI GOVERNMENT JUNIOR SCHOOL). And underneath that, also typed, the title which the Museum itself had provided: Cattle Beside Dam.

She stood rigid, suddenly appalled. This was not true. The picture was of goats, but they had thought it was cattle! She was getting a prize for a cattle picture, by false pretences.

"What is wrong?" asked her father. "You must be very pleased. Why are you looking so sad?"

She could not say anything. She was about to become a criminal, a perpetrator of fraud. She could not possibly take a prize for a cattle picture when she simply did not deserve that.

But now the Minister was standing beside her, and he was preparing to make a speech. She looked up at him, and he smiled warmly.

"You are a very good artist," he said. "Mochudi must be proud of you."

She looked at the toes of her shoes. She would have to confess.

"It is not a picture of cattle," she said. "It is a picture of goats. You cannot give me a prize for a mistake."

The Minister frowned, and looked at the label. Then he turned back to her and said: "They are the ones who have made a mistake. I also think those are goats. I do not think they are cattle."

He cleared his throat and the Director of the Museum asked for silence.

"This excellent picture of goats," said the Minister, "shows how talented are our young people in this country. This young lady will grow up to be a fine citizen and maybe a famous artist. She deserves her prize, and I am now giving it to her."

She took the wrapped parcel which he gave her, and felt his

hand upon her shoulder, and heard him whisper: "You are the most truthful child I have met. Well done."

Then the ceremony was over, and a little later they returned to Mochudi in the Principal's bumpy truck, a heroine returning, a bearer of prizes.

CHAPTER FOUR

LIVING WITH THE COUSIN AND
THE COUSIN'S HUSBAND

AT THE age of sixteen, Mma Ramotswe left school ("The best girl in this school," pronounced the Principal. "One of the best girls in Botswana.") Her father had wanted her to stay on, to do her Cambridge School Certificate, and to go even beyond that, but Mma Ramotswe was bored with Mochudi. She was bored, too, with working in the Upright Small General Dealer, where every Saturday she did the stocktaking and spent hours ticking off items on dog-eared stock lists. She wanted to go somewhere. She wanted her life to start.

"You can go to my cousin," her father said. "That is a very different place. I think that you will find lots of things happening in that house."

It cost him a great deal of pain to say this. He wanted her to stay, to look after him, but he knew that it would be selfish to expect her life to revolve around his. She wanted freedom; she wanted to feel that she was doing something with her life. And of course, at the back of his mind, was the thought of marriage. In a very short time, he knew, there would be men wanting to marry her.

He would never deny her that, of course. But what if the man who wanted to marry her was a bully, or a drunkard, or a womaniser? All of this was possible; there was any number of men like that, waiting for an attractive girl that they could latch on to and whose life they could slowly destroy. These men were like leeches; they sucked away at the goodness of a woman's heart until it was dry and all her love had been used up. That took a long time, he knew, because women seemed to have vast reservoirs of goodness in them.

If one of these men claimed Precious, then what could he, a father, do? He could warn her of the risk, but whoever listened to warnings about somebody they loved? He had seen it so often before; love was a form of blindness that closed the eyes to the most glaring faults. You could love a murderer, and simply not believe that your lover would do so much as crush a tick, let alone kill somebody. There would be no point trying to dissuade her.

The cousin's house would be as safe as anywhere, even if it could not protect her from men. At least the cousin could keep an eye on her niece, and her husband might be able to chase the most unsuitable men away. He was a rich man now, with more than five buses, and he would have that authority that rich men had. He might be able to send some of the young men packing.

THE COUSIN was pleased to have Precious in the house. She decorated a room for her, hanging new curtains of a thick yellow material which she had bought from the OK Bazaars on a shopping trip to Johannesburg. Then she filled a chest of drawers with clothes and put on top of it a framed picture of the Pope. The floor was covered with a simply patterned reed mat. It was a bright, comfortable room.

Precious settled quickly into a new routine. She was given a job in the office of the bus company, where she added invoices and checked the figures in the drivers' records. She was quick at this, and the cousin's husband noticed that she was doing as much work as the two older clerks put together. They sat at their tables and gossiped away the day, occasionally moving invoices about the desk, occasionally getting up to put on the kettle.

It was easy for Precious, with her memory, to remember how to do new things and to apply the knowledge faultlessly. She was also willing to make suggestions, and scarcely a week went past in which she failed to make some suggestion as to how the office could be more efficient.

"You're working too hard," one of the clerks said to her. "You're trying to take our jobs."

Precious looked at them blankly. She had always worked as hard as she could, at everything she did, and she simply did not understand how anybody could do otherwise. How could they sit there, as they did, and stare into the space in front of their desks when they could be adding up figures or checking the drivers' returns?

She did her own checking, often unasked, and although everything usually added up, now and then she found a small discrepancy. These came from the giving of incorrect change, the cousin explained. It was easy enough to do on a crowded bus, and as long as it was not too significant, they just ignored it. But Precious found more than this. She found a discrepancy of slightly over two thousand pula in the fuel bills invoices and she drew this to the attention of her cousin's husband.

"Are you sure?" he asked. "How could two thousand pula go missing?"

"Stolen?" said Precious.

The cousin's husband shook his head. He regarded himself as a model employer—a paternalist, yes, but that is what the men wanted, was it not? He could not believe that any of his employees would cheat him. How could they, when he was so good to them and did so much for them?

Precious showed him how the money had been taken, and they jointly pieced together how it had been moved out of the right account into another one, and had then eventually vanished altogether. Only one of the clerks had access to these funds, so it must have been him; there could be no other explanation. She did not see the confrontation, but heard it from the other room. The clerk was indignant, shouting his denial at the top of his voice. Then there was silence for a moment, and the slamming of a door.

This was her first case. This was the beginning of the career of Mma Ramotswe.

The Arrival of Note Mokoti

There were four years of working in the bus office. The cousin and her husband became accustomed to her presence and began to call her their daughter. She did not mind this; they were her people, and she loved them. She loved the cousin, even if she still treated her as a child and scolded her publicly. She loved the cousin's husband, with his sad, scarred face and his large, mechanic's hands. She loved the house, and her room with its yellow curtains. It was a good life that she had made for herself.

Every weekend she travelled up to Mochudi on one of the cousin's husband's buses and visited her father. He would be waiting outside the house, sitting on his stool, and she would curtsey before him, in the old way, and clap her hands.

Then they would eat together, sitting in the shade of the lean-to verandah which he had erected to the side of the house. She would tell him about the week's activity in the bus office and he would take in every detail, asking for names, which he would link into elaborate genealogies. Everybody was related in some way; there was nobody who could not be fitted into the far-flung corners of family.

It was the same with cattle. Cattle had their families, and after she had finished speaking, he would tell her the cattle news. Although he rarely went out to the cattle post, he had reports every week and he could run the lives of the cattle through the herd-boys. He had an eye for cattle, an uncanny ability to detect traits in calves that would blossom in maturity. He could tell, at a glance, whether a calf which seemed puny, and which was therefore cheap, could be brought on and fattened. And he backed this judgement, and bought such animals, and made them into fine, butterfat cattle (if the rains were good).

He said that people were like their cattle. Thin, wretched cattle had thin, wretched owners. Listless cattle—cattle which wandered aimlessly—had owners whose lives lacked focus. And dishonest people, he maintained, had dishonest cattle—cattle which would cheat other cattle of food or which would try to insinuate themselves into the herds of others.

Obed Ramotswe was a severe judge—of men and cattle—
and she found herself thinking: what will he say when he finds
out about Note Mokoti?

SHE HAD met Note Mokoti on a bus on the way back from
Mochudi. He was travelling down from Francistown and was
sitting in the front, his trumpet case on the seat beside him.
She could not help but notice him in his red shirt and seer-
sucker trousers; nor fail to see the high cheekbones and the
arched eyebrows. It was a proud face, the face of a man used
to being looked at and appreciated, and she dropped her eyes
immediately. She would not want him to think she was looking
at him, even if she continued to glance at him from her seat.
Who was this man? A musician, with that case beside him; a
clever person from the University perhaps?

The bus stopped in Gaborone before going south on the
road to Lobatse. She stayed in her seat, and saw him get up.
He stood up, straightened the crease of his trousers, and then
turned and looked down the bus. She felt her heart jump; he
had looked at her; no, he had not, he was looking out of the
window.

Suddenly, without thinking, she got to her feet and took her
bag down from the rack. She would get off, not because she
had anything to do in Gaborone, but because she wanted to
see what he did. He had left the bus now and she hurried,
muttering a quick explanation to the driver, one of her cousin's
husband's men. Out in the crowd, out in the late afternoon
sunlight, redolent of dust and hot travellers, she looked about
her and saw him, standing not far away. He had bought a roast
mealie from a hawker, and was eating it now, making lines

down the cob. She felt that unsettling sensation again and she stopped where she stood, as if she were a stranger who was uncertain where to go.

He was looking at her, and she turned away flustered. Had he seen her watching him? Perhaps. She looked up again, quickly glancing in his direction, and he smiled at her this time and raised his eyebrows. Then, tossing the mealie cob away, he picked up the trumpet case and walked over towards her. She was frozen, unable to walk away, mesmerised like prey before a snake.

"I saw you on that bus," he said. "I thought I had seen you before. But I haven't."

She looked down at the ground.

"I have never seen you," she said. "Ever."

He smiled. He was not frightening, she thought, and some of her awkwardness left her.

"You see most people in this country once or twice," he said. "There are no strangers."

She nodded. "That is true."

There was a silence. Then he pointed to the case at his feet.

"This is a trumpet, you know. I am a musician."

She looked at the case. It had a sticker on it; a picture of a man playing a guitar.

"Do you like music?" he asked. "Jazz? Quella?"

She looked up, and saw that he was still smiling at her.

"Yes. I like music."

"I play in a band," he said. "We play in the bar at the President Hotel. You could come and listen. I am going there now."

They walked to the bar, which was only ten minutes or so from the bus stop. He bought her a drink and sat her at a table at the back, a table with one seat at it to discourage others.

Then he played, and she listened, overcome by the sliding, slippery music, and proud that she knew this man, that she was his guest. The drink was strange and bitter; she did not like the taste of alcohol, but drinking was what you did in bars and she was concerned that she would seem out of place or too young and people would notice her.

Afterwards, when the band had its break, he came to join her, and she saw that his brow was glistening with the effort of playing.

"I'm not playing well today," he said. "There are some days when you can and some days when you can't."

"I thought you were very good. You played well."

"I don't think so. I can play better. There are days when the trumpet just talks to me. I don't have to do anything then."

She saw that people were looking at them, and that one or two women were staring at her critically. They wanted to be where she was, she could tell. They wanted to be with Note.

He put her on the late bus after they had left the bar, and stood and waved to her as the bus drew away. She waved back and closed her eyes. She had a boyfriend now, a jazz musician, and she would be seeing him again, at his request, the following Friday night, when they were playing at a braaivleis at the Gaborone Club. Members of the band, he said, always took their girlfriends, and she would meet some interesting people there, good-quality people, people she would not normally meet.

And that is where Note Mokoti proposed to Precious Ramotswe and where she accepted him, in a curious sort of way, without saying anything. It was after the band had finished and they were sitting in the darkness, away from the noise of the drinkers in the bar. He said: "I want to get married soon and I want to get married to you. You are a nice girl who will do very well for a wife."

Precious said nothing, because she was uncertain, and her silence was taken as assent.

"I will speak to your father about this," said Note. "I hope that he is not an old-fashioned man who will want a lot of cattle for you."

He was, but she did not say so. She had not agreed yet, she thought, but perhaps it was now too late.

Then Note said: "Now that you are going to be my wife, I must teach you what wives are for."

She said nothing. This is what happened, she supposed. This is how men were, just as her friends at school had told her, those who were easy, of course.

He put his arm around her and moved her back against the soft grass. They were in the shadows, and there was nobody nearby, just the noise of the drinkers shouting and laughing. He took her hand and placed it upon his stomach, where he left it, not knowing what to do. Then he started to kiss her, on her neck, her cheek, her lips, and all she heard was the thudding of her heart and her shortened breath.

He said: "Girls must learn this thing. Has anybody taught you?"

She shook her head. She had not learned and now, she felt, it was too late. She would not know what to do.

"I am glad," he said. "I knew straightaway that you were a virgin, which is a very good thing for a man. But now things will change. Right now. Tonight."

He hurt her. She asked him to stop, but he put her head back and hit her once across the cheek. But he immediately kissed her where the blow had struck, and said that he had not meant to do it. All the time he was pushing against her, and scratching at her, sometimes across her back, with his finger-nails. Then he moved her over, and he hurt her again, and struck her across her back with his belt.

She sat up, and gathered her crumpled clothes together. She was concerned, even if he was not, that somebody might come out into the night and see them.

She dressed, and as she put on her blouse, she started to weep, quietly, because she was thinking of her father, whom she would see tomorrow on his verandah, who would tell her the cattle news, and who would never imagine what had happened to her that night.

Note Mokoti visited her father three weeks later, by himself, and asked him for Precious. Obed said he would speak to his daughter, which he did when she came to see him next. He sat on his stool and looked up at her and said to her that she would never have to marry anybody she did not want to marry. Those days were over, long ago. Nor should she feel that she had to marry at all; a woman could be by herself these days—there were more and more women like that.

She could have said no at this point, which is what her father wanted her to say. But she did not want to say that. She lived for her meetings with Note Mokoti. She wanted to marry him. He was not a good man, she could tell that, but she might change him. And, when all was said and done, there remained those dark moments of contact, those pleasures he snatched from her, which were addictive. She liked that. She felt ashamed even to think of it, but she liked what he did to her, the humiliation, the urgency. She wanted to be with him, wanted him to possess her. It was like a bitter drink which bids you back. And of course she sensed that she was pregnant. It was too early to tell, but she felt that Note Mokoti's child was within her, a tiny, fluttering bird, deep within her.

THEY MARRIED on a Saturday afternoon, at three o'clock, in the church at Mochudi, with the cattle outside under the trees, for it was late October and the heat was at its worst. The country-side was dry that year, as the previous season's rains had not been good. Everything was parched and wilting; there was lit-tle grass left, and the cattle were skin and bones. It was a list-less time.

The Reformed Church Minister married them, gasping in his clerical black, mopping at his brow with a large red hand-kerchief.

He said: "You are being married here in God's sight. God places upon you certain duties. God looks after us and keeps us in this cruel world. God loves His children, but we must remember those duties He asks of us. Do you young people understand what I am saying?"

Note smiled. "I understand."

And, turning to Precious: "And do you understand?"

She looked up into the Minister's face—the face of her father's friend. She knew that her father had spoken to him about this marriage and about how unhappy he was about it, but the Minister had said that he was unable to intervene. Now his tone was gentle, and he pressed her hand lightly as he took it to place in Note's. As he did so, the child moved within her, and she winced because the movement was so sudden and so firm.

*   *   *

AFTER TWO days in Mochudi, where they stayed in the house of
a cousin of Note's, they packed their possessions into the back
of a truck and went down to Gaborone. Note had found somewhere to stay—two rooms and a kitchen in somebody's house
near Tlokweng. It was a luxury to have two rooms; one was
their bedroom, furnished with a double mattress and an old
wardrobe; the other was a living room and dining room, with a
table, two chairs, and a sideboard. The yellow curtains from
her room at the cousin's house were hung up in this room, and
they made it bright and cheerful.

Note kept his trumpet there and his collection of tapes. He
would practise for twenty minutes at a time, and then, while
his lip was resting, he would listen to a tape and pick out the
rhythms on a guitar. He knew everything about township
music—where it came from, who sang what, who played
which part with whom. He had heard the greats, too; Hugh
Masekela on the trumpet, Dollar Brand on the piano, Spokes
Machobane singing; he had heard them in person in Johannesburg, and knew every recording they had ever made.

She watched him take the trumpet from its case and fit the
mouthpiece. She watched as he raised it to his lips and then,
so suddenly, from that tiny cup of metal against his flesh, the
sound would burst out like a glorious, brilliant knife dividing
the air. And the little room would reverberate and the flies,
jolted out of their torpor, would buzz round and round as if riding the swirling notes.

She went with him to the bars, and he was kind to her there,
but he seemed to get caught up in his own circle and she felt
that he did not really want her there. There were people there
who thought of nothing but music; they talked endlessly about
music, music, music; how much could one say about music?

They didn't want her there either, she thought, and so she stopped going to the bars and stayed at home.

He came home late and he smelled of beer when he returned. It was a sour smell, like rancid milk, and she turned her head away as he pushed her down on the bed and pulled at her clothing.

"You have had a lot of beer. You have had a good evening."

He looked at her, his eyes slightly out of focus.

"I can drink if I want to. You're one of these women who stays at home and complains? Is that what you are?"

"I am not. I only meant to say that you had a good evening."

But his indignation would not be assuaged, and he said: "You are making me punish you, woman. You are making me do this thing to you."

She cried out, and tried to struggle, to push him away, but he was too strong for her.

"Don't hurt the baby."

"Baby! Why do you talk about this baby? It is not mine. I am not the father of any baby."

MALE HANDS again, but this time in thin rubber gloves, which made the hands pale and unfinished, like a white man's hands.

"Do you feel any pain here? No? And here?"

She shook her head.

"I think that the baby is all right. And up here, where these marks are. Is there pain just on the outside, or is it deeper in?"

"It is just the outside."

"I see. I am going to have to put in stitches here. All the way across here, because the skin has parted so badly. I'll spray something on to take the pain away but maybe it's better for you not to watch me while I'm sewing! Some people say men can't sew, but we doctors aren't too bad at it!"

She closed her eyes and heard a hissing sound. There was cold spray against her skin and then a numbness as the doctor worked on the wound.

"This was your husband's doing? Am I right?"

She opened her eyes. The doctor had finished the suture and had handed something to the nurse. He was looking at her now as he peeled off the gloves.

"How many times has this happened before? Is there anybody to look after you?"

"I don't know. I don't know."

"I suppose you're going to go back to him?"

She opened her mouth to speak, but he interrupted her.

"Of course you are. It's always the same. The woman goes back for more."

He sighed. "I'll probably see you again, you know. But I hope I don't. Just be careful."

SHE WENT back the next day, a scarf tied around her face to hide the bruises and the cuts. She ached in her arms and in her stomach, and the sutured wound stung sharply. They had given her pills at the hospital, and she had taken one just before she left on the bus. This seemed to help the pain, and she took another on the journey.

The door was open. She went in, her heart thumping within her chest, and saw what had happened. The room was empty, apart from the furniture. He had taken his tapes, and their new metal trunk, and the yellow curtains too. And in the bedroom, he had slashed the mattress with a knife, and there was kapok lying about, making it look like a shearing room.

She sat down on the bed and was still sitting there, staring at the floor, when the neighbour came in and said that she would get somebody to take her in a truck back to Mochudi, to Obed, to her father.

There she stayed, looking after her father, for the next fourteen years. He died shortly after her thirty-fourth birthday, and that was the point at which Precious Ramotswe, now parentless, veteran of a nightmare marriage, and mother, for a brief and lovely five days, became the first lady private detective in Botswana.

CHAPTER FIVE

WHAT YOU NEED TO OPEN
A DETECTIVE AGENCY

MMA RAMOTSWE had thought that it would not be easy to open a detective agency. People always made the mistake of thinking that starting a business was simple and then found that there were all sorts of hidden problems and unforeseen demands. She had heard of people opening businesses that lasted four or five weeks before they ran out of money or stock, or both. It was always more difficult than you thought it would be.

She went to the lawyer at Pilane, who had arranged for her to get her father's money. He had organised the sale of the cattle, and had got a good price for them.

"I have got a lot of money for you," he said. "Your father's herd had grown and grown."

She took the cheque and the sheet of paper that he handed her. It was more than she had imagined possible. But there it was—all that money, made payable to Precious Ramotswe, on presentation to Barclays Bank of Botswana.

"You can buy a house with that," said the lawyer. "And a business."

"I am going to buy both of those."

The lawyer looked interested. "What sort of business? A store? I can give you advice, you know."

"A detective agency."

The lawyer looked blank.

"There are none for sale. There are none of those."

Mma Ramotswe nodded. "I know that. I am going to have to start from scratch."

The lawyer winced as she spoke. "It's easy to lose money in business," he said. "Especially when you don't know anything about what you're doing." He stared at her hard. "Especially then. And anyway, can women be detectives? Do you think they can?"

"Why not?" said Mma Ramotswe. She had heard that people did not like lawyers, and now she thought she could see why. This man was so certain of himself, so utterly convinced. What had it to do with him what she did? It was her money, her future. And how dare he say that about women, when he didn't even know that his zip was half undone! Should she tell him?

"Women are the ones who know what's going on," she said quietly. "They are the ones with eyes. Have you not heard of Agatha Christie?"

The lawyer looked taken aback. "Agatha Christie? Of course I know her. Yes, that is true. A woman sees more than a man sees. That is well-known."

"So," said Mma Ramotswe, "when people see a sign saying

No. 1 Ladies' Detective Agency, what will they think? They'll
think those ladies will know what's going on. They're the ones."

The lawyer stroked his chin. "Maybe."

"Yes," said Mma Ramotswe. "Maybe." Adding, "Your zip,
Rra. I think you may not have noticed . . ."

SHE FOUND the house first, on a corner plot in Zebra Drive. It
was expensive, and she decided to take out a bond on part of
it, so that she could afford to buy somewhere for the business
too. That was more difficult, but at last she found a small place
near Kgale Hill, on the edge of town, where she could set up.
It was a good place, because a lot of people walked down that
road every day and would see the sign. It would be almost as
effective as having an advertisement in the *Daily News* or the
Botswana Guardian. Everybody would soon know about her.

The building she bought had originally been a general
dealer's shop, but had been converted into a dry cleaners and
finally a bottle store. For a year or so it had lain empty, and had
been lived in by squatters. They had made fires inside, and in
each of the rooms there was a part of the wall where the plaster had been charred and burned. The owner had eventually
returned from Francistown and had driven out the squatters
and placed the dejected-looking building on the market. There
had been one or two prospective purchasers, but they had
been repelled by its condition and the price had dropped.
When Mma Ramotswe had offered cash, the seller had leapt
at her offer and she received the deeds within days.

There was a lot to do. A builder was called in to replace the
damaged plaster and to repair the tin roof and, again with the
offer of cash, this was accomplished within a week. Then

Mma Ramotswe set to the task of painting, and she had soon completed the outside in ochre and the inside in white. She bought fresh yellow curtains for the windows and, in an unusual moment of extravagance, splashed out on a brand new office set of two desks and two chairs. Her friend, Mr J.L.B. Matekoni, proprietor of Tlokweng Road Speedy Motors, brought her an old typewriter which was surplus to his own requirements and which worked quite well, and with that the office was ready to open—once she had a secretary.

This was the easiest part of all. A telephone call to the Botswana College of Secretarial and Office Skills brought an immediate response. They had just the woman, they said. Mma Makutsi was the widow of a teacher and had just passed their general typing and secretarial examinations with an average grade of 97 percent; she would be ideal—they were certain of it.

Mma Ramotswe liked her immediately. She was a thin woman with a rather long face and braided hair in which she had rubbed copious quantities of henna. She wore oval glasses with wide plastic frames, and she had a fixed, but apparently quite sincere smile.

They opened the office on a Monday. Mma Ramotswe sat at her desk and Mma Makutsi sat at hers, behind the typewriter. She looked at Mma Ramotswe and smiled even more broadly.

"I am ready for work," she said. "I am ready to start."

"Mmm," said Mma Ramotswe. "It's early days yet. We've only just opened. We will have to wait for a client to come."

In her heart of hearts, she knew there would be no clients. The whole idea was a ghastly mistake. Nobody wanted a private detective, and certainly nobody would want her. Who was she, after all? She was just Precious Ramotswe from Mochudi.

She had never been to London or wherever detectives went to find out how to be private detectives. She had never even been to Johannesburg. What if somebody came in and said "You know Johannesburg of course," she would have to lie, or just say nothing.

Mma Makutsi looked at her, and then looked down at the typewriter keyboard. She opened a drawer, peered inside, and then closed it. At that moment a hen came into the room from the yard outside and pecked at something on the floor.

"Get out," shouted Mma Makutsi. "No chickens in here!"

At ten o'clock Mma Makutsi got up from her desk and went into the back room to make the tea. She had been asked to make bush tea, which was Mma Ramotswe's favourite, and she soon brought two cups back. She had a tin of condensed milk in her handbag, and she took this out and poured a small amount into each cup. Then they drank their tea, watching a small boy at the edge of the road throwing stones at a skeletal dog.

At eleven o'clock they had another cup of tea, and at twelve Mma Ramotswe rose to her feet and announced that she was going to walk down the road to the shops to buy herself some perfume. Mma Makutsi was to stay behind and answer the telephone and welcome any clients who might come. Mma Ramotswe smiled as she said this. There would be no clients, of course, and she would be closed at the end of the month. Did Mma Makutsi understand what a parlous job she had obtained for herself? A woman with an average of 97 percent deserved better than this.

Mma Ramotswe was standing at the counter of the shop looking at a bottle of perfume when Mma Makutsi hurtled through the door.

"Mma Ramotswe," she panted. "A client. There is a client in the office. It is a big case. A missing man. Come quickly. There is no time to lose."

THE WIVES of missing men are all the same, thought Mma Ramotswe. At first they feel anxiety, and are convinced that something dreadful has happened. Then doubt begins to creep in, and they wonder whether he's gone off with another woman (which he usually has), and then finally they become angry. At the anger stage, most of them don't want him back anymore, even if he's found. They just want to have a good chance to shout at him.

Mma Malatsi was in the second stage, she thought. She has begun to suspect that he is off somewhere having a good time, while she's left at home, and of course it's beginning to rankle. Perhaps there are debts to be paid, even if she looks as if she's got a fair bit of money.

"Maybe you should tell me a little bit more about your husband," she said, as Mma Malatsi began to drink the cup of strong bush tea which Mma Makutsi had brewed for her.

"His name is Peter Malatsi," Mma Malatsi said. "He's forty and he has—had—has a business selling furniture. It's a good business and he did well. So he hasn't run away from any creditors."

Mma Ramotswe nodded. "There must be another reason," she began, and then, cautiously: "You know what men are like, Mma. What about another woman? Do you think . . ."

Mma Malatsi shook her head vigorously.

"I don't think so," she said. "Maybe a year ago that would have been possible, but then he became a Christian and took up with some Church that was always singing and marching around the place in white uniforms."

Mma Ramotswe noted this down. Church. Singing. Got religion badly? Lady preacher lured him away?

"Who were these people?" she said. "Maybe they know something about him?"

Mma Malatsi shrugged. "I'm not sure," she said, slightly irritably. "In fact, I don't know. He asked me to come with him once or twice, but I refused. So he just used to go off by himself on Sundays. In fact, he disappeared on a Sunday. I thought he'd gone off to his Church."

Mma Ramotswe looked at the ceiling. This was not going to be as hard as some of these cases. Peter Malatsi had gone off with one of the Christians; that was pretty clear. All she had to do now was find which group it was and she would be on his trail. It was the old predictable story; it would be a younger Christian, she was sure of that.

BY THE end of the following day, Mma Ramotswe had compiled a list of five Christian groups which could fit the description. Over the next two days she tracked down the leaders of three of them, and was satisfied that nothing was known of Peter Malatsi. Two of the three tried to convert her; the third merely asked her for money and received a five-pula note.

When she located the leader of the fourth group, the Reverend Shadreck Mapeli, she knew that the search was over. When she mentioned the Malatsi name, the Reverend gave a shudder and glanced over his shoulder surreptitiously.

"Are you from the police?" he asked. "Are you a policeman?"

"Policewoman," she said.

"Ah!" he said mournfully. "Aee!"

"I mean, I'm not a policewoman," she said quickly. "I'm a private detective."

The Reverend appeared to calm down slightly.

"Who sent you?"

"Mma Malatsi."

"Ooh," said the Reverend. "He told us that he had no wife."

"Well, he did," said Mma Ramotswe. "And she's been wondering where he is."

"He's dead," said the Reverend. "He's gone to the Lord."

Mma Ramotswe sensed that he was telling the truth, and that the enquiry was effectively at an end. Now all that remained to be done was to find out how he had died.

"You must tell me," she said. "I won't reveal your name to anybody if you don't want me to. Just tell me how it happened."

They drove to the river in Mma Ramotswe's small white van. It was the rainy season, and there had been several storms, which made the track almost impassable. But at last they reached the river's edge and parked the van under a tree.

"This is where we have our baptisms," said the Reverend, pointing to a pool in the swollen waters of the river. "This is where I stood, here, and this is where the sinners entered the water."

"How many sinners did you have?" asked Mma Ramotswe.

"Six sinners altogether, including Peter. They all went in together, while I prepared to follow them with my staff."

"Yes?" said Mma Ramotswe. "Then what happened?"

"The sinners were standing in the water up to about here." The Reverend indicated his upper chest. "I turned round to tell the flock to start singing, and then when I turned back I noticed that there was something wrong. There were only five sinners in the water."

"One had disappeared?"

"Yes," said the Reverend, shaking slightly as he spoke. "God had taken one of them to His bosom."

Mma Ramotswe looked at the water. It was not a big river, and for much of the year it was reduced to a few stagnant pools. But in a good rainy season, such as that year's, it could be quite a torrent. A nonswimmer could easily be swept away, she reflected, and yet, if somebody were to be swept away the body would surely be found downstream. There were plenty of people who went down to the river for one purpose or another and who would be bound to notice a body. The police would have been called. There would have been something in the newspaper about an unidentified body being found in the Notwane River; the paper was always looking for stories like that. They wouldn't have let the opportunity go by.

She thought for a moment. There was another explanation, and it made her shiver. But before she went into that, she had to find out why the Reverend had kept so quiet about it all.

"You didn't tell the police," she said, trying not to sound too accusing. "Why not?"

The Reverend looked down at the ground, which, in her experience, was where people usually looked if they felt truly sorry. The shamelessly unrepentant, she found, always looked up at the sky.

"I know I should have told them. God will punish me for it. But I was worried that I would be blamed for poor Peter's accident and I thought they would take me to court. They might make me pay damages for it, and that would drive the Church into bankruptcy and put a stop to God's work." He paused. "Do you understand why I kept quiet, and told all the flock not to say anything?"

Mma Ramotswe nodded, and reached out to touch the Reverend gently on the arm.

"I do not think that what you did was bad," she said. "I'm sure that God wanted you to continue and He will not be angry. It was not your fault."

The Reverend raised his eyes and smiled.

"Those are kind words, my sister. Thank you."

THAT AFTERNOON, Mma Ramotswe asked her neighbour if she could borrow one of his dogs. He had a pack of five, and she hated every one of them for their incessant barking. These dogs barked in the morning, as if they were roosters, and at night, when the moon rose in the sky. They barked at crows, and at hammerkops; they barked at passersby; and they sometimes barked just because they had got too hot.

"I need a dog to help me on one of my cases," she explained. "I'll bring him back safe and sound."

The neighbour was flattered to have been asked.

"I'll give you this dog here," he said. "It's the senior dog, and he has a very good nose. He will make a good detective dog."

Mma Ramotswe took the dog warily. It was a large yellow creature, with a curious, offensive smell. That night, just after sunset, she put it in the back of her van, tying its neck to a handle with a piece of string. Then she set off down the track that led to the river, her headlights picking out the shapes of the thorn trees and the anthills in the darkness. In a strange way, she felt glad of the company of the dog, unpleasant though it was.

Now, beside the pool in the river, she took a thick stake from the van and drove it into the soft ground near the water's edge. Then she fetched the dog, led it down to the pool, and tied its string firmly to the stake. From a bag she had with her, she took out a large bone and put it in front of the yellow dog's nose. The animal gave a grunt of pleasure and immediately settled down to gnaw the bone.

Mma Ramotswe waited just a few yards away, a blanket tucked round her legs to keep off the mosquitoes and her old rifle over her knees. She knew it could be a long wait, and she hoped that she would not go to sleep. If she did, though, she was sure that the dog would wake her up when the time came.

Two hours passed. The mosquitoes were bad, and her skin itched, but this was work, and she never complained when she was working. Then, suddenly, there came a growling noise from the dog. Mma Ramotswe strained her eyes in the darkness. She could just make out the shape of the dog, and she could see that it was standing now, looking towards the water. The dog growled again, and gave a bark; then it was silent once more. Mma Ramotswe tossed the blanket off her knees and picked up the powerful torch at her side. Just a little bit longer, she thought.

There was a noise from the water's edge, and Mma Ramotswe knew now that it was time to switch on her torch. As the beam came on, she saw, just at the edge of the water, its head turned towards the cowering dog, a large crocodile.

The crocodile was totally unconcerned by the light, which it probably took for the moon. Its eyes were fixed on the dog, and it was edging slowly towards its quarry. Mma Ramotswe raised the rifle to her shoulder and saw the side of the crocodile's head framed perfectly in her sights. She pulled the trigger.

When the bullet struck the crocodile, it gave a great leap, a somersault in fact, and landed on its back, half in the water, half out. For a moment or two it twitched and then was still. It had been a perfectly placed shot.

Mma Ramotswe noticed that she was trembling as she put the rifle down. Her Daddy had taught her to shoot, and he had done it well, but she did not like to shoot animals, especially crocodiles. They were bad luck, these creatures, but duty had to be done. And what was it doing there anyway? These creatures were not meant to be in the Notwane River; it must have wandered for miles overland, or swum up in the flood waters from the Limpopo itself. Poor crocodile—this was the end of its adventure.

She took a knife and slit through the creature's belly. The leather was soft, and the stomach was soon exposed and its contents revealed. Inside there were pebbles, which the crocodile used for digesting its food, and several pieces of foul-smelling fish. But it was not this that interested her; she was more interested in the undigested bangles and rings and wristwatch she found. These were corroded, and one or two of them were encrusted, but they stood out amongst the stomach contents, each of them the evidence of the crocodile's sinister appetites.

"IS THIS your husband's property?" she asked Mma Malatsi, handing her the wristwatch she had claimed from the crocodile's stomach.

Mma Malatsi took the watch and looked at it. Mma Ramotswe grimaced; she hated moments like this, when she had no choice but to be the bearer of bad news.

But Mma Malatsi was extraordinarily calm. "Well at least I know that he's with the Lord," she said. "And that's much better than knowing that he's in the arms of some other woman, isn't it?"

Mma Ramotswe nodded. "I think it is," she said.

"Were you married, Mma?" asked Mma Malatsi. "Do you know what it is like to be married to a man?"

Mma Ramotswe looked out of the window. There was a thorn tree outside her window, but beyond that she could see the boulder-strewn hill.

"I had a husband," she said. "Once I had a husband. He played the trumpet. He made me unhappy and now I am glad that I no longer have a husband." She paused. "I'm sorry. I did not mean to be rude. You've lost your husband and you must be very sorry."

"A bit," said Mma Malatsi. "But I have lots to do."

CHAPTER SIX

BOY

THE BOY was eleven, and was small for his age. They had tried everything to get him to grow, but he was taking his time, and now, when you saw him, you would say that he was only eight or nine, rather than eleven. Not that it bothered him in the slightest; his father had said to him: I was a short boy too. Now I am a tall man. Look at me. That will happen to you. You just wait.

But secretly the parents feared that there was something wrong; that his spine was twisted, perhaps, and that this was preventing him from growing. When he was barely four, he had fallen out of a tree—he had been after birds' eggs—and had lain still for several minutes, the breath knocked out of him; until his grandmother had run wailing across the melon field and had lifted him up and carried him home, a shattered egg still clasped in his hand. He had recovered—or so they thought at the time—but his walk was different, they thought.

They had taken him to the clinic, where a nurse had looked at his eyes and into his mouth and had pronounced him healthy.

"Boys fall all the time. They hardly ever break anything."

The nurse placed her hands on the child's shoulders and twisted his torso.

"See. There is nothing wrong with him. Nothing. If he had broken anything, he would have cried out."

But years later, when he remained small, the mother thought of the fall and blamed herself for believing that nurse who was only good for doing bilharzia tests and checking for worms.

THE BOY was more curious than other children. He loved to look for stones in the red earth and polish them with his spittle. He found some beautiful ones too—deep-blue ones and ones which had a copper-red hue, like the sky at dusk. He kept his stones at the foot of his sleeping mat in his hut and learned to count with them. The other boys learned to count by counting cattle, but this boy did not seem to like cattle—which was another thing that made him odd.

Because of his curiosity, which sent him scuttling about the bush on mysterious errands of his own, his parents were used to his being out of their sight for hours on end. No harm could come to him, unless he was unlucky enough to step on a puff adder or a cobra. But this never happened, and suddenly he would turn up again at the cattle enclosure, or behind the goats, clutching some strange thing he had found—a vulture's feather, a dried tshongololo millipede, the bleached skull of a snake.

Now the boy was out again, walking along one of the paths that led this way and that through the dusty bush. He had found something which interested him very much—the fresh dung of a snake—and he followed the path so he might see the creature itself. He knew what it was because it had balls of fur in it, and that would only come from a snake. It was rock rabbit fur, he was sure, because of its colour and because he knew that rock rabbits were a delicacy to a big snake. If he found the snake, he might kill it with a rock, and skin it, and that would make a handsome skin for a belt for him and his father.

But it was getting dark, and he would have to give up. He would never see the snake on a night with no moon; he would leave the path and cut back across the bush towards the dirt road that wound its way back, over the dry riverbed, to the village.

He found the road easily and sat for a moment on the verge, digging his toes into soft white sand. He was hungry, and he knew that there would be some meat with their porridge that night because he had seen his grandmother preparing the stew. She always gave him more than his fair share—almost more than his father—and that angered his two sisters.

"We like meat too. We girls like meat."

But that did not persuade the grandmother.

He stood up and began to walk along the road. It was quite dark now, and the trees and bushes were black, formless shapes, merging into one another. A bird was calling somewhere—a night-hunting bird—and there were night insects screeching. He felt a small stinging pain on his right arm, and slapped at it. A mosquito.

Suddenly, on the foliage of a tree ahead, there was a band of yellow light. The light shone and dipped, and the boy turned round. There was a truck on the road behind him. It could not be a car, because the sand was far too deep and soft for a car.

He stood on the side of the road and waited. The lights were almost upon him now; a small truck, a pickup, with two bounding headlights going up and down with the bumps in the road. Now it was upon him, and he held up his hand to shade his eyes.

"Good evening, young one." The traditional greeting, called out from within the cab of the truck.

He smiled and returned the greeting. He could make out two men in the cab—a young man at the wheel and an older man next to him. He knew they were strangers, although he could not see their faces. There was something odd about the way the man spoke Setswana. It was not the way a local would speak it. An odd voice that became higher at the end of a word.

"Are you hunting for wild animals? You want to catch a leopard in this darkness?"

He shook his head. "No. I am just walking home."

"Because a leopard could catch you before you caught it!"

He laughed. "You are right, Rra! I would not like to see a leopard tonight."

"Then we will take you to your place. Is it far?"

"No. It is not far. It is just over there. That way."

THE DRIVER opened the door and got out, leaving the engine running, to allow the boy to slide in over the bench seat. Then he got back in, closed the door and engaged the gears. The boy drew his feet up—there was some animal on the floor and he had touched a soft wet nose—a dog perhaps, or a goat.

He glanced at the man to his left, the older man. It would be rude to stare and it was difficult to see much in the darkness. But he did notice the thing that was wrong with the man's lip and he saw his eyes too. He turned away. A boy should never stare at an old man like this. But why were these people here? What were they doing?

"There it is. There is my father's place. You see—over there. Those lights."

"We can see it."

"I can walk from here if you like. If you stop, I can walk. There is a path."

"We are not stopping. You have something to do for us. You can help us with something."

"They are expecting me back. They will be waiting."

"There is always somebody waiting for somebody. Always."

He suddenly felt frightened, and he turned to look at the driver. The younger man smiled at him.

"Don't worry. Just sit still. You are going somewhere else tonight."

"Where are you taking me, Rra? Why are you taking me away?"

The older man reached out and touched the boy on the shoulder.

"You will not be harmed. You can go home some other time. They will know that you are not being harmed. We are kind men, you see. We are kind men. Listen, I'm going to tell you a little story while we travel. That will make you happy and keep you quiet.

"There were some herd boys who looked after the cattle of their rich uncle. He was a rich man that one! He had more cattle than anybody else in that part of Botswana and his cattle were big, big, like this, only bigger.

"Now these boys found that one day a calf had appeared on

the edge of the herd. It was a strange calf, with many colours on it, unlike any other calf they had ever seen. And, ow! they were pleased that this calf had come.

"This calf was very unusual in another way. This calf could sing a cattle song that the boys heard whenever they went near it. They could not hear the words which this calf was using, but they were something about cattle matters.

"The boys loved this calf, and because they loved it so much they did not notice that some of the other cattle were straying away. By the time that they did notice, it was only after two of the cattle had gone for good that they saw what had happened.

"Their uncle came out. Here he comes, a tall, tall man with a stick. He shouts at the boys and he hits their calf with his stick, saying that strange calves never brought any luck.

"So the calf died, but before it died it whispered something to the boys and they were able to hear it this time. It was very special, and when the boys told their uncle what the calf had said he fell to his knees and wailed.

"The calf was his brother, you see, who had been eaten by a lion a long time before and had come back. Now this man had killed his brother and he was never happy again. He was sad. Very sad."

The boy watched the man's face as he told the story. If he had been unaware of what was happening until that moment, now he knew. He knew what was going to happen.

"Hold that boy! Take his arms! He's going to make me go off the road if you don't hold him."

"I'm trying. He is struggling like a devil."

"Just hold him. I'll stop the truck."

CHAPTER SEVEN

MMA MAKUTSI DEALS WITH THE MAIL

THE SUCCESS of the first case heartened Mma Ramotswe. She had now sent off for, and received, a manual on private detection and was going through it chapter by chapter, taking copious notes. She had made no mistakes in that first case, she thought. She had found out what information there was to be had by a simple process of listing the likely sources and seeking them out. That did not take a great deal of doing. Provided that one was methodical, there was hardly any way in which one could go wrong.

Then she had had a hunch about the crocodile and had followed it up. Again, the manual endorsed this as perfectly acceptable practice. "Don't disregard a hunch," it advised. "Hunches are another form of knowledge." Mma Ramotswe had liked that phrase and had mentioned it to Mma Makutsi. Her secretary had listened carefully, and then typed the sentence out on her typewriter and handed it to Mma Ramotswe.

Mma Makutsi was pleasant company and could type quite well. She had typed out a report which Mma Ramotswe had dictated on the Malatsi case and had typed out the bill for sending to Mma Malatsi. But apart from that she had not really been called on to do anything else and Mma Ramotswe wondered whether the business could really justify employing a secretary.

And yet one had to. What sort of private detective agency had no secretary? She would be a laughingstock without one, and clients—if there were really going to be any more, which was doubtful—could well be frightened away.

Mma Makutsi had the mail to open, of course. There was no mail for the first three days. On the fourth day, a catalogue was received, and a property tax demand, and on the fifth day a letter which was intended for the previous owner.

Then, at the beginning of the second week, she opened a white envelope dirty with finger marks and read the letter out to Mma Ramotswe.

Dear Mma Ramotswe,

I read about you in the newspaper and about how you have opened this big new agency down there in town. I am very proud for Botswana that we now have a person like you in this country.

I am the teacher at the small school at Katsana Village, thirty miles from Gaborone, which is near the place where I was born. I went to Teachers' College many years ago and I passed with a double distinction. My wife and I have two daughters and we have a son of eleven. This boy to which

I am referring has recently vanished and has not been seen for two months.

We went to the police. They made a big search and asked questions everywhere. Nobody knew anything about our son. I took time off from the school and searched the land around our village. We have some *kopjes* not too far away and there are boulders and caves over there. I went into each one of those caves and looked into every crevice. But there was no sign of my son.

He was a boy who liked to wander, because he had a strong interest in nature. He was always collecting rocks and things like that. He knew a lot about the bush and he would never get into danger from stupidity. There are no leopards in these parts anymore and we are too far away from the Kalahari for lions to come.

I went everywhere, calling, calling, but my son never answered me. I looked in every well of every farmer and village nearby and asked them to check the water. But there was no sign of him.

How can a boy vanish off the face of the Earth like this? If I were not a Christian, I would say that some evil spirit had lifted him up and carried him off. But I know that things like that do not really happen.

I am not a wealthy man. I cannot afford the services of a private detective, but I ask you, Mma, in the name of Jesus Christ, to help me in one small way. Please, when you are making your enquiries about other things, and talking to people who might know what goes on, please ask them if they have heard anything about a boy called Thobiso, aged eleven years and four months, who is the son of the teacher at Katsana Village. Please just ask them, and if you hear anything at all, please address a note to the undersigned, myself, the teacher.

In God's name, Ernest Molai Pakotati, Dip.Ed.

Mma Makutsi stopped reading and looked across the room at Mma Ramotswe. For a moment, neither spoke. Then Mma Ramotswe broke the silence.

"Do you know anything about this?" she asked. "Have you heard anything about a boy going missing?"

Mma Makutsi frowned. "I think so. I think there was something in the newspaper about a search for a boy. I think they thought he might have run away from home for some reason."

Mma Ramotswe rose to her feet and took the letter from her secretary. She held it as one might hold an exhibit in court—gingerly, so as not to disturb the evidence. It felt to her as if the letter—a mere scrap of paper, so light in itself—was weighted with pain.

"I don't suppose there's much I can do," she said quietly. "Of course I can keep my ears open. I can tell the poor daddy that, but what else can I do? He will know the bush around Katsana. He will know the people. I can't really do very much for him."

Mma Makutsi seemed relieved. "No," she said. "We can't help that poor man."

A letter was dictated by Mma Ramotswe, and Mma Makutsi typed it carefully into the typewriter. Then it was sealed in an envelope, a stamp stuck on the outside, and it was placed in the new red out-tray Mma Ramotswe had bought from the Botswana Book Centre. It was the second letter to leave the No. 1 Ladies' Detective Agency, the first being Mma Malatsi's bill for two hundred and fifty pula—the bill on the top of which Mma Makutsi had typed: "Your late husband— the solving of the mystery of his death."

THAT EVENING, in the house in Zebra Drive, Mma Ramotswe prepared herself a meal of stew and pumpkin. She loved standing in the kitchen, stirring the pot, thinking over the events of the day, sipping at a large mug of bush tea which she balanced on the edge of the stove. Several things had happened that day, apart from the arrival of the letter. A man had come in with a query about a bad debt and she had reluctantly agreed to help him recover it. She was not sure whether this was the sort of thing which a private detective should do—there was nothing in the manual about it—but he was persistent and she found it difficult to refuse. Then there had been a visit from a woman who was concerned about her husband.

"He comes home smelling of perfume," she said, "And smiling too. Why would a man come home smelling of perfume and smiling?"

"Perhaps he is seeing another woman," ventured Mma Ramotswe.

The woman had looked at her aghast.

"Do you think he would do that? My husband?"

They had discussed the situation and it was agreed that the woman would tackle her husband on the subject.

"It's possible that there is another explanation," said Mma Ramotswe reassuringly.

"Such as?"

"Well . . ."

"Many men wear perfume these days," offered Mma Makutsi. "They think it makes them smell good. You know how men smell."

The client had turned in her chair and stared at Mma Makutsi.

"My husband does not smell," she said. "He is a very clean man."

Mma Ramotswe had thrown Mma Makutsi a warning look. She would have to have a word with her about keeping out of the way when clients were there.

But whatever else had happened that day, her thoughts kept returning to the teacher's letter and the story of the missing boy. How the poor man must have fretted—and the mother, too. He did not say anything about a mother, but there must have been one, or a grandmother of course. What thoughts would have been in their minds as each hour went past with no sign of the boy, and all the time he could be in danger, stuck in an old mine shaft, perhaps, too hoarse to cry out anymore while rescuers beat about above him. Or stolen perhaps—whisked away by somebody in the night. What cruel heart could do such a thing to an innocent child? How could anybody resist the boy's cries as he begged to be taken home? That such things could happen right there, in Botswana of all places, made her shiver with dread.

She began to wonder whether this was the right job for her after all. It was all very well thinking that one might help people to sort out their difficulties, but then these difficulties could be heartrending. The Malatsi case had been an odd one. She had expected Mma Malatsi to be distraught when she showed her the evidence that her husband had been eaten by a crocodile, but she had not seemed at all put out. What had she said? But then I have lots to do. What an extraordinary, unfeeling thing for somebody to say when she had just lost her husband. Did she not value him more than that?

Mma Ramotswe paused, her spoon dipped half below the surface of the simmering stew. When people were unmoved in that way, Mma Christie expected the reader to be suspicious. What would Mma Christie have thought if she had seen Mma Malatsi's cool reaction, her virtual indifference? She would have thought: This woman killed her husband! That's why she's unmoved by the news of his death. She knew all along that he was dead!

But what about the crocodile and the baptism, and the other sinners? No, she must be innocent. Perhaps she wanted him dead, and then her prayer was answered by the crocodile. Would that make you a murderer in God's eyes if something then happened? God would know, you see, that you had wanted somebody dead because there are no secrets that you can keep from God. Everybody knew that.

She stopped. It was time to take the pumpkin out of the pot and eat it. In the final analysis, that was what solved these big problems of life. You could think and think and get nowhere, but you still had to eat your pumpkin. That brought you down to earth. That gave you a reason for going on. Pumpkin.

CHAPTER EIGHT

A CONVERSATION WITH
MR J.L.B. MATEKONI

THE BOOKS did not look good. At the end of the first month of its existence, the No. 1 Ladies' Detective Agency was making a convincing loss. There had been three paying clients, and two who came for advice, received it, and declined to pay. Mma Malatsi had paid her bill for two hundred and fifty pula; Happy Bapetsi had paid two hundred pula for the exposure of her false father; and a local trader had paid one hundred pula to find out who was using his telephone to make unauthorised long-distance calls to Francistown. If one added this up it came to five hundred and fifty pula; but then Mma Makutsi's wages were five hundred and eighty pula a month. This meant that there was a loss of thirty pula, without even taking into account other overheads, such as the cost of petrol for the tiny white van and the cost of electricity for the office.

Of course, businesses took some time to get established—Mma Ramotswe understood this—but how long could one go on at a loss? She had a certain amount of money left over from her father's estate, but she could not live on that forever. She should have listened to her father; he had wanted her to buy a butchery, and that would have been so much safer. What was the expression they used? A blue-chip investment, that was it. But where was the excitement in that?

She thought of Mr J.L.B. Matekoni, proprietor of Tlokweng Road Speedy Motors. Now that was a business which would be making a profit. There was no shortage of customers, as everybody knew what a fine mechanic he was. That was the difference between them, she thought; he knew what he was doing, whereas she did not.

Mma Ramotswe had known Mr J.L.B. Matekoni for years. He came from Mochudi, and his uncle had been a close friend of her father. Mr J.L.B. Matekoni was forty-five—ten years older than Mma Ramotswe, but he regarded himself as being a contemporary and often said, when making an observation about the world: "For people of our age . . ."

He was a comfortable man, and she wondered why he had never married. He was not handsome, but he had an easy, reassuring face. He would have been the sort of husband that any woman would have liked to have about the house. He would fix things and stay in at night and perhaps even help with some of the domestic chores—something that so few men would ever dream of doing.

But he had remained single, and lived alone in a large house near the old airfield. She sometimes saw him sitting on his verandah when she drove past—Mr J.L.B. Matekoni by himself, sitting on a chair, staring out at the trees that grew in his garden. What did a man like that think about? Did he sit there and reflect on how nice it would be to have a wife, with children running around the garden, or did he sit there and think about the garage and the cars he had fixed? It was impossible to tell.

She liked to call on him at the garage and talk to him in his greasy office with its piles of receipts and orders for spare parts. She liked to look at the calendars on the wall, with their simple pictures of the sort that men liked. She liked to drink tea from one of his mugs with the greasy fingerprints on the outside while his two assistants raised cars on jacks and cluttered and banged about underneath.

Mr J.L.B. Matekoni enjoyed these sessions. They would talk about Mochudi, or politics, or just exchange the news of the day. He would tell her who was having trouble with his car, and what was wrong with it, and who had bought petrol that day, and where they said they were going.

But that day they talked about finances, and about the problems of running a paying business.

"Staff costs are the biggest item," said Mr J.L.B. Matekoni. "You see those two young boys out there under that car? You've no idea what they cost me. Their wages, their taxes, the insurance to cover them if that car were to fall on their heads. It all adds up. And at the end of the day there are just one or two pula left for me. Never much more."

"But at least you aren't making a loss," said Mma Ramotswe. "I'm thirty pula down on my first month's trading. And I'm sure it'll get worse."

Mr J.L.B. Matekoni sighed. "Staff costs," he said. "That secretary of yours—the one with those big glasses. That's where the money will be going."

Mma Ramotswe nodded. "I know," she said. "But you need a secretary if you have an office. If I didn't have a secretary, then I'd be stuck there all day. I couldn't come over here and talk to you. I couldn't go shopping."

Mr J.L.B. Matekoni reached for his mug. "Then you need to get better clients," he said. "You need a couple of big cases. You need somebody rich to give you a case."

"Somebody rich?"

"Yes. Somebody like . . . like Mr Patel, for example."

"Why would he need a private detective?"

"Rich men have their problems," said Mr J.L.B. Matekoni. "You never know."

They lapsed into silence, watching the two young mechanics remove a wheel from the car on which they were working.

"Stupid boys," said Mr J.L.B. Matekoni. "They don't need to do that."

"I've been thinking," said Mma Ramotswe. "I had a letter the other day. It made me very sad, and I wondered whether I should be a detective after all."

She told him of the letter about the missing boy, and she explained how she had felt unable to help the father.

"I couldn't do anything for him," she said. "I'm not a miracle worker. But I felt so sorry for him. He thought that his son had fallen in the bush or been taken by some animal. How could a father bear that?"

Mr J.L.B. Matekoni snorted. "I saw that in the paper," he said. "I read about that search. And I knew it was hopeless from the beginning."

"Why?" asked Mma Ramotswe.

For a moment, Mr J.L.B. Matekoni was silent. Mma Ramotswe looked at him, and past him, through the window to the thorn tree outside. The tiny grey-green leaves, like blades of grass, were folded in upon themselves, against the heat; and beyond them the empty sky, so pale as to be white; and the smell of dust.

"Because that boy's dead," said Mr J.L.B. Matekoni, tracing an imaginary pattern in the air with his finger. "No animal took him, or at least no ordinary animal. A santawana maybe, a thokolosi. Oh yes."

Mma Ramotswe was silent. She imagined the father—the father of the dead boy, and for a brief moment she remembered that awful afternoon in Mochudi, at the hospital, when the nurse had come up to her, straightening her uniform, and she saw that the nurse was crying. To lose a child, like that, was something that could end one's world. One could never get back to how it was before. The stars went out. The moon disappeared. The birds became silent.

"Why do you say he's dead?" she asked. "He could have got lost and then . . ."

Mr J.L.B. Matekoni shook his head. "No," he said. "That boy would have been taken for witchcraft. He's dead now."

She put her empty mug down on the table. Outside, in the workshop, a wheel brace was dropped with a loud, clanging sound.

She glanced at her friend. This was a subject that one did not talk about. This was the one subject which would bring fear to the most resolute heart. This was the great taboo.

"How can you be sure?"

Mr J.L.B. Matekoni smiled. "Come on, now, Mma Ramotswe. You know as well as I do what goes on. We don't like to talk about it do we? It's the thing we Africans are most ashamed of. We know it happens but we pretend it doesn't. We know all right what happens to children who go missing. We know."

She looked up at him. Of course he was telling the truth,

because he was a truthful, good man. And he was probably right—no matter how much everybody would like to think of other, innocent explanations as to what had happened to a missing boy, the most likely thing was exactly what Mr J.L.B. Matekoni said. The boy had been taken by a witch doctor and killed for medicine. Right there, in Botswana, in the late twentieth century, under that proud flag, in the midst of all that made Botswana a modern country, this thing had happened, this heart of darkness had thumped out like a drum. The little boy had been killed because some powerful person somewhere had commissioned the witch doctor to make strengthening medicine for him.

She cast her eyes down.

"You may be right," she said. "That poor boy . . ."

"Of course I'm right," said Mr J.L.B. Matekoni. "And why do you think that poor man had to write that letter to you? It's because the police will be doing nothing to find out how and where it happened. Because they're scared. Every one of them. They're just as scared as I am and those two boys out there under that car are. Scared, Mma Ramotswe. Frightened for our lives. Every one of us—maybe even you."

MMA RAMOTSWE went to bed at ten that night, half an hour later than usual. She liked to lie in bed sometimes, with her reading lamp on, and read a magazine. Now she was tired, and the magazine kept slipping from her hands, defeating her struggles to keep awake.

She turned out the light and said her prayers, whispering the words although there was nobody in the house to hear her. It was always the same prayer, for the soul of her father, Obed, for Botswana and for rain that would make the crops grow and the cattle fat, and for her little baby, now safe in the arms of Jesus.

In the early hours of the morning she awoke in terror, her heartbeat irregular, her mouth dry. She sat up and reached for the light switch, but when she turned it on nothing happened. She pushed her sheet aside—there was no need for a blanket in the hot weather—and slipped off the bed.

The light in the corridor did not work either, nor that in the kitchen, where the moon made shadows and shapes on the floor. She looked out of the window, into the night. There were no lights anywhere; a power cut.

She opened the back door and stepped out into the yard in her bare feet. The town was in darkness, the trees obscure, indeterminate shapes, clumps of black.

"Mma Ramotswe!"

She stood where she was, frozen in terror. There was somebody in the yard, watching her. Somebody had whispered her name.

She opened her mouth to speak, but no sound came. And it would be dangerous to speak, anyway. So she backed away, slowly, inch by inch, towards the kitchen door. Once inside, she slammed the door shut behind her and reached for the lock. As she turned the key the electricity came on and the kitchen was flooded with light. The fridge started to purr; a light from the cooker winked on and off at her: 3:04; 3:04

CHAPTER NINE

THE BOYFRIEND

THERE WERE three quite exceptional houses in the country, and Mma Ramotswe felt some satisfaction that she had been invited to two of them. The best-known of these was Mokolodi, a rambling chateau-like building placed in the middle of the bush to the south of Gaborone. This house, which had a gate-house with gates on which hornbills had been worked in iron, was probably the grandest establishment in the country, and was certainly rather more impressive than Phakadi House, to the north, which was rather too close to the sewage ponds for Mma Ramotswe's taste. This had its compensations, though, as the sewage ponds attracted a great variety of bird life, and from the verandah of Phakadi one could watch flights of flamingos landing on the murky green water. But you could not do this if the wind was in the wrong direction, which it often was.

The third house could only be suspected of being a house of distinction, as very few people were invited to enter it, and

Gaborone as a whole had to rely on what could be seen of the house from the outside—which was not much, as it was surrounded by a high white wall—or on reports from those who were summoned into the house for some special purpose. These reports were unanimous in their praise for the sheer opulence of the interior.

"Like Buckingham Palace," said one woman who had been called to arrange flowers for some family occasion. "Only rather better. I think that the Queen lives a bit more simply than those people in there."

The people in question were the family of Mr Paliwalar Sundigar Patel, the owner of eight stores—five in Gaborone and three in Francistown—a hotel in Orapa, and a large outfitters in Lobatse. He was undoubtedly one of the wealthiest men in the country, if not the wealthiest, but amongst the Batswana this counted for little, as none of the money had gone into cattle, and money which was not invested in cattle, as everybody knew, was but dust in the mouth.

Mr Paliwalar Patel had come to Botswana in 1967, at the age of twenty-five. He had not had a great deal in his pocket then, but his father, a trader in a remote part of Zululand, had advanced him the money to buy his first shop in the African Mall. This had been a great success; Mr Patel bought goods for virtually nothing from traders in distress and then sold them on at minimal profit. Trade blossomed and shop was added to shop, all of them run on the same commercial philosophy. By his fiftieth birthday, he stopped expanding his empire, and concentrated on the improvement and education of his family.

There were four children—a son, Wallace, twin daughters, Sandri and Pali, and the youngest, a daughter called Nandira. Wallace had been sent to an expensive boarding school in Zimbabwe, in order to satisfy Mr Patel's ambition that he become a gentleman. There he had learned to play cricket, and to be cruel. He had been admitted to dental school, after a large donation by Mr Patel, and had then returned to Durban, where he set up a practice in cosmetic dentistry. At some point he had shortened his name—"for convenience's sake"—and had become Mr Wallace Pate BDS (Natal).

Mr Patel had protested at the change. "Why are you now this Mr Wallace Pate BDS (Natal) may I ask? Why? You ashamed, or something? You think I'm just a Mr Paliwalar Patel BA (Failed) or something?"

The son had tried to placate his father.

"Short names are easier, father. Pate, Patel—it's the same thing. So why have an extra letter at the end? The modern idea is to be brief. We must be modern these days. Everything is modern, even names."

There had been no such pretensions from the twins. They had both been sent back to the Natal to meet husbands, which they had done in the manner expected by their father. Both sons-in-law had now been taken into the business and were proving to have good heads for figures and a sound understanding of the importance of tight profit margins.

Then there was Nandira, who was sixteen at the time and a pupil at Maru-a-Pula School in Gaborone, the best and most expensive school in the country. She was bright academically, was consistently given glowing reports from the school, and was expected to make a good marriage in the fullness of time—probably on her twentieth birthday, which Mr Patel had felt was precisely the right time for a girl to marry.

The entire family, including the sons-in-law, the grandparents, and several distant cousins, lived in the Patel mansion

near the old Botswana Defence Force Club. There had been
several houses on the plot, old colonial-style houses with wide
verandahs and fly screens, but Mr Patel had knocked them
down and built his new house from scratch. In fact, it was several houses linked together, all forming the family compound.

"We Indians like to live in a compound," Mr Patel had
explained to the architect. "We like to be able to see what's
going on in the family, you know."

The architect, who was given a free rein, designed a house
in which he indulged every architectural whimsy which more
demanding and less well-funded clients had suppressed over
the years. To his astonishment, Mr Patel accepted everything,
and the resulting building proved to be much to his taste. It
was furnished in what could only be called Delhi Rococo, with
a great deal of gilt in furniture and curtains, and on the walls
expensive pictures of Hindu saints and mountain deer with
eyes that followed one about the room.

When the twins married, at an expensive ceremony in Durban to which over fifteen hundred guests were invited, they
were each given their own quarters, the house having been
considerably expanded for the purpose. The sons-in-law were
also each given a red Mercedes-Benz, with their initials on the
driver's door. This required the Patel garage to be expanded as
well, as there were now four Mercedes-Benz cars to be housed
there; Mr Patel's, Mrs Patel's car (driven by a driver), and the
two belonging to the sons-in law.

An elderly cousin had said to him at the wedding in Durban:
"Look, man, we Indians have got to be careful. You shouldn't
go flashing your money around the place. The Africans don't
like that, you know, and when they get the chance they'll take
it all away from us. Look at what happened in Uganda. Listen

to what some of the hotheads are saying in Zimbabwe. Imagine what the Zulus would do to us if they had half a chance. We've got to be discreet."

Mr Patel had shaken his head. "None of that applies in Botswana. There's no danger there, I'm telling you. They're stable people. You should see them; with all their diamonds. Diamonds bring stability to a place, believe me."

The cousin appeared to ignore him. "Africa's like that, you see," he continued. "Everything's going fine one day, just fine, and then the next morning you wake up and discover your throat's been cut. Just watch out."

Mr Patel had taken the warning to heart, to an extent, and had added to the height of the wall surrounding his house so that people could not look in the windows and see the luxury. And if they continued to drive around in their big cars, well, there were plenty of those in town and there was no reason why they should be singled out for special attention.

MMA RAMOTSWE was delighted when she received the telephone call from Mr Patel asking her whether she could possibly call on him, in his house, some evening in the near future. They agreed upon that very evening, and she went home to change into a more formal dress before presenting herself at the gates of the Patel mansion. Before she went out, she telephoned Mr J.L.B. Matekoni.

"You said I should get a rich client," she said. "And now I have. Mr Patel."

Mr J.L.B. Matekoni drew in his breath. "He is a very rich man," he said. "He has four Mercedes-Benzes. Four. Three of them are all right, but one has had bad problems with its transmission. There was a coupling problem, one of the worst I've seen, and I had to spend days trying to get a new casing . . ."

YOU COULD not just push open the gate at the Patel house; nor could you park outside and hoot your horn, as everybody did with other houses. At the Patel house you pressed a bell in the wall, and a high-pitched voice issued from a small speaker above your head.

"Yes. Patel place here. What do you want?"

"Mma Ramotswe," she said. "Private . . ."

A crackling noise came from the speaker.

"Private? Private what?"

She was about to answer, when there was another crackling sound and the gate began to swing open. Mma Ramotswe had left her tiny white van round the corner, to keep up appearances, and so she entered the compound by foot. Inside, she found herself in a courtyard which had been transformed by shade netting into a grove of lush vegetation. At the far end of the courtyard was the entrance to the house itself, a large doorway flanked by tall white pillars and tubs of plants. Mr Patel appeared before the open door and waved to her with his walking stick.

She had seen Mr Patel before, of course, and knew that he had an artificial leg, but she had never seen him at really close quarters and had not expected him to be so small. Mma Ramotswe was not tall—being blessed with generous girth, rather than height—but Mr Patel still found himself looking up at her when he shook her hand and gestured for her to come inside.

"Have you been in my house before?" he asked, knowing, of

course, that she had not. "Have you been at one of my parties?"

This was a lie as well, she knew. Mr Patel never gave parties, and she wondered why he should pretend to do so.

"No," she said simply. "You have never asked me."

"Oh dear," he said, chuckling as he spoke. "I have made a big mistake."

He led her through an entrance hall, a long room with a shiny black and white marble floor. There was a lot of brass in this room—expensive, polished brass—and the overall effect was one of glitter.

"We shall go through to my study," he said. "That is my private room in which none of the family are ever allowed. They know not to disturb me there, even if the house is burning down."

The study was another large room, dominated by a large desk on which there were three telephones and an elaborate pen and ink stand. Mma Ramotswe looked at the stand, which consisted of several glass shelves for the pens, the shelves being supported by miniature elephant tusks, carved in ivory.

"Sit down, please," said Mr Patel, pointing to a white leather armchair. "It takes me a little time to sit because I am missing one leg. There, you see. I am always on the lookout for a better leg. This one is Italian and cost me a lot of money, but I think there are better legs to be had. Maybe in America."

Mma Ramotswe sank into the chair and looked at her host.

"I'll get straight to the point," said Mr Patel. "There's no point in beating about the bush and chasing all sorts of rabbits, is there? No, there isn't."

He paused, waiting for Mma Ramotswe's confirmation. She nodded her head slightly.

"I am a family man, Mma Ramotswe," he said. "I have a happy family who all live in this house, except for my son, who is a gentleman dentist in Durban. You may have heard of him. People call him Pate these days."

"I know of him," said Mma Ramotswe. "People speak highly of him, even here."

Mr Patel beamed. "Well, my goodness, that's a very pleasing thing to be told. But my other children are also very important to me. I make no distinction between my children. They are all the same. Equal-equal."

"That's the best way to do it," said Mma Ramotswe. "If you favour one, then that leads to a great deal of bitterness."

"You can say that again, oh yes," said Mr Patel. "Children notice when their parents give two sweets to one and one to another. They can count same as us."

Mma Ramotswe nodded again, wondering where the conversation was leading.

"Now," said Mr Patel. "My big girls, the twins, are well married to good boys and are living here under this roof. That is all very excellent. And that leaves just one child, my little Nandira. She is sixteen and she is at Maru-a-Pula. She is doing well at school, but . . ."

He paused, looking at Mma Ramotswe through narrowed eyes. "You know about teenagers, don't you? You know how things are with teenagers in these modern days?"

Mma Ramotswe shrugged. "They are often bad trouble for their parents. I have seen parents crying their eyes out over their teenagers."

Mr Patel suddenly lifted his walking stick and hit his artificial leg for emphasis. The sound was surprisingly hollow and tinny.

"That's what is worrying me," he said vehemently. "That's what is happening. And I will not have that. Not in my family."

"What?" asked Mma Ramotswe. "Teenagers?"

"Boys," said Mr Patel bitterly. "My Nandira is seeing some boy in secret. She denies it, but I know that there is a boy. And this cannot be allowed, whatever these modern people are saying about the town. It cannot be allowed in this family—in this house."

AS MR Patel spoke, the door to his study, which had been closed behind them when they had entered, opened and a woman came into the room. She was a local woman and she greeted Mma Ramotswe politely in Setswana before offering her a tray on which various glasses of fruit juice were set. Mma Ramotswe chose a glass of guava juice and thanked the servant. Mr Patel helped himself to orange juice and then impatiently waved the servant out of the room with his stick, waiting until she had gone before he continued to speak.

"I have spoken to her about this," he said. "I have made it very clear to her. I told her that I don't care what other children are doing—that is their parents' business, not mine. But I have made it very clear that she is not to go about the town with boys or see boys after school. That is final."

He tapped his artificial leg lightly with his walking stick and then looked at Mma Ramotswe expectantly.

Mma Ramotswe cleared her throat. "You want me to do something about this?" she said quietly. "Is this why you have asked me here this evening?"

Mr Patel nodded. "That is precisely why. I want you to find out who this boy is, and then I will speak to him."

Mma Ramotswe stared at Mr Patel. Had he the remotest idea, she wondered, how young people behaved these days, especially at a school like Maru-a-Pula, where there were all those foreign children, even children from the American Embassy and such places? She had heard about Indian fathers trying to arrange marriages, but she had never actually encountered such behaviour. And here was Mr Patel assuming that she would agree with him; that she would take exactly the same view.

"Wouldn't it be better to speak to her?" she asked gently. "If you asked her who the young man was, then she might tell you."

Mr Patel reached for his stick and tapped his tin leg.

"Not at all," he said sharply, his voice becoming shrill. "Not at all. I have already been asking her for three weeks, maybe four weeks. And she gives no answer. She is dumb insolent."

Mma Ramotswe sat and looked down at her feet, aware of Mr Patel's expectant gaze upon her. She had decided to make it a principle of her professional life never to turn anybody away, unless they asked her to do something criminal. This rule appeared to be working; she had already found that her ideas about a request for help, about its moral rights and wrongs, had changed when she had become more aware of all the factors involved. It might be the same with Mr Patel; but even if it were not, were there good enough reasons for turning him down? Who was she to condemn an anxious Indian father when she really knew very little about how these people ran their lives? She felt a natural sympathy for the girl, of course; what a terrible fate to have a father like this one, intent on keeping one in some sort of gilded cage. Her own Daddy had never stood in her way over anything; he had trusted her and she, in turn, had never kept anything from him—apart from the truth about Note perhaps.

She looked up. Mr Patel was watching her with his dark eyes, the tip of his walking stick tapping almost imperceptibly on the floor.

"I'll find out for you," she said. "Although I must say I don't really like doing this. I don't like the idea of watching a child."

"But children must be watched!" expostulated Mr Patel. "If parents don't watch their children, then what happens? You answer that!"

"There comes a time when they must have their own lives," said Mma Ramotswe. "We have to let go."

"Nonsense!" shouted Mr Patel. "Modern nonsense. My father beat me when I was twenty-two! Yes, he beat me for making a mistake in the shop. And I deserved it. None of this modern nonsense."

Mma Ramotswe rose to her feet.

"I am a modern lady," she said. "So perhaps we have different ideas. But that has nothing to do with it. I have agreed to do as you have asked me. Now all that you need to do is to let me see a photograph of this girl, so that I can know who it is I am going to be watching."

Mr Patel struggled to his feet, straightening the tin leg with his hands as he did so.

"No need for a photograph," he said. "I can produce the girl herself. You can look at her."

Mma Ramotswe raised her hands in protest. "But then she will know me," she said. "I must be able to be unobserved."

"Ah!" said Mr Patel. "A very good idea. You detectives are very clever men."

"Women," said Mma Ramotswe.

Mr Patel looked at her sideways, but said nothing. He had no time for modern ideas.

As she left the house, Mma Ramotswe thought: He has four children; I have none. He is not a good father this man, because he loves his children too much—he wants to own them. You have to let go. You have to let go.

And she thought of that moment when, not even supported by Note, who had made some excuse, she had laid the tiny body of their premature baby, so fragile, so light, into the earth and had looked up at the sky and wanted to say something to God, but couldn't because her throat was blocked with sobs and no words, nothing, would come.

IT SEEMED to Mma Ramotswe that it would be a rather easy case. Watching somebody could always be difficult, as you had to be aware of what they were doing all the time. This could mean long periods of waiting outside houses and offices, doing nothing but watching for somebody to appear. Nandira would be at school for most of the day, of course, and that meant that Mma Ramotswe could get on with other things until three o'clock came round and the school day drew to an end. That was the point at which she would have to follow her and see where she went.

Then the thought occurred to Mma Ramotswe that following a child could be problematic. It was one thing to follow somebody driving a car—all you had to do was tail them in the little white van. But if the person you were watching was riding a bicycle—as many children did on their way home from school—then it would look rather odd if the little white van were to be seen crawling along the road. If she walked home, of course, then Mma Ramotswe could herself walk, keeping a reasonable distance behind her. She could even borrow one of her neighbour's dreadful yellow dogs and pretend to be taking that for a walk.

On the day following her interview with Mr Patel, Mma Ramotswe parked the tiny white van in the school car park shortly before the final bell of the day sounded. The children came out in dribs and drabs, and it was not until shortly after twenty past three that Nandira walked out of the school entrance, carrying her schoolbag in one hand and a book in the other. She was by herself, and Mma Ramotswe was able to get a good look at her from the cab of her van. She was an attractive child, a young woman really; one of those sixteen-year-olds who could pass for nineteen, or even twenty.

She walked down the path and stopped briefly to talk to another girl, who was waiting under a tree for her parents to collect her. They chatted for a few minutes, and then Nandira walked off towards the school gates.

Mma Ramotswe waited a few moments, and then got out of the van. Once Nandira was out on the road, Mma Ramotswe followed her slowly. There were several people about, and there was no reason why she should be conspicuous. On a late winter afternoon it was quite pleasant to walk down the road; a month or so later it would be too hot, and then she could well appear out of place.

She followed the girl down the road and round the corner. It had become clear to her that Nandira was not going directly home, as the Patel house was in the opposite direction to the route she had chosen. Nor was she going into town, which meant that she must be going to meet somebody at a house somewhere. Mma Ramotswe felt a glow of satisfaction. All she would probably have to do was to find the house and then it would be child's play to get the name of the owner, and the boy. Perhaps she could even go to Mr Patel this evening and reveal the boy's identity. That would impress him, and it would be a very easily earned fee.

Nandira turned another corner. Mma Ramotswe held back a little before following her. It would be easy to become over-confident following an innocent child, and she had to remind herself of the rules of pursuit. The manual on which she relied, *The Principles of Private Investigation* by Clovis Andersen, stressed that one should never crowd one's subject. "Keep a long rein," wrote Mr Andersen, "even if it means losing the subject from time to time. You can always pick up the trail later. And a few minutes of non-eye contact is better than an angry confrontation."

Mma Ramotswe judged that it was now time to go round the corner. She did so, expecting to see Nandira several hundred yards down the road, but when she looked down it, the road was empty—non-eye contact, as Clovis Andersen called it, had set in. She turned round, and looked in the other direction. There was a car in the distance, coming out of the driveway of a house, and nothing else.

Mma Ramotswe was puzzled. It was a quiet road, and there were not more than three houses on either side of it—at least in the direction in which Nandira had been going. But these houses all had gates and driveways, and bearing in mind that she had only been out of view for a minute or so, Nandira would not have had time to disappear into one of these houses. Mma Ramotswe would have seen her in a driveway or going in through a front door.

If she has gone into one of the houses, thought Mma

Ramotswe, then it must be one of the first two, as she would certainly not have been able to reach the houses farther along the road. So perhaps the situation was not as bad as she had thought it might be; all she would have to do would be to check up on the first house on the right-hand side of the road and the first house on the left.

She stood still for a moment, and then she made up her mind. Walking as quickly as she could, she made her way back to the tiny white van and drove back along the route on which she had so recently followed Nandira. Then, parking the van in front of the house on the right, she walked up the driveway towards the front door.

When she knocked on the door, a dog started to bark loudly inside the house. Mma Ramotswe knocked again, and there came the sound of somebody silencing the dog. "Quiet, Bison; quiet, I know, I know!" Then the door opened and a woman looked out at her. Mma Ramotswe could tell that she was not a Motswana. She was a West African, probably a Ghanaian, judging by the complexion and the dress. Ghanaians were Mma Ramotswe's favourite people; they had a wonderful sense of humor and were almost inevitably in a good mood.

"Hallo Mma," said Mma Ramotswe. "I'm sorry to disturb you, but I'm looking for Sipho."

The woman frowned.

"Sipho? There's no Sipho here."

Mma Ramotswe shook her head.

"I'm sure it was this house. I'm one of the teachers from the secondary school, you see, and I need to get a message to one of the form four boys. I thought that this was his house."

The woman smiled. "I've got two daughters," she said. "But no son. Could you find me a son, do you think?"

"Oh dear," said Mma Ramotswe, sounding harassed. "Is it the house over the road then?"

The woman shook her head. "That's that Ugandan family," she said. "They've got a boy, but he's only six or seven, I think."

Mma Ramotswe made her apologies and walked back down the drive. She had lost Nandira on the very first afternoon, and she wondered whether the girl had deliberately shrugged her off. Could she possibly have known that she was being followed? This seemed most unlikely, which meant that it was no more than bad luck that she had lost her. Tomorrow she would be more careful. She would ignore Clovis Andersen for once and crowd her subject a little more.

At eight o'clock that night she received a telephone call from Mr Patel.

"You have anything to report to me yet?" he asked. "Any information?"

Mma Ramotswe told him that she unfortunately had not been able to find out where Nandira went after school, but that she hoped that she might be more successful the following day.

"Not very good," said Mr Patel. "Not very good. Well, I at least have something to report to you. She came home three hours after school finished—three hours—and told me that she had just been at a friend's house. I said: what friend? and she just answered that I did not know her. Her. Then my wife found a note on the table, a note which our Nandira must have dropped. It said: "See you tomorrow, Jack." Now who is this Jack, then? Who is this person? Is that a girl's name, I ask you?"

"No," said Mma Ramotswe. "It sounds like a boy."

"There!" said Mr Patel, with the air of one producing the

elusive answer to a problem. "That is the boy, I think. That is the one we must find. Jack who? Where does he live? That sort of thing—you must tell me it all."

Mma Ramotswe prepared herself a cup of bush tea and went to bed early. It had been an unsatisfactory day in more than one respect, and Mr Patel's crowing telephone call merely set the seal on it. So she lay in bed, the bush tea on her bedside table, and read the newspaper before her eyelids began to droop and she drifted off to sleep.

THE NEXT afternoon she was late in reaching the school car park. She was beginning to wonder whether she had lost Nandira again when she saw the girl come out of the school, accompanied by another girl. Mma Ramotswe watched as the two of them walked down the path and stood at the school gate. They seemed deep in conversation with one another, in that exclusive way which teenagers have of talking to their friends, and Mma Ramotswe was sure that if only she could hear what was being said, then she would know the answers to more than one question. Girls talked about their boyfriends in an easy, conspiratorial way, and she was certain that this was the subject of conversation between Nandira and her friend.

Suddenly a blue car drew up opposite the two girls. Mma Ramotswe stiffened and watched as the driver leant over the passenger seat and opened the front door. Nandira got in, and her friend got into the back. Mma Ramotswe started the engine of the little white van and pulled out of the school car park, just as the blue car drew away from the school. She followed at a safe distance, but ready to close the gap between them if there was any chance of losing them. She would not repeat yesterday's mistake and see Nandira vanish into thin air.

The blue car was taking its time, and Mma Ramotswe did not have to strain to keep up. They drove past the Sun Hotel and made their way towards the Stadium roundabout. There they turned in towards town and drove past the hospital and the Anglican Cathedral towards the Mall. Shops, thought Mma Ramotswe. They're just going shopping; or are they? She had seen teenagers meeting one another after school in places like the Botswana Book Centre. They called it "hanging around," she believed. They stood about and chatted and cracked jokes and did everything except buy something. Perhaps Nandira was going off to hang around with this Jack.

The blue car nosed into a parking place near the President Hotel. Mma Ramotswe parked several cars away and watched as the two girls got out of the car, accompanied by an older woman, presumably the mother of the other girl. She said something to her daughter, who nodded, and then detached herself from the girls and walked off in the direction of the hardware stores.

Nandira and her friend walked past the steps of the President Hotel and then slowly made their way up to the Post Office. Mma Ramotswe followed them casually, stopping to look at a rack of African print blouses which a woman was displaying in the square.

"Buy one of these Mma," said the woman. "Very good blouses. They never run. Look, this one I'm wearing has been washed ten, twenty times, and hasn't run. Look."

Mma Ramotswe looked at the woman's blouse—the colours had certainly not run. She glanced out of the corner of her eye at the two girls. They were looking in the shoe shop window, taking their time about wherever they were going.

"You wouldn't have my size," said Mma Ramotswe. "I need a very big blouse."

The trader checked her rack and then looked at Mma Ramotswe again.

"You're right," she said. "You are too big for these blouses. Far too big."

Mma Ramotswe smiled. "But they are nice blouses, Mma, and I hope you sell them to some nice small person."

She moved on. The girls had finished with the shoe shop and were strolling up towards the Book Centre. Mma Ramotswe had been right; they were planning to hang about.

THERE WERE very few people in the Botswana Book Centre. Three or four men were paging through magazines in the periodical section, and one or two people were looking at books. The assistants were leaning over the counters, gossiping idly, and even the flies seemed lethargic.

Mma Ramotswe noticed that the two girls were at the far end of the shop, looking at a shelf of books in the Setswana section. What were they doing there? Nandira could be learning Setswana at school, but she would hardly be likely to be buying any of the schoolbooks or biblical commentaries that dominated that section. No, they must be waiting for somebody.

Mma Ramotswe walked purposefully to the African section and reached for a book. It was *The Snakes of Southern Africa,* and it was well illustrated. She gazed at a picture of a short brown snake and asked herself whether she had seen one of these. Her cousin had been bitten by a snake like that years ago, when they were children, and had come to no harm. Was that the snake? She looked at the text below the picture and read. It could well have been the same snake, because it was described as nonvenomous and not at all aggressive. But it had attacked her cousin; or had her cousin attacked it? Boys attacked snakes. They threw stones at them and seemed unable to leave them alone. But she was not sure whether Putoke had done that; it was so long ago, and she could not really remember.

She looked over at the girls. They were standing there, talking to one another again, and one of them was laughing. Some story about boys, thought Mma Ramotswe. Well, let them laugh; they'll realise soon enough that the whole subject of men was not very funny. In a few years' time it would be tears, not laughter, thought Mma Ramotswe grimly.

She returned to her perusal of *The Snakes of Southern Africa*. Now this was a bad snake, this one. There it was. Look at the head! Ow! And those evil eyes! Mma Ramotswe shuddered, and read: "The above picture is of an adult male black mamba, measuring 1.87 metres. As is shown in the distribution map, this snake is to be found throughout the region, although it has a certain preference for open veld. It differs from the green mamba, both in distribution, habitat, and toxicity of venom. The snake is one of the most dangerous snakes to be found in Africa, being outranked in this respect only by the Gaboon Viper, a rare, forest-dwelling snake found in certain parts of the eastern districts of Zimbabwe.

"Accounts of attacks by black mambas are often exaggerated,

and stories of the snake's attacking men on galloping horses, and overtaking them, are almost certainly apocryphal. The mamba can manage a considerable speed over a very short distance, but could not compete with a horse. Nor are the stories of virtually instantaneous death necessarily true, although the action of the venom can be speeded if the victim of the bite should panic, which of course he often does on realising that he has been bitten by a mamba.

"In one reliably recorded case, a twenty-six-year-old man in good physical condition sustained a mamba bite on his right ankle after he had inadvertently stepped on the snake in the bush. There was no serum immediately available, but the victim possibly succeeded in draining off some of the venom when he inflicted deep cuts on the site of the bite (not a course of action which is today regarded as helpful). He then walked some four miles through the bush to seek help and was admitted to hospital within two hours. Antivenom was administered and the victim survived unscathed; had it been a puff-adder bite, of course, there would have been considerable necrotic damage within that time and he may even have lost the leg . . ."

Mma Ramotswe paused. One leg. He would need to have an artificial leg. Mr Patel. Nandira. She looked up sharply. The snake book had so absorbed her that she had not been paying attention to the girls and now—where were they?—gone. They were gone.

She pushed *The Snakes of Southern Africa* back onto the shelf and rushed out into the square. There were more people about now, as many people did their shopping in the latter part of the afternoon, to escape the heat. She looked about her. There were some teenagers a little way away, but they were boys. No, there was a girl. But was it Nandira? No. She looked in the other direction. There was a man parking his bicycle under a tree and she noticed that the bicycle had a car aerial on it. Why?

She set off in the direction of the President Hotel. Perhaps the girls had merely gone back to the car to rejoin the mother, in which case, everything would be all right. But when she got to the car park, she saw the blue car going out at the other end, with just the mother in it. So the girls were still around, somewhere in the square.

Mma Ramotswe went back to the steps of the President Hotel and looked out over the square. She moved her gaze systematically—as Clovis Andersen recommended—looking at each group of people, scrutinising each knot of shoppers outside each shop window. There was no sign of the girls. She noticed the woman with the rack of blouses. She had a packet of some sort in her hand and was extracting what looked like a Mopani worm from within it.

"Mopani worms?" asked Mma Ramotswe.

The woman turned round and looked at her.

"Yes." She offered the bag to Mma Ramotswe, who helped herself to one of the dried tree worms and popped it into her mouth. It was a delicacy she simply could not resist.

"You must see everything that goes on, Mma," she said, as she swallowed the worm. "Standing here like this."

The woman laughed. "I see everybody. Everybody."

"Did you see two girls come out of the Book Centre?" asked Mma Ramotswe. "One Indian girl and one African girl. The Indian one about so high?"

The trader picked out another worm from her bag and popped it into her mouth.

"I saw them," she said. "They went over to the cinema. Then they went off somewhere else. I didn't notice where they were going."

Mma Ramotswe smiled. "You should be a detective," she said.

"Like you," said the woman simply.

This surprised Mma Ramotswe. She was quite well-known, but she had not necessarily expected a street trader to know who she was. She reached into her handbag and extracted a ten-pula note, which she pressed into the woman's hand.

"Thank you," she said. "That's a fee from me. And I hope you will be able to help me again some time."

The woman seemed delighted.

"I can tell you everything," she said. "I am the eyes of this place. This morning, for example, do you want to know who was talking to whom just over there? Do you know? You'd be surprised if I told you."

"Some other time," said Mma Ramotswe. "I'll be in touch."

There was no point in trying to find where Nandira had got to now, but there was every point in following up the information that she already had. So Mma Ramotswe went to the cinema and enquired as to the time of that evening's performance, which is what she concluded the two girls had been doing. Then she returned to the little white van and drove home, to prepare herself for an early supper and an outing to the cinema. She had seen the name of the film; it was not something that she wanted to sit through, but it had been at least a year since she had been to the cinema and she found that she was looking forward to the prospect.

Mr Patel telephoned before she left.

"My daughter has said that she is going out to see a friend about some homework," he said peevishly. "She is lying to me again."

"Yes," said Mma Ramotswe. "I'm afraid that she is. But I know where she's going and I shall be there, don't you worry."

"She is going to see this Jack?" shouted Mr Patel. "She is meeting this boy?"

"Probably," said Mma Ramotswe. "But there is no point in your upsetting yourself. I will give you a report tomorrow."

"Early-early, please," said Mr Patel. "I am always up at six, sharp-sharp."

THERE WERE very few people in the cinema when Mma Ramotswe arrived. She chose a seat in the penultimate row, at the back. This gave her a good view of the door through which anybody entering the auditorium would have to pass, and even if Nandira and Jack came in after the lights had gone down, it would still be possible for Mma Ramotswe to pick them out.

Mma Ramotswe recognised several of the customers. Her butcher arrived shortly after she did, and he and his wife gave her a friendly wave. Then there was one of the teachers from the school and the woman who ran the aerobics class at the President Hotel. Finally there was the Catholic bishop, who arrived by himself and ate popcorn loudly in the front row.

Nandira arrived five minutes before the first part of the programme was about to start. She was by herself, and she stood for a moment in the door, looking around her. Mma Ramotswe felt her eyes rest on her, and she looked down quickly, as if inspecting the floor for something. After a moment or two she looked up again, and saw that the girl was still looking at her.

Mma Ramotswe looked down at the floor again, and saw a discarded ticket, which she reached down to pick up.

Nandira walked purposefully across the auditorium to Mma Ramotswe's row and sat down in the seat next to her.

"Evening, Mma," she said politely. "Is this seat taken?"

Mma Ramotswe looked up, as if surprised.

"There is nobody there," she said. "It is quite free."

Nandira sat down.

"I am looking forward to this film," she said pleasantly. "I have wanted to see it for a long time."

"Good," said Mma Ramotswe. "It is nice to see a film that you've always wanted to see."

There was a silence. The girl was looking at her, and Mma Ramotswe felt quite uncomfortable. What would Clovis Andersen have done in such circumstances? She was sure that he said something about this sort of thing, but she could not quite remember what it was. This was where the subject crowded you, rather than the other way round.

"I saw you this afternoon," said Nandira. "I saw you at Maru-a-Pula."

"Ah, yes," said Mma Ramotswe. "I was waiting for somebody."

"Then I saw you in the Book Centre," Nandira continued. "You were looking at a book."

"That's right," said Mma Ramotswe. "I was thinking of buying a book."

"Then you asked Mma Bapitse about me," Nandira said quietly. "She's that trader. She told me that you were asking about me."

Mma Ramotswe made a mental note to be careful of Mma Bapitse in the future.

"So, why are you following me?" asked Nandira, turning in her seat to stare at Mma Ramotswe.

Mma Ramotswe thought quickly. There was no point in denying it, and she may as well try to make the most of a difficult situation. So she told Nandira about her father's anxieties and how he had approached her.

"He wants to find out whether you're seeing boys," she said. "He's worried about it."

Nandira looked pleased.

"Well, if he's worried, he's only got himself to blame if I keep going out with boys."

"And are you?" asked Mma Ramotswe. "Are you going out with lots of boys?"

Nandira hesitated. Then, quietly: "No. Not really."

"But what about this Jack?" asked Mma Ramotswe. "Who's he?"

For a moment it seemed as if Nandira was not going to reply. Here was another adult trying to pry into her private life, and yet there was something about Mma Ramotswe that she trusted. Perhaps she could be useful; perhaps . . .

"Jack doesn't exist," she said quietly. "I made him up."

"Why?"

Nandira shrugged. "I want them—my family—to think I've got a boyfriend," she said. "I want them to think there's somebody I chose, not somebody they thought right for me." She paused. "Do you understand that?"

Mma Ramotswe thought for a moment. She felt sorry for this poor, overprotected girl, and imagined just how in such circumstances one might want to pretend to have a boyfriend.

"Yes," she said, laying a hand on Nandira's arm. "I understand."

Nandira fidgeted with her watchstrap.

"Are you going to tell him?" she asked.

"Well, do I have much choice?" asked Mma Ramotswe. "I can hardly say that I've seen you with a boy called Jack when he doesn't really exist."

Nandira sighed. "Well, I suppose I've asked for it. It's been a silly game." She paused. "But once he realises that there's nothing in it, do you think that he might let me have a bit more freedom? Do you think that he might let me live my life for a little without having to tell him how I spend every single minute?"

"I could try to persuade him," said Mma Ramotswe. "I don't know whether he'll listen to me. But I could try."

"Please do," said Nandira. "Please try."

They watched the film together, and both enjoyed it. Then Mma Ramotswe drove Nandira back in her tiny white van, in a companionable silence, and dropped her at the gate in the high white wall. The girl stood and watched as the van drove off, and then she turned and pressed the bell.

"Patel place here. What do you want?"

"Freedom," she muttered under her breath, and then, more loudly: "It's me, Papa. I'm home now."

MMA RAMOTSWE telephoned Mr Patel early the next morning, as she had promised to do. She explained to him that it would be better for her to speak to him at home, rather than to explain matters over the telephone.

"You've got bad news for me," he said, his voice rising. "You are going to be telling me something bad-bad. Oh my God! What is it?"

Mma Ramotswe reassured him that the news was not bad,

but she still found him looking anxious when she was shown into his study half an hour later.

"I am very worried," he said. "You will not understand a father's worries. It is different for a mother. A father feels a special sort of worry."

Mma Ramotswe smiled reassuringly.

"The news is good," she said. "There is no boyfriend."

"And what about this note?" he said. "What about this Jack person? Is that all imagination?"

"Yes," said Mma Ramotswe simply. "Yes, it is."

Mr Patel looked puzzled. He lifted his walking stick and tapped his artificial leg several times. Then he opened his mouth to speak, but said nothing.

"You see," said Mma Ramotswe, "Nandira has been inventing a social life for herself. She made up a boyfriend for herself just to bring a bit of . . . of freedom into her life. The best thing you can do is just to ignore it. Give her a bit more time to lead her own life. Don't keep asking her to account for her time. There's no boyfriend and there may not even be one for some time."

Mr Patel put his walking stick down on the floor. Then he closed his eyes and appeared deep in thought.

"Why should I do this?" he said after a while. "Why should I give in to these modern ideas?"

Mma Ramotswe was ready with her answer. "Because if you don't, then the imaginary boyfriend may turn into a real one. That's why."

Mma Ramotswe watched him as he wrestled with her advice. Then, without warning he stood up, tottered for a while before he got his balance, and then turned to face her.

"You are a very clever woman," he said. "And I'm going to

take your advice. I will leave her to get on with her life, and then I am sure that in two or three years she will agree with us and allow me to arra . . . to help her to find a suitable man to marry."

"That could easily happen," said Mma Ramotswe, breathing a sigh of relief.

"Yes," said Mr Patel warmly. "And I shall have you to thank for it all!"

MMA RAMOTSWE often thought about Nandira when she drove past the Patel compound, with its high white wall. She expected to see her from time to time, now that she knew what she looked like, but she never did, at least not until a year later, when, while taking her Saturday morning coffee on the verandah of the President Hotel, she felt somebody tap her shoulder. She turned round in her seat, and there was Nandira, with a young man. The young man was about eighteen, she thought, and he had a pleasant, open expression.

"Mma Ramotswe," said Nandira in a friendly way. "I thought it was you."

Mma Ramotswe shook Nandira's hand. The young man smiled at her.

"This is my friend," said Nandira. "I don't think you've met him."

The young man stepped forward and held out his hand.

"Jack," he said.

MMA RAMOTSWE THINKS ABOUT THE LAND WHILE DRIVING HER TINY WHITE VAN TO FRANCISTOWN

MMA RAMOTSWE drove her tiny white van before dawn along the sleeping roads of Gaborone, past the Kalahari Breweries, past the Dry Lands Research Station, and out onto the road that led north. A man leaped out from bushes at the side of the road and tried to flag her down; but she was unwilling to stop in the dark, for you never knew who might be wanting a lift at such an hour. He disappeared into the shadows again, and in her mirror she saw him deflate with disappointment. Then, just past the Mochudi turnoff, the sun came up, rising over the wide plains that stretched away towards the course of the Limpopo. Suddenly it was there, smiling on Africa, a slither of golden red ball, inching up, floating effortlessly free of the horizon to dispel the last wisps of morning mist.

The thorn trees stood clear in the sharp light of morning, and there were birds upon them, and in flight—hoopoes,

louries, and tiny birds which she could not name. Here and there cattle stood at the fence which followed the road for mile upon mile. They raised their heads and stared, or ambled slowly on, tugging at the tufts of dry grass that clung tenaciously to the hardened earth.

This was a dry land. Just a short distance to the west lay the Kalahari, a hinterland of ochre that stretched off, for unimaginable miles, to the singing emptinesses of the Namib. If she turned her tiny white van off on one of the tracks that struck off from the main road, she could drive for perhaps thirty or forty miles before her wheels would begin to sink into the sand and spin hopelessly. The vegetation would slowly become sparser, more desert-like. The thorn trees would thin out and there would be ridges of thin earth, through which the omnipresent sand would surface and crenellate. There would be patches of bareness, and scattered grey rocks, and there would be no sign of human activity. To live with this great dry interior, brown and hard, was the lot of the Batswana, and it was this that made them cautious, and careful in their husbandry.

If you went there, out into the Kalahari, you might hear lions by night. For the lions were there still, on these wide landscapes, and they made their presence known in the darkness, in coughing grunts and growls. She had been there once as a young woman, when she had gone with her friend to visit a remote cattle post. It was as far into the Kalahari as cattle could go, and she had felt the utter loneliness of a place without people. This was Botswana distilled; the essence of her country.

It was the rainy season, and the land was covered with green. Rain could transform it so quickly, and had done so;

now the ground was covered with shoots of sweet new grass, Namaqualand daisies, the vines of Tsama melons, and aloes with stalk flowers of red and yellow.

They had made a fire at night, just outside the crude huts which served as shelter at the cattle post, but the light from the fire seemed so tiny under the great empty night sky with its dipping constellations. She had huddled close to her friend, who had told her that she should not be frightened, because lions would keep away from fires, as would supernatural beings, *tokoloshes* and the like.

She awoke in the small hours of the morning, and the fire was low. She could make out its embers through the spaces between the branches that made up the wall of the hut. Somewhere, far away, there was a grunting sound, but she was not afraid, and she walked out of the hut to stand underneath the sky and draw the dry, clear air into her lungs. And she thought: I am just a tiny person in Africa, but there is a place for me, and for everybody, to sit down on this earth and touch it and call it their own. She waited for another thought to come, but none did, and so she crept back into the hut and the warmth of the blankets on her sleeping mat.

Now, driving the tiny white van along those rolling miles, she thought that one day she might go back into the Kalahari, into those empty spaces, those wide grasslands that broke and broke the heart.

CHAPTER ELEVEN

BIG CAR GUILT

I T WAS three days after the satisfactory resolution of the Patel case. Mma Ramotswe had put in her bill for two thousand pula, plus expenses, and had been paid by return of post. This astonished her. She could not believe that she would be paid such a sum without protest, and the readiness, and apparent cheerfulness with which Mr Patel had settled the bill induced pangs of guilt over the sheer size of the fee.

It was curious how some people had a highly developed sense of guilt, she thought, while others had none. Some people would agonise over minor slips or mistakes on their part, while others would feel quite unmoved by their own gross acts of betrayal or dishonesty. Mma Pekwane fell into the former category, thought Mma Ramotswe. Note Mokoti fell into the latter.

Mma Pekwane had seemed anxious when she had come into the office of the No. 1 Ladies' Detective Agency. Mma Ramotswe had given her a strong cup of bush tea, as she always did with nervous clients, and had waited for her to be ready to speak. She was anxious about a man, she thought; there were all the signs. What would it be? Some piece of masculine bad behaviour, of course, but what?

"I'm worried that my husband has done a dreadful thing," said Mma Pekwane eventually. "I feel very ashamed for him."

Mma Ramotswe nodded her head gently. Masculine bad behaviour.

"Men do terrible things," she said. "All wives are worried about their husbands. You are not alone."

Mma Pekwane sighed. "But my husband has done a terrible thing," she said. "A very terrible thing."

Mma Ramotswe stiffened. If Rra Pekwane had killed somebody she would have to make it quite clear that the police should be called in. She would never dream of helping anybody conceal a murderer.

"What is this terrible thing?" she asked.

Mma Pekwane lowered her voice. "He has a stolen car."

Mma Ramotswe was relieved. Car theft was rife, almost unremarkable, and there must be many women driving around the town in their husbands' stolen cars. Mma Ramotswe could never imagine herself doing that, of course, and nor, it seemed, could Mma Pekwane.

"Did he tell you it's stolen?" she asked. "Are you sure of it?"

Mma Pekwane shook her head. "He said a man gave it to him. He said that this man had two Mercedes-Benzes and only needed one."

Mma Ramotswe laughed. "Do men really think they can fool us that easily?" she said. "Do they think we're fools?"

"I think they do," said Mma Pekwane.

Mma Ramotswe picked up her pencil and drew several lines

on her blotter. Looking at the scribbles, she saw that she had drawn a car.

She looked at Mma Pekwane. "Do you want me to tell you what to do?" she asked. "Is that what you want?"

Mma Pekwane looked thoughtful. "No," she replied. "I don't want that. I've decided what I want to do."

"And that is?"

"I want to give the car back. I want to give it back to its owner."

Mma Ramotswe sat up straight. "You want to go to the police then? You want to inform on your husband?"

"No. I don't want to do that. I just want the car to get back to its owner without the police knowing. I want the Lord to know that the car's back where it belongs."

Mma Ramotswe stared at her client. It was, she had to admit, a perfectly reasonable thing to want. If the car were to be returned to the owner, then Mma Pekwane's conscience would be clear, and she would still have her husband. On mature reflection, it seemed to Mma Ramotswe to be a very good way of dealing with a difficult situation.

"But why come to me about this?" asked Mma Ramotswe. "How can I help?"

Mma Pekwane gave her answer without hesitation.

"I want you to find out who owns that car," she said. "Then I want you to steal it from my husband and give it back to the rightful owner. That's all I want you to do."

LATER THAT evening, as she drove home in her little white van, Mma Ramotswe thought that she should never have agreed to help Mma Pekwane; but she had, and now she was committed. Yet it was not going to be a simple matter—unless, of course, one went to the police, which she clearly could not do. It may be that Rra Pekwane deserved to be handed over, but her client had asked that this should not happen, and her first loyalty was to the client. So some other way would have to be found.

That evening, after her supper of chicken and pumpkin, Mma Ramotswe telephoned Mr J.L.B. Matekoni.

"Where do stolen Mercedes-Benzes come from?" asked Mma Ramotswe.

"From over the border," said Mr J.L.B. Matekoni. "They steal them in South Africa, bring them over here, respray them, file off the original engine number, and then sell them cheaply or send them up to Zambia. I know who does all this, by the way. We all know."

"I don't need to know that," said Mma Ramotswe. "What I need to know is how you identify them after all this has happened."

Mr J.L.B. Matekoni paused. "You have to know where to look," he said. "There's usually another serial number somewhere—on the chassis—or under the bonnet. You can usually find it if you know what you're doing."

"You know what you're doing," said Mma Ramotswe. "Can you help me?"

Mr J.L.B. Matekoni sighed. He did not like stolen cars. He preferred to have nothing to do with them, but this was a request from Mma Ramotswe, and so there was only one answer to give.

"Tell me where and when," he said.

*   *   *

THEY ENTERED the Pekwane garden the following evening, by arrangement with Mma Pekwane, who had promised that at the agreed time she would make sure that the dogs were inside and her husband would be busy eating a special meal she would prepare for him. So there was nothing to stop Mr J.L.B. Matekoni from wriggling under the Mercedes-Benz parked in the yard and flashing his torch up into the bodywork. Mma Ramotswe offered to go under the car as well, but Mr J.L.B. Matekoni doubted whether she would fit and declined her offer. Ten minutes later, he had a serial number written on a piece of paper and the two of them slipped out of the Pekwane yard and made their way to the small white van parked down the road.

"Are you sure that's all I'll need?" asked Mma Ramotswe. "Will they know from that?"

"Yes," said Mr J.L.B. Matekoni. "They'll know."

She dropped him off outside his gate and he waved goodbye in the darkness. She would be able to repay him soon, she knew.

THAT WEEKEND, Mma Ramotswe drove her tiny white van over the border to Mafikeng and went straight to the Railway Café. She bought a copy of the *Johannesburg Star* and sat at a table near the window reading the news. It was all bad, she decided, and so she laid the paper to one side and passed the time by looking at her fellow customers.

"Mma Ramotswe!"

She looked up. There he was, the same old Billy Pilani, older now, of course, but otherwise the same. She could just see him at the Mochudi Government School, sitting at his desk, dreaming.

She bought him a cup of coffee and a large doughnut and explained to him what she needed.

"I want you to find out who owns this car," she said, passing the slip of paper with the serial number written on it in the handwriting of Mr J.L.B. Matekoni. "Then, when you've found out, I want you to tell the owner, or the insurance company, or whoever, that they can come up to Gaborone and they will find their car ready for them in an agreed place. All they have to do is to bring South African number plates with the original number on them. Then they can drive the car home."

Billy Pilani looked surprised.

"All for nothing?" he asked. "Nothing to be paid?"

"Nothing," said Mma Ramotswe. "It's just a question of returning property to its rightful owner. That's all. You believe in that, don't you Billy?"

"Of course," said Billy Pilani quickly. "Of course."

"And Billy I want you to forget you're a policeman while all this is going on. There's not going to be any arrest for you."

"Not even a small one?" asked Billy in a disappointed tone.

"Not even that."

BILLY PILANI telephoned the following day.

"I've got the details from our list of stolen vehicles," he said. "I've spoken to the insurance company, who've already paid out. So they'd be very happy to get the car back. They can send one of their men over the border to pick it up."

"Good," said Mma Ramotswe. "They are to be in the African

Mall in Gaborone at seven o'clock in the morning next Tuesday, with the number plates."

Everything was agreed, and at five o'clock on the Tuesday morning, Mma Ramotswe crept into the yard of the Pekwane house and found, as she had been expecting, the keys of the Mercedes-Benz lying on the ground outside the bedroom window, where Mma Pekwane had tossed them the previous night. She had been assured by Mma Pekwane that her husband was a sound sleeper and that he never woke up until Radio Botswana broadcast the sound of cowbells at six.

He did not hear her start the car and drive out onto the road, and indeed it was not until almost eight o'clock that he noticed that his Mercedes-Benz was stolen.

"Call the police," shouted Mma Pekwane. "Quick, call the police!"

She noticed that her husband was hesitating.

"Maybe later," he said. "In the meantime, I think I shall look for it myself."

She looked him directly in the eye, and for a moment she saw him flinch. He's guilty, she thought. I was right all along. Of course he can't go to the police and tell them that his stolen car has been stolen.

She saw Mma Ramotswe later that day and thanked her.

"You've made me feel much better," she said. "I shall now be able to sleep at night without feeling guilty for my husband."

"I'm very pleased," said Mma Ramotswe. "And maybe he's learned a lesson too. A very interesting lesson."

"What would that be?" asked Mma Pekwane.

"That lightning always strikes in the same place twice," said Mma Ramotswe. "Whatever people say to the contrary."

CHAPTER TWELVE

MMA RAMOTSWE'S HOUSE IN ZEBRA DRIVE

THE HOUSE had been built in 1968, when the town inched out from the shops and the Government Buildings. It was on a corner site, which was not always a good thing, as people would sometimes stand on that corner, under the thorn trees that grew there, and spit into her garden, or throw their rubbish over her fence. At first, when she saw them doing that, she would shout from the window, or bang a dustbin lid at them, but they seemed to have no shame, these people, and they just laughed. So she gave up, and the young man who did her garden for her every third day would just pick up the rubbish and put it away. That was the only problem with that house. For the rest, Mma Ramotswe was fiercely proud of it, and daily reflected on her good fortune in being able to buy it when she did, just before house prices went so high that honest people could no longer pay them.

The yard was a large one, almost two-thirds of an acre, and

it was well endowed with trees and shrubs. The trees were nothing special—thorn trees for the most part—but they gave good shade, and they never died if the rains were bad. Then there were the purple bougainvillaeas which had been enthusiastically planted by the previous owners, and which had almost taken over by the time Mma Ramotswe came. She had to cut these back, to give space for her pawpaws and her pumpkins.

At the front of the house there was a verandah, which was her favourite place, and which was where she liked to sit in the mornings, when the sun rose, or in the evenings, before the mosquitoes came out. She had extended it by placing an awning of shade netting supported by rough-hewn poles. This filtered out many of the rays of the sun and allowed plants to grow in the green light it created. There she had elephant-ear and ferns, which she watered daily, and which made a lush patch of green against the brown earth.

Behind the verandah was the living room, the largest room in the house, with its big window that gave out onto what had once been a lawn. There was a fireplace here, too large for the room, but a matter of pride for Mma Ramotswe. On the mantelpiece she had placed her special china, her Queen Elizabeth II teacup and her commemoration plate with the picture of Sir Seretse Khama, President, *Kgosi* of the Bangwato people, Statesman. He smiled at her from the plate, and it was as if he gave a blessing, as if he knew. As did the Queen, for she loved Botswana too, and understood.

But in pride of place was the photograph of her Daddy, taken just before his sixtieth birthday. He was wearing the suit which he had bought in Bulawayo on his visit to his cousin there, and he was smiling, although she knew that by then he was in pain. Mma Ramotswe was a realist, who inhabited the present, but one nostalgic thought she allowed herself, one indulgence, was to imagine her Daddy walking through the door and greeting her again, and smiling at her, and saying: "My Precious! You have done well! I am proud of you!" And she imagined driving him round Gaborone in her tiny white van and showing him the progress that had been made, and she smiled at the pride he would have felt. But she could not allow herself to think like this too often, for it ended in tears, for all that was passed, and for all the love that she had within her.

The kitchen was cheerful. The cement floor, sealed and polished with red floor paint, was kept shining by Mma Ramotswe's maid, Rose, who had been with her for five years. Rose had four children, by different fathers, who lived with her mother at Tlokweng. She worked for Mma Ramotswe, and did knitting for a knitting cooperative, and brought her children up with the little money that there was. The oldest boy was a carpenter now, and was giving his mother money, which helped, but the little ones were always needing shoes and new trousers, and one of them could not breathe well and needed an inhaler. But Rose still sang, and this was how Mma Ramotswe knew she had arrived in the morning, as the snatches of song came drifting in from the kitchen.

CHAPTER THIRTEEN

WHY DON'T YOU MARRY ME?

HAPPINESS? MMA Ramotswe was happy enough. With her detective agency and her house in Zebra Drive, she had more than most, and was aware of it. She was also aware of how things had changed. When she had been married to Note Mokoti she had been conscious of a deep, overwhelming unhappiness that followed her around like a black dog. That had gone now.

If she had listened to her father, if she had listened to the cousin's husband, she would never have married Note and the years of unhappiness would never have occurred. But they did, because she was headstrong, as everybody is at the age of twenty, and when we simply cannot see, however much we may think we can. The world is full of twenty-year-olds, she thought, all of them blind.

Obed Ramotswe had never taken to Note, and had told her that, directly. But she had responded by crying and by saying that he was the only man she would ever find and that he would make her happy.

"He will not," said Obed. "That man will hit you. He will use you in all sorts of ways. He thinks only of himself and what he wants. I can tell, because I have been in the mines and you see all sorts of men there. I have seen men like that before."

She had shaken her head and rushed out of the room, and he had called out after her, a thin, pained, cry. She could hear it now, and it cut and cut at her. She had hurt the man who loved her more than any other, a good, trusting man who only wanted to protect her. If only one could undo the past; if one could go back and avoid the mistakes, make different choices . . .

"If we could go back," said Mr J.L.B. Matekoni, pouring tea into Mma Ramotswe's mug. "I have often thought that. If we could go back and know then what we know now . . ." He shook his head in wonderment. "My goodness! I would live my life differently!"

Mma Ramotswe sipped at her tea. She was sitting in the office of Tlokweng Road Speedy Motors, underneath Mr J.L.B. Matekoni's spares suppliers' calendar, passing the time of day with her friend, as she sometimes did when her own office was quiet. This was inevitable; sometimes people simply did not want to find things out. Nobody was missing, nobody was cheating on their wives, nobody was embezzling. At such times, a private detective may as well hang a closed sign on the office door and go off to plant melons. Not that she intended to plant melons; a quiet cup of tea followed by a shopping trip to the African Mall was as good a way of spending the afternoon as any. Then she might go to the Book Centre and see if any interesting magazines had arrived. She loved magazines. She loved their smell and their bright pictures. She loved interior design magazines which showed how people lived in faraway countries. They had so much in their houses, and such beautiful things too. Paintings, rich curtains, piles of velvet cushions which would have been wonderful for a fat person to sit upon, strange lights at odd angles . . .

Mr J.L.B. Matekoni warmed to his theme.

"I have made hundreds of mistakes in my lifetime," he said, frowning at the recollection. "Hundreds and hundreds."

She looked at him. She had thought that everything had gone rather well in his life. He had served his apprenticeship as a mechanic, saved up his money, and then bought his own garage. He had built a house, married a wife (who had unfortunately died), and become the local chairman of the Botswana Democratic Party. He knew several ministers (very slightly) and was invited to one of the annual garden parties at State House. Everything seemed rosy.

"I can't see what mistakes you've made," she said. "Unlike me."

Mr J.L.B. Matekoni looked surprised.

"I can't imagine you making any mistakes," she said. "You're too clever for that. You would look at all the possibilities and then choose the right one. Every time."

Mma Ramotswe snorted.

"I married Note," she said simply.

Mr J.L.B. Matekoni looked thoughtful.

"Yes," he said. "That was a bad mistake."

They were silent for a moment. Then he rose to his feet. He was a tall man, and he had to be careful not to bump his head when he stood erect. Now, with the calendar behind him and the fly paper dangling down from the ceiling above, he cleared his throat and spoke.

"I would like you to marry me," he said. "That would not be a mistake."

Mma Ramotswe hid her surprise. She did not give a start, nor drop her mug of tea, nor open her mouth and make no sound. She smiled instead, and stared at her friend.

"You are a good kind man," she said. "You are like my Daddy . . . a bit. But I cannot get married again. Ever. I am happy as I am. I have got the agency, and the house. My life is full."

Mr J.L.B. Matekoni sat down. He looked crestfallen, and Mma Ramotswe reached out to touch him. He moved it away instinctively, as a burned man will move away from fire.

"I am very sorry," she said. "I should like you to know that if I were ever to marry anybody, which I shall not do, I would choose a man like you. I would even choose you. I am sure of this."

Mr J.L.B. Matekoni took her mug and poured her more tea. He was silent now—not out of anger, or resentment—but because it had cost him all his energy to make his declaration of love and he had no more words for the time being.

HANDSOME MAN

ALICE BUSANG was nervous about consulting Mma Ramotswe, but was soon put at ease by the comfortable, overweight figure sitting behind the desk. It was rather like speaking to a doctor or a priest, she thought; in such consultations nothing that one could possibly say would shock.

"I am suspicious of my husband," she said. "I think that he is carrying on with ladies."

Mma Ramotswe nodded. All men carried on with ladies, in her experience. The only men who did not were ministers of religion and headmasters.

"Have you seen him doing this?" she asked.

Alice Busang shook her head. "I keep watching out but I never see him with other women. I think he is too cunning."

Mma Ramotswe wrote this down on a piece of paper.

"He goes to bars, does he?"

"Yes."

"That's where they meet them. They meet these women who hang about in bars waiting for other women's husbands. This city is full of women like that."

She looked at Alice, and there flowed between them a brief current of understanding. All women in Botswana were the victims of the fecklessness of men. There were virtually no men these days who would marry a woman and settle down to look after her children; men like that seemed to be a thing of the past.

"Do you want me to follow him?" she said. "Do you want me to find out whether he picks up other women?"

Alice Busang nodded. "Yes," she said. "I want proof. Just for myself. I want proof so that I can know what sort of man I married."

MMA RAMOTSWE was too busy to take on the Busang case until the following week. That Wednesday, she stationed herself in her small white van outside the office in the Diamond Sorting Building where Kremlin Busang worked. She had been given a photograph of him by Alice Busang and she glanced at this on her knee; this was a handsome man, with broad shoulders and a wide smile. He was a ladies' man by the look of him, and she wondered why Alice Busang had married him if she wanted a faithful husband. Hopefulness, of course; a naïve hope that he would be unlike other men. Well, you only had to look at him to realise that this would not be so.

She followed him, her white van trailing his old blue car through the traffic to the Go Go Handsome Man's Bar down by the bus station. Then, while he strolled into the bar, she sat for a moment in her van and put a little more lipstick on her lips and a dab of cream on her cheeks. In a few minutes she would go in and begin work in earnest.

IT WAS not crowded inside the Go Go Handsome Man's Bar and there were only one or two other women there. Both of them she recognised as bad women. They stared at her, but she ignored them and took a seat at the bar, just two stools from Kremlin Busang.

She bought a beer and looked about her, as if taking in the surroundings of the bar for the first time.

"You've not been here before, my sister," said Kremlin Busang. "It's a good bar, this one."

She met his gaze. "I only come to bars on big occasions," she said. "Such as today."

Kremlin Busang smiled. "Your birthday?"

"Yes," she said. "Let me buy you a drink to celebrate."

She bought him a beer, and he moved over to the stool beside her. She saw that he was a good-looking man, exactly as his photograph had revealed him, and his clothes were well chosen. They drank their beers together, and then she ordered him another one. He began to tell her about his job.

"I sort diamonds," he said. "It's a difficult job, you know. You need good eyesight."

"I like diamonds," she said. "I like diamonds a lot."

"We are very lucky to have so many diamonds in this country," he said. "My word! Those diamonds!"

She moved her left leg slightly, and it touched his. He noticed this, as she saw him glance down, but he did not move his leg away.

"Are you married?" she asked him quietly.

He did not hesitate. "No. I've never been married. It's better to be single these days. Freedom, you know."

She nodded. "I like to be free too," she said. "Then you can decide how to spend your own time."

"Exactly," he said. "Dead right."

She drained her glass.

"I must go," she said, and then, after a short pause: "Maybe you'd like to come back for a drink at my place. I've got some beer there."

He smiled. "Yes. That's a good idea. I had nothing to do either."

He followed her home in his car and together they went into her house and turned on some music. She poured him a beer, and he drank half of it in one gulp. Then he put his arm around her waist, and told her that he liked good, fat women. All this business about being thin was nonsense and was quite wrong for Africa.

"Fat women like you are what men really want," he said.

She giggled. He was charming, she had to admit it, but this was work and she must be quite professional. She must remember that she needed evidence, and that might be more difficult to get.

"Come and sit by me," she said. "You must be tired after standing up all day, sorting diamonds."

SHE HAD her excuses ready, and he accepted them without protest. She had to be at work early the next morning and he could not stay. But it would be a pity to end such a good evening and have no memento of it.

"I want to take a photograph of us, just for me to keep. So that I can look at it and remember tonight."

He smiled at her and pinched her gently.

"Good idea."

So she set up her camera, with its delayed switch, and leapt back on the sofa to join him. He pinched her again and put his arm around her and kissed her passionately as the flash went off.

"We can publish that in the newspapers if you like," he said. "Mr Handsome with his friend Miss Fatty."

She laughed. "You're a ladies' man all right, Kremlin. You're a real ladies' man. I knew it first time I saw you."

"Well somebody has to look after the ladies," he said.

ALICE BUSANG returned to the office that Friday and found Mma Ramotswe waiting for her.

"I'm afraid that I can tell you that your husband is unfaithful," she said. "I've got proof."

Alice closed her eyes. She had expected this, but she had not wanted it. She would kill him, she thought; but no, I still love him. I hate him. No, I love him.

Mma Ramotswe handed her the photograph. "There's your proof," she said.

Alice Busang stared at the picture. Surely not! Yes, it was her! It was the detective lady.

"You . . ." she stuttered. "You were with my husband?"

"He was with me," said Mma Ramotswe. "You wanted proof, didn't you? I got the best proof you could hope for."

Alice Busang dropped the photograph.

"But you . . . you went with my husband. You . . ."

Mma Ramotswe frowned. "You asked me to trap him, didn't you?"

Alice Busang's eyes narrowed. "You bitch!" she screamed. "You fat bitch! You took my Kremlin! You husband-stealer! Thief!"

Mma Ramotswe looked at her client with dismay. This would be a case, she thought, where she might have to waive the fee.

CHAPTER FIFTEEN

MR J.L.B. MATEKONI'S DISCOVERY

ALICE BUSANG was ushered out of the agency still shouting her insults at Mma Ramotswe.

"You fat tart! You think you're a detective! You're just man hungry, like all those bar girls! Don't be taken in everyone! This woman isn't a detective. No. 1 Husband Stealing Agency, that's what this is!"

When the row had died away, Mma Ramotswe and Mma Makutsi looked at one another. What could one do but laugh? That woman had known all along what her husband was up to, but had insisted on proof. And when she got the proof, she blamed the messenger.

"Look after the office while I go off to the garage," said Mma Ramotswe. "I just have to tell Mr J.L.B. Matekoni about this."

He was in his glass-fronted office cubicle, tinkering with a distributor cap.

"Sand gets everywhere these days," he said. "Look at this."

He extracted a fragment of silica from a metal duct and showed it triumphantly to his visitor.

"This little thing stopped a large truck in its tracks," he said. "This tiny piece of sand."

"For want of a nail, the shoe was lost," said Mma Ramotswe, remembering a distant afternoon in the Mochudi Government School when the teacher had quoted this to them. "For want of a shoe, the . . ." She stopped. It refused to come back.

"The horse fell down," volunteered Mr J.L.B. Matekoni. "I was taught that too."

He put the distributor cap down on his table and went off to fill the kettle. It was a hot afternoon, and a cup of tea would make them both feel better.

She told him about Alice Busang and her reaction to the proof of Kremlin's activities.

"You should have seen him," she said. "A real ladies' man. Stuff in his hair. Dark glasses. Fancy shoes. He had no idea how funny he looked. I much prefer men with ordinary shoes and honest trousers."

Mr J.L.B. Matekoni cast an anxious glance down at his shoes—scruffy old suede boots covered with grease—and at his trousers. Were they honest?

"I couldn't even charge her a fee," Mma Ramotswe went on. "Not after that."

Mr J.L.B. Matekoni nodded. He seemed preoccupied by something. He had not picked up the distributor cap again and was staring out of the window.

"You're worried about something?" She wondered whether her refusal of his proposal had upset him more than she imagined. He was not the sort to bear grudges, but did he resent her? She did not want to lose his friendship—he was her best

friend in town, in a way, and life without his comforting presence would be distinctly the poorer. Why did love—and sex—
complicate life so much? It would be far simpler for us not to
have to worry about them. Sex played no part in her life now
and she found that a great relief. She did not have to worry
how she looked; what people thought of her. How terrible to
be a man, and to have sex on one's mind all the time, as men
are supposed to do. She had read in one of her magazines that
the average man thought about sex over sixty times a day! She
could not believe that figure, but studies had apparently revealed
it. The average man, going about his daily business, had all
those thoughts in his mind; thoughts of pushing and shoving,
as men do, while he was actually doing something else! Did
doctors think about it as they took your pulse? Did lawyers
think about it as they sat at their desks and plotted? Did pilots
think about it as they flew their aeroplanes? It simply beggared
belief.

And Mr J.L.B. Matekoni, with his innocent expression and
his plain face, was he thinking about it while he looked into
distributor caps or heaved batteries out of engines? She looked
at him; how could one tell? Did a man thinking about sex start
to leer, or open his mouth and show his pink tongue, or . . .
No. That was impossible.

"What are you thinking about, Mr J.L.B. Matekoni?" The
question slipped out, and she immediately regretted it. It was
as if she had challenged him to confess that he was thinking
about sex.

He stood up and closed the door, which had been slightly
ajar. There was nobody to overhear them. The two mechanics
were at the other end of the garage, drinking their afternoon
tea, thinking about sex, thought Mma Ramotswe.

"If you hadn't come to see me, I would have come to see you," said Mr J.L.B. Matekoni. "I have found something, you see."

She felt relieved; so he was not upset about her turning him down. She looked at him expectantly.

"There was an accident," said Mr J.L.B. Matekoni. "It was not a bad one. Nobody was hurt. Shaken a bit, but not hurt. It was at the old four-way stop. A truck coming along from the roundabout didn't stop. It hit a car coming from the Village. The car was pushed into the storm ditch and was quite badly dented. The truck had a smashed headlight and a little bit of damage to the radiator. That's all."

"And?"

Mr J.L.B. Matekoni sat down and stared at his hands.

"I was called to pull the car out of the ditch. I took my rescue truck and we winched it up. Then we towed it back here and left it round the back. I'll show it to you later."

He paused for a moment before continuing. The story seemed simple enough, but it appeared to be costing him a considerable effort to tell it.

"I looked it over. It was a panel-beating job and I could easily get my panel-beater to take it off to his workshop and sort it out. But there were one or two things I would have to do first. I had to check the electrics, for a start. These new expensive cars have so much wiring that a little knock here or there can make everything go wrong. You won't be able to lock your doors if the wires are nicked. Or your antitheft devices will freeze everything solid. It's very complicated, as those two boys out there drinking their tea on my time are only just finding out."

"Anyway, I had to get at a fuse box under the dashboard, and while I was doing this, I inadvertently opened the glove compartment. I looked inside—I don't know why—but something made me do it. And I found something. A little bag."

Mma Ramotswe's mind was racing ahead. He had stumbled upon illicit diamonds—she was sure of it.

"Diamonds?"

"No," said Mr J.L.B. Matekoni. "Worse than that."

SHE LOOKED at the small bag which he had taken out of his safe and placed on the table. It was made of animal skin—a pouch really—and was similar to the bags which the Basarwa ornamented with fragments of ostrich shell and used to store herbs and pastes for their arrows.

"I'll open it," he said. "I don't want to make you touch it."

She watched as he untied the strings that closed the mouth of the bag. His expression was one of distaste, as if he were handling something with an offensive smell.

And there was a smell, a dry, musty odour, as he extracted the three small objects from the bag. Now she understood. He need say nothing further. Now she understood why he had seemed so distracted and uncomfortable. Mr J.L.B. Matekoni had found muti. He had found medicine.

She said nothing as the objects were laid out on the table. What could one say about these pitiful remnants, about the bone, about the piece of skin, about the little wooden bottle, stoppered, and its awful contents?

Mr J.L.B. Matekoni, reluctant to touch the objects, poked at the bone with a pencil.

"See," he said simply. "That's what I found."

Mma Ramotswe got up from her chair and walked towards the door. She felt her stomach heave, as one does when confronted with a nauseous odour, a dead donkey in a ditch, the overpowering smell of carrion.

The feeling passed and she turned round.

"I'm going to take that bone and check," she said. "We could be wrong. It could be an animal. A duiker. A hare."

Mr J.L.B. Matekoni shook his head. "It won't be," he said. "I know what they'll say."

"Even so," said Mma Ramotswe. "Put it in an envelope and I'll take it."

Mr J.L.B. Matekoni opened his mouth to speak, but thought better of it. He was going to warn her, to tell her that it was dangerous to play around with these things, but that would imply that one believed in their power, and he did not. Did he?

She put the envelope in her pocket and smiled.

"Nothing can happen to me now," she said. "I'm protected."

Mr J.L.B. Matekoni tried to laugh at her joke, but found that he could not. It was tempting Providence to use those words and he hoped that she would not have cause to regret them.

"There's one thing I'd like to know," said Mma Ramotswe, as she left the office. "That car—who owned it?"

Mr J.L.B. Matekoni glanced at the two mechanics. They were both out of earshot, but he lowered his voice nonetheless while he told her.

"Charlie Gotso," he said. "Him. That one."

Mma Ramotswe's eyes widened.

"Gotso? The important one?"

Mr J.L.B. Matekoni nodded. Everyone knew Charlie Gotso. He was one of the most influential men in the country. He had the ear of . . . well, he had the ear of just about everyone who counted. There was no door in the country closed to him, nobody who would turn down a request for a favour. If Charlie Gotso asked you to do something for him, you did it. If you did not, then you might find that life became more difficult later on. It was always very subtly done—your application for a licence for your business may encounter unexpected delays; or you may find that there always seemed to be speed traps on your particular route to work; or your staff grew restless and went to work for somebody else. There was never anything you could put your finger on—that was not the way in Botswana, but the effect would be very real.

"Oh dear," said Mma Ramotswe.

"Exactly," said Mr J.L.B. Matekoni. "Oh dear."

CHAPTER SIXTEEN

THE CUTTING OF FINGERS
AND SNAKES

IN THE beginning, which in Gaborone really means thirty years ago, there were very few factories. In fact, when Princess Marina watched as the Union Jack was hauled down in the stadium on that windy night in 1966 and the Bechuanaland Protectorate ceased to exist, there were none. Mma Ramotswe had been an eight-year-old girl then, a pupil at the Government School at Mochudi, and only vaguely aware that anything special was happening and that something which people called freedom had arrived. But she had not felt any different the next day, and she wondered what this freedom meant. Now she knew of course, and her heart filled with pride when she thought of all they had achieved in thirty short years. The great swathe of territory which the British really had not known what to do with had prospered to become the best-run state in Africa, by far. Well could people shout Pula! Pula! Rain! Rain! with pride.

Gaborone had grown, changing out of all recognition. When she first went there as a little girl there had been little more than several rings of houses about the Mall and the few government offices—much bigger than Mochudi, of course, and so much more impressive, with the government buildings and Seretse Khama's house. But it was still quite small, really, if you had seen photographs of Johannesburg, or even Bulawayo. And no factories. None at all.

Then, little by little, things had changed. Somebody built a furniture workshop which produced sturdy living-room chairs. Then somebody else decided to set up a small factory to make breeze-blocks for building houses. Others followed, and soon there was a block of land on the Lobatse Road which people began to call the Industrial Sites. This caused a great stir of pride; so this is what freedom brought, people thought. There was the Legislative Assembly and the House of Chiefs, of course, where people could say what they liked—and did— but there were also these little factories and the jobs that went with them. Now there was even a truck factory on the Francistown Road, assembling ten trucks a month to send up as far as the Congo; and all of this started from nothing!

Mma Ramotswe knew one or two factory managers, and one factory owner. The factory owner, a Motswana who had come into the country from South Africa to enjoy the freedom denied him on the other side, had set up his bolt works with a tiny amount of capital, a few scraps of secondhand machinery bought from a bankruptcy sale in Bulawayo, and a workforce consisting of his brother-in-law, himself, and a mentally handicapped boy whom he had found sitting under a tree and who had proved to be quite capable of sorting bolts. The business had prospered, largely because the idea behind it was so simple. All that the factory made was a single sort of bolt, of the sort which was needed for fixing galvanised tin roof sheeting onto roof beams. This was a simple process, which required only one sort of machine—a machine of a sort that never seemed to break down and rarely needed servicing.

Hector Lepodise's factory grew rapidly, and by the time Mma Ramotswe got to know him, he was employing thirty people and producing bolts that held roofs onto their beams as far north as Malawi. At first all his employees had been his relatives, with the exception of the mentally handicapped boy, who had subsequently been promoted to tea-boy. As the business grew, however, the supply of relatives dwindled, and Hector began to employ strangers. He maintained his earlier paternalistic employment habits, though—there was always plenty of time off for funerals as well as full pay for those who were genuinely sick—and his workers, as a result, were usually fiercely loyal to him. Yet with a staff of thirty, of whom only twelve were relatives, it was inevitable that there would be some who would attempt to exploit his kindness, and this is where Mma Ramotswe came in.

"I can't put my finger on it," said Hector, as he drank coffee with Mma Ramotswe on the verandah of the President Hotel, "but I've never trusted that man. He only came to me about six months ago, and now this."

"Where had he been working before?" asked Mma Ramotswe. "What did they say about him?"

Hector shrugged. "He had a reference from a factory over the border. I wrote to them but they didn't bother to reply. Some of them don't take us seriously, you know. They treat us as one of their wretched Bantustans. You know what they're like."

Mma Ramotswe nodded. She did. They were not all bad, of course. But many of them were awful, which somehow eclipsed the better qualities of some of the nice ones. It was very sad.

"So he came to me just six months ago," Hector continued. "He was quite good at working the machinery, and so I put him on the new machine I bought from that Dutchman. He worked it well, and I upped his pay by fifty pula a month. Then suddenly he left me, and that was that."

"Any reason?" asked Mma Ramotswe.

Hector frowned. "None that I could make out. He collected his pay on a Friday and just did not come back. That was about two months ago. Then the next I heard from him was through an attorney in Mahalapye. He wrote me a letter saying that his client, Mr Solomon Moretsi, was starting a legal action against me for four thousand pula for the loss of a finger owing to an industrial accident in my factory."

Mma Ramotswe poured another cup of coffee for them both while she digested this development. "And was there an accident?"

"We have an incident book in the works," said Hector. "If anybody gets hurt, they have to enter the details in the book. I looked at the date which the attorney mentioned and I saw that there had been something. Moretsi had entered that he had hurt a finger on his right hand. He wrote that he had put a bandage on it and it seemed all right. I asked around, and somebody said that he had mentioned to them that he was leaving his machine for a while to fix his finger which he had cut. They thought it had not been a big cut, and nobody had bothered any more about it."

"Then he left?"

"Yes," said Hector. "That was a few days before he left."

Mma Ramotswe looked at her friend. He was an honest man, she knew, and a good employer. If anybody had been hurt she was sure that he would have done his best for them.

Hector took a sip of his coffee. "I don't trust that man," he said. "I don't think I ever did. I simply don't believe that he lost a finger in my factory. He may have lost a finger somewhere else, but that has nothing to do with me."

Mma Ramotswe smiled. "You want me to find this finger for you? Is that why you asked me to the President Hotel?"

Hector laughed. "Yes. And I also asked you because I enjoy sitting here with you and I would like to ask you to marry me. But I know that the answer will always be the same."

Mma Ramotswe reached out and patted her friend on the arm.

"Marriage is all very well," she said. "But being the No. 1 lady detective in the country is not an easy life. I couldn't sit at home and cook—you know that."

Hector shook his head. "I've always promised you a cook. Two cooks, if you like. You could still be a detective."

Mma Ramotswe shook her head. "No," she said. "You can carry on asking me, Hector Lepodise, but I'm afraid that the answer is still no. I like you as a friend, but I do not want a husband. I am finished with husbands for good."

MMA RAMOTSWE examined the papers in the office of Hector's factory. It was a hot and uncomfortable room, unprotected from the noise of the factory, and with barely enough space for the two filing cabinets and two desks which furnished it. Papers lay scattered on the surface of each desk; receipts, bills, technical catalogues.

"If only I had a wife," said Hector. "Then this office would not be such a mess. There would be places to sit down and flowers in a vase on my desk. A woman would make all the difference."

Mma Ramotswe smiled at his remark, but said nothing. She picked up the grubby exercise book which he had placed in front of her and paged through it. This was the incident book, and there, sure enough, was the entry detailing Moretsi's injury, the words spelled out in capitals in a barely literate hand:

MORETSI CUT HIS FINGER. NO. 2 FINGER COUNTING FROM THUMB. MACHINE DID IT. RIGHT HAND. BANDAGE PUT ON BY SAME. SIGNED: SOLOMON MORETSI. WITNESS: JESUS CHRIST.

She reread the entry and then looked at the attorney's letter. The dates tallied: "My client says that the accident occurred on 10th May last. He attended at the Princess Marina Hospital the following day. The wound was dressed, but osteomyelitis set in. The following week surgery was performed and the damaged finger was amputated at the proximal phalangeal joint (see attached hospital report). My client claims that this accident was due entirely to your negligence in failing adequately to fence working parts of machinery operated in your factory and has instructed me to raise an action for damages on his behalf. It would clearly be in the interests of all concerned if this action were to be settled promptly and my client has accordingly been advised that the sum of four thousand pula will be acceptable to him in lieu of court-awarded damages."

Mma Ramotswe read the remainder of the letter, which as far as she could make out was meaningless jargon which the attorney had been taught at law school. They were impossible, these people; they had a few years of lectures at the University of Botswana and they set themselves up as experts on everything. What did they know of life? All they knew was how to parrot the stock phrases of their profession and to continue to be obstinate until somebody, somewhere, paid up. They won by attrition in most cases, but they themselves concluded it was skill. Few of them would survive in her profession, which required tact and perspicacity.

She looked at the copy of the medical report. It was brief and said exactly what the attorney had paraphrased. The date was right; the headed note paper looked authentic; and there was the doctor's signature at the bottom. It was a name she knew.

Mma Ramotswe looked up from the papers to see Hector staring at her expectantly.

"It seems straightforward," she said. "He cut his finger and it became infected. What do your insurance people say?"

Hector sighed. "They say I should pay up. They say that they'll cover me for it and it would be cheaper in the long run. Once one starts paying lawyers to defend it, then the costs can very quickly overtake the damages. Apparently they'll settle up to ten thousand pula without fighting, although they asked me not to tell anybody about that. They would not like people to think they're an easy touch."

"Shouldn't you do what they say?" asked Mma Ramotswe. It seemed to her that there was no real point in denying that the accident had happened. Obviously this man had lost a finger and deserved some compensation; why should Hector make such a fuss about this when he did not even have to pay?

Hector guessed what she was thinking. "I won't," he said. "I just refuse. Refuse. Why should I pay money to somebody who

I think is trying to cheat me? If I pay him this time, then he'll go on to somebody else. I'd rather give that four thousand pula to somebody who deserved it."

He pointed to the door that linked the office to the factory floor.

"I've got a woman in there," he said, "with ten children. Yes, ten. She's a good worker too. Think what she could do with four thousand pula."

"But she hasn't lost a finger," interrupted Mma Ramotswe. "He might need that money if he can't work so well anymore."

"Bah! Bah! He's a crook, that man. I couldn't sack him because I had nothing on him. But I knew he was no good. And some of the others didn't like him either. The boy who makes the tea, the one with a hole in his brain, he can always tell. He wouldn't take tea to him. He said that the man was a dog and couldn't drink tea. You see, he knew. These people sense these things."

"But there's a big difference between entertaining suspicions and being able to prove something," said Mma Ramotswe. "You couldn't stand up in the High Court in Lobatse and say that there was something about this man which was not quite right. The judge would just laugh at you. That's what judges do when people say that sort of thing. They just laugh."

Hector was silent.

"Just settle," said Mma Ramotswe quietly. "Do what the insurance people tell you to do. Otherwise you'll end up with a bill for far more than four thousand pula."

Hector shook his head. "I won't pay for something I didn't do," he said through clenched teeth. "I want you to find out what this man is up to. But if you come back to me in a week's time and say that I am wrong, then I will pay without a murmur. Will that do?"

Mma Ramotswe nodded. She could understand his reluctance to pay damages he thought he didn't owe, and her fee for a week's work would not be high. He was a wealthy man, and he was entitled to spend his own money in pursuit of a principle; and, if Moretsi was lying, then a fraudster would have been confounded in the process. So she agreed to act, and she drove away in her little white van wondering how she could prove that the missing finger had nothing to do with Hector's factory. As she parked the van outside her office and walked into the cool of her waiting room, she realised that she had absolutely no idea how to proceed. It had all the appearances of a hopeless case.

THAT NIGHT, as she lay in the bedroom of her house in Zebra Drive, Mma Ramotswe found that sleep eluded her. She got up, put on the pink slippers which she always wore since she had been stung by a scorpion while walking through the house at night, and went through to the kitchen to make a pot of bush tea.

The house seemed so different at night. Everything was in its correct place, of course, but somehow the furniture seemed more angular and the pictures on the wall more one-dimensional. She remembered somebody saying that at night we are all strangers, even to ourselves, and this struck her as being true. All the familiar objects of her daily life looked as if they belonged to somebody else, somebody called Mma Ramotswe, who was not quite the person walking about in pink slippers.

Even the photograph of her Daddy in his shiny blue suit seemed different. This was a person called Daddy Ramotswe, of course, but not the Daddy she had known, the Daddy who had sacrificed everything for her, and whose last wish had been to see her happily settled in a business. How proud he would have been to have seen her now, the owner of the No. 1 Ladies' Detective Agency, known to everybody of note in town, even to permanent secretaries and Government ministers. And how important he would have felt had he seen her that very morning almost bumping into the Malawian High Commissioner as she left the President Hotel and the High Commissioner saying: "Good morning, Mma Ramotswe, you almost knocked me down there, but there's nobody I would rather be knocked down by than you, my goodness!" To be known to a High Commissioner! To be greeted by name by people like that! Not that she was impressed by them, of course, even high commissioners; but her Daddy would have been, and she regretted that he had not lived to see his plans for her come to fruition.

She made her tea and settled down to drink it on her most comfortable chair. It was a hot night and the dogs were howling throughout the town, egging one another on in the darkness. It was not a sound you really noticed anymore, she thought. They were always there, these howling dogs, defending their yards against all sorts of shadows and winds. Stupid creatures!

She thought of Hector. He was a stubborn man—famously so—but she rather respected him for it. Why should he pay? What was it he had said: If I pay him this time then he'll go on to somebody else. She thought for a moment, and then put the mug of bush tea down on the table. The idea had come to her suddenly, as all her good ideas seemed to come. Perhaps Hector was the somebody else. Perhaps he had already made claims elsewhere. Perhaps Hector was not the first!

Sleep proved easier after that, and she awoke the next morning confident that a few enquiries, and perhaps a trip up to Mahalapye, would be all that was required to dispose of Moretsi's spurious claim. She breakfasted quickly and then drove directly to the office. It was getting towards the end of winter, which meant that the temperature of the air was just right, and the sky was bright, pale blue, and cloudless. There was a slight smell of wood-smoke in the air, a smell that tugged at her heart because it reminded her of mornings around the fire in Mochudi. She would go back there, she thought, when she had worked long enough to retire. She would buy a house, or build one perhaps, and ask some of her cousins to live with her. They would grow melons on the lands and might even buy a small shop in the village; and every morning she could sit in front of her house and sniff at the wood-smoke and look forward to spending the day talking with her friends. How sorry she felt for white people, who couldn't do any of this, and who were always dashing around and worrying themselves over things that were going to happen anyway. What use was it having all that money if you could never sit still or just watch your cattle eating grass? None, in her view; none at all, and yet they did not know it. Every so often you met a white person who understood, who realised how things really were; but these people were few and far between and the other white people often treated them with suspicion.

The woman who swept her office was already there when she arrived. She asked after her family, and the woman told her of their latest doings. She had one son who was a warder at the prison and another who was a trainee chef at the Sun Hotel. They were both doing well, in their ways, and Mma Ramotswe was always interested to hear of their achievements. But that morning she cut the cleaner short—as politely as she could—and got down to work.

The trade directory gave her the information she needed. There were ten insurance companies doing business in Gaborone; four of these were small, and probably rather specialised; the other six she had heard of and had done work for four of them. She listed them, noted down their telephone numbers, and made a start.

The Botswana Eagle Company was the first she telephoned. They were willing to help, but could not come up with any information. Nor could the Mutual Life Company of Southern Africa, or the Southern Star Insurance Company. But at the fourth, Kalahari Accident and Indemnity, which asked for an hour or so to search the records, she found out what she needed to know.

"We've found one claim under that name," said the woman on the other end of the line. "Two years ago we had a claim from a garage in town. One of their petrol attendants claimed to have injured his finger while replacing the petrol pump dispenser in its holder. He lost a finger and they claimed under their employer's policy."

Mma Ramotswe's heart gave a leap. "Four thousand pula?" she asked.

"Close enough," said the clerk. "We settled for three thousand eight hundred."

"Right hand?" pressed Mma Ramotswe. "Second finger counting from the thumb?"

The clerk shuffled through some papers.

"Yes," she said. "There's a medical report. It says something about . . . I'm not sure how to pronounce it . . . osteomy . . ."

"Elitis," prompted Mma Ramotswe. "Requiring amputation of the finger at the proximal phalangeal joint?"

"Yes," said the clerk. "Exactly."

There were one or two details to be obtained, and Mma Ramotswe did that before thanking the clerk and ringing off. For a few moments she sat quite still, savouring the satisfaction of having revealed the fraud so quickly. But there were still several loose ends to be sorted out, and for these she would have to go up to Mahalapye. She would like to meet Moretsi, if she could, and she was also looking forward to an interview with his attorney. That, she thought, would be a pleasure that would more or less justify the two-hour drive up that awful Francistown Road.

The attorney proved to be quite willing to see her that afternoon. He assumed that she had been engaged by Hector to settle, and he imagined that it would be quite easy to browbeat her into settling on his terms. They might try for a little bit more than four thousand, in fact; he could say that there were new factors in the assessment of damages which made it necessary to ask for more. He would use the word quantum, which was Latin, he believed, and he might even refer to a recent decision of the Court of Appeal or even the Appellate Division in Bloemfontein. That would intimidate anyone, particularly a woman! And yes, he was sure that Mr Moretsi would be able to be there. He was a busy man, of course; no, he wasn't in fact, he couldn't work, poor man, as a result of his injury, but he would make sure that he was there.

Mma Ramotswe chuckled as she put down the telephone.

The attorney would be going to fetch his client out of some bar, she imagined, where he was probably already celebrating prematurely the award of four thousand pula. Well, he was due for an unpleasant surprise, and she, Mma Ramotswe, would be the agent of Nemesis.

She left her office in the charge of her secretary and set off to Mahalapye in the tiny white van. The day had heated up, and now, at noon, it was really quite hot. In a few months' time it would be impossible at midday and she would hate to have to drive any distance through the heat. She travelled with her window open and the rushing air cooled the van. She drove past the Dry Lands Research Station and the road that led off to Mochudi. She drove past the hills to the east of Mochudi and down into the broad valley that lay beyond. All around her there was nothing—just endless bush that stretched away to the bounds of the Kalahari on the one side and the plains of the Limpopo on the other. Empty bush, with nothing in it, but some cattle here and there and the occasional creaking wind-mill bringing up a tiny trickle of water for the thirsty beasts; nothing, nothing, that was what her country was so rich in— emptiness.

She was half an hour from Mahalapye when the snake shot across the road. The first she saw of it was when its body was about halfway out onto the road—a dart of green against the black tar; and then she was upon it, and the snake was beneath the van. She drew in her breath and slowed the car, looking behind her in the mirror as she did so. Where was the snake? Had it succeeded in crossing the road in time? No, it had not; she had seen it go under the van and she was sure that she had heard something, a dull thump.

She drew to a halt at the edge of the road, and looked in the mirror again. There was no sign of the snake. She looked at the steering wheel and drummed her fingers lightly against it. Perhaps it had been too quick to be seen; these snakes could move with astonishing speed. But she had looked almost immediately, and it was far too big a snake to disappear just like that. No, the snake was in the van somewhere, in the works or under her seat perhaps. She had heard of this happening time and time again. People picked up snakes as passengers and the first thing they knew about it was when the snake bit them. She had heard of people dying at the wheel, as they drove, bitten by snakes that had been caught up in the pipes and rods that ran this way and that under a car.

Mma Ramotswe felt a sudden urge to leave the van. She opened her door, hesitantly at first, but then threw it back and leaped out, to stand, panting, beside the vehicle. There was a snake under the tiny white van, she was now sure of that; but how could she possibly get it out? And what sort of snake was it? It had been green, as far as she remembered, which meant at least it wasn't a mamba. It was all very well people talking about green mambas, which certainly existed, but Mma Ramotswe knew that they were very restricted in their distribution and they were certainly not to be found in any part of Botswana. They were tree-dwelling snakes, for the most part, and they did not like sparse thorn bush. It was more likely to be a cobra, she thought, because it was large enough and she could think of no other green snake that long.

Mma Ramotswe stood quite still. The snake could have been watching her at that very moment, ready to strike if she approached any closer; or it could have insinuated itself into the cab of the van and was even now settling in under her seat. She bent forward and tried to look under the van, but she could not get low enough without going onto her hands and knees. If she did that, and if the snake should choose to move, she was worried that she would be unable to get away quickly enough. She stood up again and thought of Hector. This was what husbands were for. If she had accepted him long ago, then she would not be driving alone up to Mahalapye. She would have a man with her, and he would be getting under the van to poke the snake out of its place.

The road was very quiet, but there was a car or a truck every so often, and now she was aware of a car coming from the Mahalapye direction. The car slowed down as it approached her and then stopped. There was a man in the driver's seat and a young boy beside him.

"Are you in trouble, Mma?" he called out politely. "Have you broken down?"

Mma Ramotswe crossed the road and spoke to him through his open window. She explained about the snake, and he turned off his engine and got out, instructing the boy to stay where he was.

"They get underneath," he said. "It can be dangerous. You were right to stop."

The man approached the van gingerly. Then, leaning through the open door of the cab, he reached for the lever which released the bonnet and he gave it a sharp tug. Satisfied that it had worked, he walked slowly round to the front of the van and very carefully began to open the bonnet. Mma Ramotswe joined him, peering over his shoulder, ready to flee at the first sight of the snake.

The man suddenly froze.

"Don't make any sudden movement," he said very softly. "There it is. Look."

Mma Ramotswe peered into the engine space. For a few moments she could make out nothing unusual, but then the snake moved slightly and she saw it. She was right; it was a cobra, twined about the engine, its head moving slowly to right and left, as if seeking out something.

The man was quite still. Then he touched Mma Ramotswe on the forearm.

"Walk very carefully back to the door," he said. "Get into the cab, and start the engine. Understand?"

Mma Ramotswe nodded. Then, moving as slowly as she could, she eased herself into the driving seat and reached forward to turn the key.

The engine came into life immediately, as it always did. The tiny white van had never failed to start first time.

"Press the accelerator," yelled the man. "Race the engine!"

Mma Ramotswe did as she was told, and the engine roared throatily. There was a noise from the front, another thump, and then the man signalled to her to switch off. Mma Ramotswe did so, and waited to be told whether it was safe to get out.

"You can come out," he called. "That's the end of the cobra."

Mma Ramotswe got out of the cab and walked round to the front. Looking into the engine, she saw the cobra in two pieces, quite still.

"It had twined itself through the blades of the fan," said the man, making a face of disgust. "Nasty way to go, even for a snake. But it could have crept into the cab and bitten you, you know. So there we are. You are still alive."

Mma Ramotswe thanked him and drove off, leaving the cobra on the side of the road. It would prove to be an eventful journey, even if nothing further were to happen during the final half hour. It did not.

"NOW," SAID Mr Jameson Mopotswane, the Mahalapye attorney, sitting back in his unprepossessing office next to the butchery. "My poor client is going to be a little late, as the message only got to him a short time ago. But you and I can discuss details of the settlement before he arrives."

Mma Ramotswe savoured the moment. She leaned back in her chair and looked about his poorly furnished room.

"So business is not so good these days," she said, adding: "Up here."

Jameson Mopotswane bristled.

"It's not bad," he said. "In fact, I'm very busy. I get in here at seven o'clock, you know, and I'm on the go until six."

"Every day?" asked Mma Ramotswe innocently.

Jameson Mopotswane glared at her.

"Yes," he said. "Every day, including Saturdays. Sometimes Sundays."

"You must have a lot to do," said Mma Ramotswe.

The attorney took this in a reconciliatory way and smiled, but Mma Ramotswe continued: "Yes, a lot to do, sorting out the lies your clients tell you from the occasional—occasional—truth."

Jameson Mopotswane put his pen down on his desk and glared at her. Who was this pushy woman, and what right did she have to talk about his clients like that? If this is the way she wanted to play it, then he would be quite happy not to settle. He could do with fees, even if taking the matter to court would delay his client's damages.

"My clients do not lie," he said slowly. "Not more than anybody else, anyway. And you have no business, if I may say so, to suggest that they are liars."

Mma Ramotswe raised an eyebrow.

"Oh no?" she challenged. "Well, let's just take your Mr Moretsi, for example. How many fingers has he got?"

Jameson Mopotswane looked at her disdainfully.

"It's cheap to make fun of the afflicted," he sneered. "You know very well that he's got nine, or nine and a half if you want to split hairs."

"Very interesting," said Mma Ramotswe. "And if that's the case, then how can he possibly have made a successful claim to Kalahari Accident and Indemnity, about three years ago, for the loss of a finger in an accident in a petrol station? Could you explain that?"

The attorney sat quite still.

"Three years ago?" he said faintly. "A finger?"

"Yes," said Mma Ramotswe. "He asked for four thousand—a bit of a coincidence—and settled for three thousand eight hundred. The company have given me the claim number, if you want to check up. They're always very helpful, I find, when there's any question of insurance fraud being uncovered. Remarkably helpful."

Jameson Mopotswane said nothing, and suddenly Mma Ramotswe felt sorry for him. She did not like lawyers, but he was trying to earn a living, like everybody else, and perhaps she was being too hard on him. He might well have been supporting elderly parents, for all she knew.

"Show me the medical report," she said, almost kindly. "I'd be interested to see it."

The attorney reached for a file on his desk and took out a report.

"Here," he said. "It all seemed quite genuine."

Mma Ramotswe looked at the piece of headed paper and then nodded.

"There we are," she said. "It's just as I thought. Look at the date there. It's been whited out and a new date typed in. Our friend did have a finger removed once, and it may even have been as a result of an accident. But then all that he's done is to get a bottle of correction fluid, change the date, and create a new accident, just like that."

The attorney took the sheet of paper and held it up to the light. He need not even have done that; the correction fluid could be seen clearly enough at first glance.

"I'm surprised that you did not notice that," said Mma Ramotswe. "It doesn't exactly need a forensic laboratory to see what he's done."

It was at this point in the shaming of the attorney that Moretsi arrived. He walked into the office and reached out to shake hands with Mma Ramotswe. She looked at the hand and saw the stub of the finger. She rejected the proffered hand.

"Sit down," said Jameson Mopotswane coldly.

Moretsi looked surprised, but did as he was told.

"So you're the lady who's come to pay . . ."

The attorney cut him short.

"She has not come to pay anything," he said. "This lady has come all the way from Gaborone to ask you why you keep claiming for lost fingers."

Mma Ramotswe watched Moretsi's expression as the attorney spoke. Even if there had not been the evidence of the changed date on the hospital report, his crestfallen look would have convinced her. People always collapsed when confronted with the truth; very, very few could brave it out.

"Keep claiming . . . ?" he said limply.

"Yes," said Mma Ramotswe. "You claim, I believe, to have lost three fingers. And yet if I look at your hand today I see that two have miraculously grown back! This is wonderful! Perhaps you have discovered some new drug that enables fingers to grow back once they have been chopped off?"

"Three?" said the attorney, puzzled.

Mma Ramotswe looked at Moretsi.

"Well," she said. "There was Kalahari Accident. Then there was . . . Could you refresh my memory? I've got it written down somewhere."

Moretsi looked to his attorney for support, but saw only anger.

"Star Insurance," he said quietly.

"Ah!" said Mma Ramotswe. "Thank you for that."

The attorney picked up the medical report and waved it at his client.

"And you expected to be able to fool me with this . . . crude alteration? You expected to get away with that?"

Moretsi said nothing, as did Mma Ramotswe. She was not surprised, of course; these people were utterly slippery, even if they had a law degree to write after their names.

"Anyway," said Jameson Mopotswane, "that's the end of your tricks. You'll be facing fraud charges, you know, and you'll have to get somebody else to defend you. You won't get me, my friend."

Moretsi looked at Mma Ramotswe, who met his gaze directly.

"Why did you do it?" she asked. "Just tell me why you thought you could get away with it?"

Moretsi took a handkerchief out of his pocket and blew his nose.

"I am looking after my parents," he said. "And I have a sister who is sick with a disease that is killing everybody these days. You know what I'm talking about. She has children. I have to support them."

Mma Ramotswe looked into his eyes. She had always been able to rely on her ability to tell whether a person was telling the truth or not, and she knew that Moretsi was not lying. She thought quickly. There was no point in sending this man to prison. What would it achieve? It would merely add to the suffering of others—of the parents and of the poor sister. She knew what he was talking about and she understood what it meant.

"Very well," she said. "I will not tell the police about any of this. And my client will not either. But in return, you will promise that there will be no more lost fingers. Do you understand?"

Moretsi nodded rapidly.

"You are a good Christian lady," he said. "God is going to make it very easy for you in heaven."

"I hope so," said Mma Ramotswe. "But I am also a very nasty lady sometimes. And if you try any more of this nonsense with insurance people, then you will find that I will become very unpleasant."

"I understand," said Moretsi. "I understand."

"You see," said Mma Ramotswe, casting a glance at the

attentive attorney, "there are some people in this country, some men, who think that women are soft and can be twisted this way and that. Well I'm not. I can tell you, if you are interested, that I killed a cobra, a big one, on my way here this afternoon."

"Oh?" said Jameson Mopotswane. "What did you do?"

"I cut it in two," said Mma Ramotswe. "Two pieces."

CHAPTER SEVENTEEN

THE THIRD METACARPAL

ALL THAT was a distraction. It was gratifying to deal with a case like that so quickly, and to the clear satisfaction of the client, but one could not put out of one's mind the fact that there was a small brown envelope in the drawer with contents that could not be ignored.

She took it out discreetly, not wanting Mma Makutsi to see it. She thought that she could trust her, but this was a matter which was very much more confidential than any other matter they had encountered so far. This was dangerous.

She left the office, telling Mma Makutsi that she was going to the bank. Several cheques had come in, and needed to be deposited. But she did not go to the bank, or at least not immediately. She drove instead to the Princess Marina Hospital and followed the signs that said PATHOLOGY.

A nurse stopped her.

"Are you here to identify a body, Mma?"

Mma Ramotswe shook her head. "I have come to see Dr Gulubane. He is not expecting me, but he will see me. I am his neighbour."

The nurse looked at her suspiciously, but told her to wait while she went to fetch the doctor. A few minutes after she returned and said that the doctor would be with her shortly.

"You should not disturb these doctors at the hospital," she said disapprovingly. "They are busy people."

Mma Ramotswe looked at the nurse. What age was she? Nineteen, twenty? In her father's day, a girl of nineteen would not have spoken to a woman of thirty-five like that—spoken to her as if she was a child making an irritating request. But things were different now. Upstarts showed no respect for people who were older, and bigger too, than they were. Should she tell her that she was a private detective? No, there was no point in engaging with a person like this. She was best ignored.

Dr Gulubane arrived. He was wearing a green apron— heaven knows what awful task he had been performing—and he seemed quite pleased to have been disturbed.

"Come with me to my office," he said. "We can talk there."

Mma Ramotswe followed him down a corridor to a small office furnished with a completely bare table, a telephone, and a battered grey filing cabinet. It was like the office of a minor civil servant, and it was only the medical books on a shelf which gave away its real purpose.

"As you know," she began, "I'm a private detective these days."

Dr Gulubane beamed a broad smile. He was remarkably cheerful, she thought, given the nature of his job.

"You won't get me to talk about my patients," he said. "Even if they're all dead."

She shared the joke. "That's not what I want," she said. "All I would like you to do is to identify something for me. I have it with me." She took out the envelope and spilled its contents on the desk.

Dr Gulubane immediately stopped smiling and picked up the bone. He adjusted his spectacles.

"Third metacarpal," he muttered. "Child. Eight. Nine. Something like that."

Mma Ramotswe could hear her own breathing.

"Human?"

"Of course," said Dr Gulubane. "As I said, it's from a child. An adult's bone would be bigger. You can tell at a glance. A child of about eight or nine. Possibly a bit older."

The doctor put the bone down on the table and looked up at Mma Ramotswe.

"Where did you get it?"

Mma Ramotswe shrugged. "Somebody showed it to me. And you won't get me to talk about my clients either."

Dr Gulubane made an expression of distaste.

"These things shouldn't be handed round like that," he said. "People show no respect."

Mma Ramotswe nodded her agreement. "But can you tell me anything more? Can you tell me when the . . . when the child died?"

Dr Gulubane opened a drawer and took out a magnifying glass, with which he examined the bone further, turning it round in the palm of his hand.

"Not all that long ago," he said. "There's a small amount of tissue here at the top. It doesn't look entirely dessicated. Maybe a few months, maybe less. You can't be sure."

Mma Ramotswe shuddered. It was one thing to handle bone, but to handle human tissue was quite a different matter.

"And another thing," said Dr Gulubane. "How do you know that the child whose bone this is is dead? I thought you were the detective—surely you would have thought: this is an extremity—people can lose extremities and still live! Did you think that, Mrs Detective? I bet you didn't!"

SHE CONVEYED the information to Mr J.L.B. Matekoni over dinner in her house. He had readily accepted her invitation and she had prepared a large pot of stew and a combination of rice and melons. Halfway through the meal she told him of her visit to Dr Gulubane. Mr J.L.B. Matekoni stopped eating.

"A child?" There was dismay in his voice.

"That's what Dr Gulubane said. He couldn't be certain about the age. But he said it was about eight or nine."

Mr J.L.B. Matekoni winced. It would have been far better never to have found the bag. These things happened—they all knew that—but one did not want to get mixed up in them. They could only mean trouble—particularly if Charlie Gotso was involved in them.

"What do we do?" asked Mma Ramotswe.

Mr J.L.B. Matekoni closed his eyes and swallowed hard.

"We can go to the police," he said. "And if we do that, Charlie Gotso will get to hear about my finding the bag. And that will be me done for, or just about."

Mma Ramotswe agreed. The police had a limited interest in pursuing crime, and certain sorts of crime interested them not at all. The involvement of the country's most powerful figures in witchcraft would certainly be in the latter category.

"I don't think we should go to the police," said Mma Ramotswe.

"So we just forget about it?" Mr J.L.B. Matekoni fixed Mma Ramotswe with a look of appeal.

"No. We can't do that," she said. "People have been forgetting about this sort of thing for long enough, haven't they? We can't do that."

Mr J.L.B. Matekoni lowered his eyes. His appetite seemed to have deserted him now, and the stew was congealing on his plate.

"The first thing we do," she said, "is to arrange for Charlie Gotso's windscreen to be broken. Then you telephone him and tell him that thieves have broken into his car while it was in the garage. You tell him that there does not appear to have been anything stolen, but that you will willingly pay for a new windscreen yourself. Then you wait and see."

"To see what?"

"To see if he comes back and tells you something's missing. If he does, you tell him that you will personally undertake to recover this thing, whatever it is. You tell him that you have a contact, a lady private detective, who is very good at recovering stolen property. That's me, of course."

Mr J.L.B. Matekoni's jaw had dropped. One did not simply go up to Charlie Gotso just like that. You had to pull strings to see him.

"And then?"

"Then I take the bag back to him and you leave it up to me. I'll get the name of the witch doctor from him and then, well, we'll think about what to do then."

She made it sound so simple that he found himself convinced that it would work. That was the wonderful thing about confidence—it was infectious.

Mr J.L.B. Matekoni's appetite returned. He finished the stew, had a second helping, and then drank a large cup of tea before Mma Ramotswe walked with him to his car and said good-night.

She stood in the drive and watched the lights of his car disappear. Through the darkness, she could see the lights of Dr Gulubane's house. The curtains of his living room were open, and the doctor was standing at the open window, looking out into the night. He could not see her, as she was in darkness and he was in the light, but it was almost as if he was watching her.

CHAPTER EIGHTEEN

A LOT OF LIES

NE OF the young mechanics tapped him on the shoulder, leaving a greasy fingerprint. He was always doing this, that young man, and it annoyed Mr J.L.B. Matekoni intensely.

"If you want to attract my attention," he had said on more than one occasion, "you can always speak to me. I have a name. I am Mr J.L.B. Matekoni, and I answer to that. You don't have to come and put your dirty fingers on me."

The young man had apologised, but had tapped him on the shoulder the next day, and Mr J.L.B. Matekoni had realised that he was fighting a losing battle.

"There's a man to see you, Rra," said the mechanic. "He's waiting in the office."

Mr J.L.B. Matekoni put down his spanner and wiped his hands on a cloth. He had been involved in a particularly delicate operation—fine-tuning the engine of Mrs Grace Mapondwe, who was well-known for her sporty style of driving. It was a matter of pride to Mr J.L.B. Matekoni that people knew that Mrs Mapondwe's roaring engine note could be put down to his efforts; it was a free advertisement in a way. Unfortunately, she had ruined her car and it was becoming more and more difficult for him to coax life out of the increasingly sluggish engine.

The visitor was sitting in the office, in Mr J.L.B. Matekoni's chair. He had picked up a tyre brochure and was flipping through it when Mr J.L.B. Matekoni entered the room. Now he tossed it down casually and stood up.

Mr J.L.B. Matekoni rapidly took in the other man's appearance. He was dressed in khaki, as a soldier might be, and he had an expensive, snakeskin belt. There was also a fancy watch, with multiple dials and a prominent second hand. It was the sort of watch worn by those who feel that seconds are important, thought Mr J.L.B. Matekoni.

"Mr Gotso sent me," he said. "You telephoned him this morning."

Mr J.L.B. Matekoni nodded. It had been easy to break the windscreen and scatter the fragments of glass about the car. It had been easy to telephone Mr Gotso's house and report that the car had been broken into; but this part was more difficult—this was lying to somebody's face. It's Mma Ramotswe's fault, he thought. I am a simple mechanic. I didn't ask to get involved in these ridiculous detective games. I am just too weak.

And he was—when it came to Mma Ramotswe. She could ask anything of him, and he would comply. Mr J.L.B. Matekoni even had a fantasy, unconfessed, guiltily enjoyed in which he helped Mma Ramotswe. They were in the Kalahari together and Mma Ramotswe was threatened by a lion. He called out, drawing the lion's attention to him, and the animal turned and snarled. This gave her the chance to escape, while he dispatched the lion with a hunting knife; an innocent enough fantasy, one might have thought, except for one thing: Mma Ramotswe was wearing no clothes.

He would have loved to save her, naked or otherwise, from a lion, but this was different. He had even had to make a false report to the police, which had really frightened him, even if they had not even bothered to come round to investigate. He was a criminal now, he supposed, and it was all because he was weak. He should have said no. He should have told Mma Ramotswe that it was not her job to be a crusader.

"Mr Gotso is very angry," said the visitor. "You have had that car for ten days. Now you telephone us and tell us that it is broken into. Where's your security? That's what Mr Gotso says: where's your security?"

Mr J.L.B. Matekoni felt a trickle of sweat run down his back. This was terrible.

"I'm very sorry, Rra. The panel-beaters took a long time. Then I had to get a new part. These expensive cars, you can't put anything in them . . ."

Mr Gotso's man looked at his watch.

"All right, all right. I know how slow these people are. Just show me the car."

Mr J.L.B. Matekoni led the way out of the office. The man seemed less threatening now; was it really that easy to turn away wrath?

They stood before the car. He had already replaced the windscreen, but had propped what remained of the shattered one against a nearby wall. He had also taken the precaution of leaving a few pieces of broken glass on the driver's seat.

The visitor opened the front door and peered inside.

"I have replaced the windscreen free of charge," said Mr J.L.B. Matekoni. "I will also make a big reduction in the bill."

The other man said nothing. He was leaning across now and had opened the glove compartment. Mr J.L.B. Matekoni watched quietly.

The man got out of the car and brushed his hand against his trousers; he had cut himself on one of the small pieces of glass.

"There is something missing from the glove compartment. Do you know anything about that?"

Mr J.L.B. Matekoni shook his head—three times.

The man put his hand to his mouth and sucked at the cut.

"Mr Gotso forgot that he had something there. He only remembered when you told him about the car being broken into. He is not going to be pleased to hear that this item has gone."

Mr J.L.B. Matekoni passed the man a piece of rag.

"I'm sorry you've cut yourself. Glass gets everywhere when a windscreen goes. Everywhere."

The man snorted. "It doesn't matter about me. What matters is that somebody has stolen something belonging to Mr Gotso."

Mr J.L.B. Matekoni scratched his head.

"The police are useless. They didn't even come. But I know somebody who can look into this."

"Oh yes? Who can do that?"

"There's a lady detective these days. She has an office over that way, near Kgale Hill. Have you seen it?"

"Maybe. Maybe not."

Mr J.L.B. Matekoni smiled. "She's an amazing lady! She

knows everything that's going on. If I ask her, she'll be able to find out who did this thing. She might even be able to get the property back. What was it, by the way?"

"Property. A small thing belonging to Mr Charlie Gotso."

"I see."

The man took the rag off his wound and flung it on the floor.

"Can you ask that lady then," he said grudgingly. "Ask her to get this thing back to Mr Gotso."

"I will," said Mr J.L.B. Matekoni. "I will speak to her this evening, and I am sure she will get results. In the meantime, that car is ready and Mr Gotso can collect it anytime. I will clear up the last bits of glass."

"You'd better," said the visitor. "Mr Gotso doesn't like to cut his hand."

Mr Gotso doesn't like to cut his hand! You're a little boy, thought Mr J.L.B. Matekoni. You're just like a truculent little boy. I know your type well enough! I remember you—or somebody very like you—in the playground at Mochudi Government School—bullying other boys, breaking things, pretending to be tough. Even when the teacher whipped you, you made much about being too brave to cry.

And this Mr Charlie Gotso, with his expensive car and sinister ways—he's a boy too. Just a little boy.

HE WAS determined that Mma Ramotswe should not get away with it. She seemed to assume that he would do whatever she told him to do and very rarely asked him whether he wanted to take part in her schemes. And of course he had been far too meek in agreeing with her; that was the problem, really—she thought that she could get away with it because he never stood up to her. Well, he would show her this time. He would put an end to all this detective nonsense.

He left the garage, still smarting, busy rehearsing in his mind what he would say to her when he reached the office.

"Mma Ramotswe, you've made me lie. You've drawn me into a ridiculous and dangerous affair which is quite simply none of our business. I am a mechanic. I fix cars—I cannot fix lives."

The last phrase struck him for its forcefulness. Yes—that was the difference between them. She was a fixer of lives—as so many women are—whereas he was a fixer of machines. He would tell her this, and she would have to accept its truth. He did not want to destroy their friendship, but he could not continue with this posturing and deception. He had never lied—never—even in the face of the greatest of temptations, and now here he was enmeshed in a whole web of deceit involving the police and one of Botswana's most powerful men!

She met him at the door of the No. 1 Ladies' Detective Agency. She was throwing the dregs from a teapot into the yard as he drew up in his garage van.

"Well?" she said. "Did everything go as planned?"

"Mma Ramotswe, I really think . . ."

"Did he come round himself, or did he send one of his men?"

"One of his men. But, listen, you are a fixer of lives, I am just . . ."

"And did you tell him that I could get the thing back? Did he seem interested?"

"I fix machines. I cannot . . . You see, I have never lied. I have never lied before, even when I was a small boy. My tongue would go stiff if I tried to lie, and I couldn't."

Mma Ramotswe upended the teapot for a final time.

"You've done very well this time. Lies are quite all right if you are lying for a good cause. Is it not a good cause to find out who killed an innocent child? Are lies worse than murder, Mr J.L.B. Matekoni? Do you think that?"

"Murder is worse. But . . ."

"Well there you are. You didn't think it through, did you? Now you know."

She looked at him and smiled, and he thought: I am lucky. She is smiling at me. There is nobody to love me in this world. Here is somebody who likes me and smiles at me. And she's right about murder. It's far worse than lies.

"Come in for tea," said Mma Ramotswe. "Mma Makutsi has boiled the kettle and we can drink tea while we decide what to do next."

CHAPTER NINETEEN

MR CHARLIE GOTSO, BA

MR CHARLIE Gotso looked at Mma Ramotswe. He respected fat women, and indeed had married one five years previously. She had proved to be a niggling, troublesome woman and eventually he had sent her down to live on a farm near Lobatse, with no telephone and a road that became impassable in wet weather. She had complained about his other women, insistently, shrilly, but what did she expect? Did she seriously think that he, Mr Charlie Gotso, would restrict himself to one woman, like a clerk from a Government department? When he had all that money and influence? And a BA as well? That was the trouble with marrying an uneducated woman who knew nothing of the circles in which he moved. He had been to Nairobi and Lusaka. He knew what people were thinking in places like that. An intelligent woman, a woman with a BA, would have known better; but then, he reminded himself, this fat woman down in Lobatse had borne him five children already and one had to acknowledge that fact. If only she would not carp on about other women.

"You are the woman from Matekoni?"

She did not like his voice. It was sandpaper-rough, and he slurred the ends of the words lazily, as if he could not be bothered to make himself clear. This came from contempt, she felt; if you were as powerful as he was, then why bother to communicate properly with your inferiors? As long as they understood what you wanted—that was the essential thing.

"Mr J.L.B. Matekoni asked me to help him, Rra. I am a private detective."

Mr Gotso stared at her, a slight smile playing on his lips.

"I have seen this place of yours. I saw a sign when I was driving past. A private detective agency for ladies, or something like that."

"Not just for ladies, Rra," said Mma Ramotswe. "We are lady detectives but we work for men too. Mr Patel, for example. He consulted us."

The smile became broader. "You think you can tell men things?"

Mma Ramotswe answered calmly. "Sometimes. It depends. Sometimes men are too proud to listen. We can't tell that sort of man anything."

He narrowed his eyes. The remark was ambiguous. She could have been suggesting he was proud, or she could be talking about other men. There were others, of course . . .

"So anyway," said Mr Gotso. "You know that I lost some property from my car. Matekoni says that you might know who took it and get it back for me?"

Mma Ramotswe inclined her head in agreement. "I have done that," she said. "I found out who broke into your car. They were just boys. A couple of boys."

Mr Gotso raised an eyebrow. "Their names? Tell me who they are."

"I cannot do that," said Mma Ramotswe.

"I want to smack them. You will tell me who they are."

Mma Ramotswe looked up at Mr Gotso and met his gaze. For a moment neither said anything. Then she spoke: "I gave them my word I would not give their names to anybody if they gave me back what they had stolen. It was a bargain." As she spoke, she looked around Mr Gotso's office. It was just behind the Mall, in an unprepossessing side street, marked on the outside with a large blue sign, GOTSO HOLDING ENTER-PRISES. Inside, the room was simply furnished, and if it were not for the photographs on the wall, you would hardly know that this was the room of a powerful man. But the photographs gave it away: Mr Gotso with Moeshoeshoe, King of the Basotho; Mr Gotso with Hastings Banda; Mr Gotso with Sobhuza II. This was a man whose influence extended beyond their borders.

"You made a promise on my behalf?"

"Yes, I did. It was the only way I could get the item back."

Mr Gotso appeared to think for a moment; Mma Ramotswe looked at one of the pictures more closely. Mr Gotso was giving a cheque to some good cause and everybody was smiling; "Big cheque handed over for charity" ran the cut-out newspaper headline below.

"Very well," he said. "I suppose that was all you could do. Now, where is this item of property?"

Mma Ramotswe reached into her handbag and took out the small leather pouch.

"This is what they gave me."

She put it on the table and he reached across and took it in his hand.

"This is not mine, of course. This is something which one of my men had. I was looking after it for him. I have no idea what it is."

"Muti, Rra. Medicine from a witch doctor."

Mr Gotso's look was steely.

"Oh yes? Some little charm for the superstitious?"

Mma Ramotswe shook her head.

"No, I don't think so. I think that is powerful stuff. I think that was probably rather expensive."

"Powerful?" His head stayed absolutely still as he spoke, she noticed. Only the lips moved as the unfinished words slid out.

"Yes. That is good. I would like to be able to get something like that myself. But I do not know where I can find it."

Mr Gotso moved slightly now, and the eyes slid down Mma Ramotswe's figure.

"Maybe I could help you, Mma."

She thought quickly, and then gave her answer. "I would like you to help me. Then maybe I could help you in some way."

He had reached for a cigarette from a small box on his table and was now lighting it. Again the head did not move.

"In what way could you help me, Mma? Do you think I'm a lonely man?"

"You are not lonely. I have heard that you are a man with many women friends. You don't need another."

"Surely I'm the best judge of that."

"No, I think you are a man who likes information. You need that to keep powerful. You need muti too, don't you?"

He took the cigarette out of his mouth and laid it on a large glass ashtray.

"You should be careful about saying things like that," he said. The words were well articulated now; he could speak clearly when he wanted to. "People who accuse others of witchcraft can regret it. Really regret it."

"But I am not accusing you of anything. I told you myself that I used it, didn't I? No, what I was saying was that you are a man who needs to know what's going on in this town. You can easily miss things if your ears are blocked with wax."

He picked up the cigarette again and drew on it.

"You can tell me things?"

Mma Ramotswe nodded. "I hear some very interesting things in my business. For example, I can tell you about that man who is trying to build a shop next to your shop in the Mall. You know him? Would you like to hear about what he did before he came to Gaborone? He wouldn't like people to know that, I think."

Mr Gotso opened his mouth and picked a fragment of tobacco from his teeth.

"You are a very interesting woman, Mma Ramotswe. I think I understand you very well. I will give you the name of the witch doctor if you give me this useful information. Would that suit you?"

Mma Ramotswe clicked her tongue in agreement. "That is very good. I shall be able to get something from this man which will help me get even better information. And if I hear anything else, well I shall be happy to let you know."

"You are a very good woman," said Mr Gotso, picking up a

small pad of paper. "I'm going to draw you a sketch-map. This man lives out in the bush not far from Molepolole. It is difficult to find his place, but this will show you just where to go. I warn you, by the way—he's not cheap. But if you say that you are a friend of Mr Charlie Gotso, then you will find that he takes off twenty percent. Which isn't at all bad, is it?"

CHAPTER TWENTY

MEDICAL MATTERS

SHE HAD the information now. She had a map to find a murderer, and she would find him. But there was still the detective agency to run, and cases which needed to be dealt with—including a case which involved a very different sort of doctor, and a hospital.

Mma Ramotswe had no stomach for hospitals; she disliked the smell of them; she shuddered at the sight of the patients sitting on benches in the sun, silenced by their suffering; she was frankly depressed by the pink day-pyjamas they gave to those who had come with TB. Hospitals were to her a *memento mori* in bricks and mortar; an awful reminder of the inevitable end that was coming to all of us but which she felt was best ignored while one got on with the business of life.

Doctors were another matter altogether, and Mma Ramotswe had always been impressed by them. She admired, in particu-lar, their sense of the confidential and she took comfort in the fact that you could tell a doctor something and, like a priest, he would carry your secret to the grave. You never found this amongst lawyers, who were boastful people, on the whole, always prepared to tell a story at the expense of a client, and, when one came to think of it, some accountants were just as indiscreet in discussing who earned what. As far as doctors were concerned, though, you might try as hard as you might to get information out of them, but they were inevitably tight-lipped.

Which was as it should be, thought Mma Ramotswe. I should not like anybody else to know about my . . . What had she to be embarrassed about? She thought hard. Her weight was hardly a confidential matter, and anyway, she was proud of being a traditionally built African lady, unlike these terrible, stick-like creatures one saw in the advertisements. Then there were her corns—well, those were more or less on public display when she wore her sandals. Really, there was nothing that she felt she had to hide.

Now constipation was quite a different matter. It would be dreadful for the whole world to know about troubles of that nature. She felt terribly sorry for people who suffered from constipation, and she knew that there were many who did. There were probably enough of them to form a political party—with a chance of government perhaps—but what would such a party do if it was in power? Nothing, she imagined. It would try to pass legislation, but would fail.

She stopped her reverie, and turned to the business in hand. Her old friend, Dr Maketsi, had telephoned her from the hospital and asked if he could call in at her office on his way home that evening. She readily agreed; she and Dr Maketsi were both from Mochudi, and although he was ten years her senior she felt extremely close to him. So she cancelled her hair-braiding appointment in town and stayed at her desk, catching up on some tedious paperwork until Dr Maketsi's familiar voice called out: Ko! Ko! and he came into the office.

They exchanged family gossip for a while, drinking bush tea and reflecting on how Mochudi had changed since their day. She asked after Dr Maketsi's aunt, a retired teacher to whom half the village still turned for advice. She had not run out of steam, he said, and was now being pressed to stand for Parliament, which she might yet do.

"We need more women in public life," said Dr Maketsi. "They are very practical people, women. Unlike us men."

Mma Ramotswe was quick to agree. "If more women were in power, they wouldn't let wars break out," she said. "Women can't be bothered with all this fighting. We see war for what it is—a matter of broken bodies and crying mothers."

Dr Maketsi thought for a moment. He was thinking of Mrs Ghandi, who had a war, and Mrs Golda Meir, who also had a war, and then there was . . .

"Most of the time," he conceded. "Women are gentle most of the time, but they can be tough when they need to be."

Dr Maketsi was eager to change the subject now, as he feared that Mma Ramotswe might go on to ask him whether he could cook, and he did not want a repetition of the conversation he had had with a young woman who had returned from a year in the United States. She had said to him, challengingly, as if the difference in their ages were of no consequence: "If you eat, you should cook. It's as simple as that." These ideas came from America and may be all very well in theory, but had they made the Americans any happier? Surely there had to be some limits to all this progress, all this unsettling change. He had heard recently of men who were obliged by their wives to change the nappies of their babies. He shuddered at the thought; Africa was not ready for that, he reflected. There were some aspects of the old arrangements in Africa which were very appropriate and comfortable—if you were a man, which of course Dr Maketsi was.

"But these are big issues," he said jovially. "Talking about pumpkins doesn't make them grow." His mother-in-law said this frequently, and although he disagreed with almost everything she said, he found himself echoing her words only too often.

Mma Ramotswe laughed. "Why have you come to see me?" she said. "Do you want me to find you a new wife, maybe?"

Dr Maketsi clicked his tongue in mock disapproval. "I have come about a real problem," he said. "Not just about a little question of wives."

Mma Ramotswe listened as the doctor explained just how delicate his problem was and she assured him that she, like him, believed in confidentiality.

"Not even my secretary will get to hear what you tell me," she said.

"Good," said Dr Maketsi. "Because if I am wrong about this, and if anybody hears about it, I shall be very seriously embarrassed—as will the whole hospital. I don't want the Minister coming looking for me."

"I understand," said Mma Ramotswe. Her curiosity was thoroughly aroused now, and she was anxious to hear what juicy matter was troubling her friend. She had been burdened with several rather mundane cases recently, including a very demeaning one which involved tracing a rich man's dog. A dog! The only lady detective in the country should not have to stoop to such depths and indeed Mma Ramotswe would not have done so, had it not been for the fact that she needed the fee. The little white van had developed an ominous rattle in the engine and Mr J.L.B. Matekoni, called upon to consider the problem, had gently broken the news to her that it needed expensive repairs. And what a terrible, malodorous dog it had turned out to be; when she eventually found the animal being dragged along on a string by the group of urchins which had stolen it, the dog had rewarded its liberator with a bite on the ankle.

"I am worried about one of our young doctors," said Dr Maketsi. "He is called Dr Komoti. He's Nigerian."

"I see."

"I know that some people are suspicious of Nigerians," said Dr Maketsi.

"I believe that there are some people like that," said Mma Ramotswe, catching the doctor's eye and then looking away again quickly, almost guiltily.

Dr Maketsi drank the last of his bush tea and replaced his mug on the table.

"Let me tell you about our Dr Komoti," he said. "Starting from the time he first turned up for interview. It was my job to interview him, in fact, although I must admit that it was rather a formality. We were desperately short of people at the time and needed somebody who would be able to lend a hand in casualty. We can't really be too choosy, you know. Anyway, he seemed to have a reasonable C.V. and he had brought several references with him. He had been working in Nairobi for a few years, and so I telephoned the hospital he was at and they confirmed that he was perfectly all right. So I took him on.

"He started about six months ago. He was pretty busy in

casualty. You probably know what it's like in there. Road accidents, fights, the usual Friday evening business. Of course a lot of the work is just cleaning up, stopping the bleeding, the occasional resuscitation—that sort of thing.

"Everything seemed to be going well, but after Dr Komoti had been there about three weeks the consultant in charge had a word with me. He said that he thought that the new doctor was a bit rusty and that some of the things he did seemed a bit surprising. For example, he had sewed several wounds up quite badly and the stitching had to be redone.

"But sometimes he was really quite good. For example, a couple of weeks ago we had a woman coming in with a tension pneumothorax. That's a pretty serious matter. Air gets into the space round the lungs and makes the lung collapse, like a popped balloon. If this happens, you have to drain the air out as quickly as you can so that the lung can expand again.

"This is quite a tricky job for an inexperienced doctor. You've got to know where to put in the drain. If you get it wrong you could even puncture the heart or do all sorts of other damage. If you don't do it quickly, the patient can die. I almost lost somebody myself with one of these a few years ago. I got quite a fright over it.

"Dr Komoti turned out to be pretty good at this, and he undoubtedly saved this woman's life. The consultant turned up towards the end of the procedure and he let him finish it. He was impressed, and mentioned it to me. But at the same time, this is the same doctor who had failed to spot an obvious case of enlarged spleen the day before."

"He's inconsistent?" said Mma Ramotswe.

"Exactly," said Dr Maketsi. "One day he'll be fine, but the next day he'll come close to killing some unfortunate patient."

Mma Ramotswe thought for a moment, remembering a news item in *The Star*. "I was reading the other day about a bogus surgeon in Johannesburg," she said. "He practised for almost ten years and nobody knew that he had no qualifications. Then somebody spotted something by chance and they exposed him."

"It's extraordinary," said Dr Maketsi. "These cases crop up from time to time. And these people often get away with it for a long time—for years sometimes."

"Did you check up on his qualifications?" asked Mma Ramotswe. "It's easy enough to forge documents these days with photocopiers and laser printers—anybody can do it. Maybe he's not a doctor at all. He could have been a hospital porter or something like that."

Dr Maketsi shook his head. "We went through all that," he said. "We checked with his Medical School in Nigeria—that was a battle, I can tell you—and we also checked with the General Medical Council in Britain, where he did a registrar's job for two years. We even obtained a photograph from Nairobi, and it's the same man. So I'm pretty sure that he's exactly who he says he is."

"Couldn't you just test him?" asked Mma Ramotswe. "Couldn't you try to find out how much he knows about medicine by just asking him some tricky questions?"

Dr Maketsi smiled. "I've done that already. I've taken the opportunity to speak to him about one or two difficult cases. On the first occasion he coped quite well, and he gave a fairly good answer. He clearly knew what he was talking about. But on the second occasion, he seemed evasive. He said that he wanted to think about it. This annoyed me, and so I mentioned something about the case we had discussed before.

This took him off his guard, and he just mumbled something inconsequential. It was as if he had forgotten what he'd said to me three days before."

Mma Ramotswe looked up at the ceiling. She knew about forgetfulness. Her poor Daddy had become forgetful at the end and had sometimes barely remembered her. That was understandable in the old, but not in a young doctor. Unless he was ill, of course, and in that case something could have gone wrong with his memory.

"There's nothing wrong with him mentally," said Dr Maketsi, as if predicting her question. "As far as I can tell, that is. This isn't a case of pre-senile dementia or anything like that. What I'm afraid of is drugs. I think that he's possibly abusing drugs and that half the time he's treating patients he's not exactly there."

Dr Maketsi paused. He had delivered his bombshell, and he sat back, as if silenced by the implications of what he had said. This was almost as bad as if they had been allowing an unqualified doctor to practise. If the Minister heard that a doctor was treating patients in the hospital while high on drugs, he might begin to question the closeness of supervision in the hospital.

He imagined the interview. "Now Dr Maketsi, could you not see from the way this man was behaving that he was drugged? Surely you people should be able to spot things like that. If it's obvious enough to me when I walk down the street that somebody has been smoking *dagga,* then surely it should be obvious enough to somebody like you. Or am I fondly imagining that you people are more perceptive than you really are . . ."

"I can see why you're worried," said Mma Ramotswe. "But I'm not sure whether I can help. I don't really know my way around the drug scene. That's really a police matter."

Dr Maketsi was dismissive. "Don't talk to me about the police," he said. "They never keep their mouths shut. If I went to them to get this looked into, they'd treat it as a straightforward drugs enquiry. They'd barge in and search his house and then somebody would talk about it. In no time at all word would be all about town that he was a drug addict." He paused, concerned that Mma Ramotswe should understand the subtleties of his dilemma. "And what if he isn't? What if I'm wrong? Then I would have as good as killed his reputation for no reason. He may be incompetent from time to time, but that's no reason for destroying him."

"But if we did find out that he was using drugs," said Mma Ramotswe. "And I'm not sure how we could do this, what then? Would you dismiss him?"

Dr Maketsi shook his head vigorously. "We don't think about drugs in those terms. It isn't a question of good behaviour and bad behaviour. I'd look on it as a medical problem and I'd try to help him. I'd try to sort out the problem."

"But you can't 'sort out' with those people," said Mma Ramotswe. "Smoking *dagga* is one thing, but using pills and all the rest is another. Show me one reformed drug addict. Just one. Maybe they exist; I've just never seen them."

Dr Maketsi shrugged. "I know they can be very manipulative people," he said. "But some of them get off it. I can show you some figures."

"Well, maybe, maybe not," said Mma Ramotswe. "The point is: what do you want me to do?"

"Find out about him," said Dr Maketsi. "Follow him for a few days. Find out whether he's involved in the drug scene. If he is, find out whether he's supplying others with drugs while you are about it. Because that will be another problem for us.

We keep a tight rein on drugs in the hospital, but things can go missing, and the last thing we want is a doctor who's passing hospital drug supplies to addicts. We can't have that."

"You'd sack him then?" goaded Mma Ramotswe. "You wouldn't try to help him?"

Dr Maketsi laughed. "We'd sack him good and proper."

"Good," said Mma Ramotswe. "And proper too. Now I have to tell you about my fee."

Dr Maketsi's face fell. "I was worried about that. This is such a delicate enquiry, I could hardly get the hospital to pay for it."

Mma Ramotswe nodded knowingly. "You thought that as an old friend . . ."

"Yes," said Dr Maketsi quietly. "I thought that as an old friend you might remember how when your Daddy was so ill at the end . . ."

Mma Ramotswe did remember. Dr Maketsi had come unfailingly to the house every evening for three weeks and eventually had arranged for her Daddy to be put in a private room at the hospital, all for nothing.

"I remember very well," she said. "I only mentioned the fee to tell you that there would be none."

SHE HAD all the information she needed to start her investigation of Dr Komoti. She had his address in Kaunda Way; she had a photograph, supplied by Dr Maketsi; and she had a note of the number of the green station wagon which he drove. She had also been given his telephone number, and the number of his postal box at the Post Office, although she could not imagine the circumstances in which she might need these. Now all she had to do was to start to watch Dr Komoti and to learn as much as she could about him in the shortest possible time.

Dr Maketsi had thoughtfully provided her with a copy of the duty rota in the casualty department for the following four months. This meant that Mma Ramotswe would know exactly when he might be expected to leave the hospital to return home and also when he might be on night duty. This would save a great deal of time and effort in sitting waiting in the street in the tiny white van.

She started two days later. She was there when Dr Komoti drove out of the staff car park at the hospital that afternoon and she followed him discreetly into town, parking a few cars away from him and waiting until he was well away from the car park before she got out of the van. He visited one or two shops and picked up a newspaper from the Book Centre. Then he returned to his car, drove straight home, and stayed there—blamelessly, she assumed—until the lights went out in the house just before ten that evening. It was a dull business sitting in the tiny white van, but Mma Ramotswe was used to it and never complained once she had agreed to take on a matter. She would sit in her van for a whole month, even more, if asked to do so by Dr Maketsi; it was the least she could do after what he had done for her Daddy.

Nothing happened that evening, nor the next evening. Mma Ramotswe was beginning to wonder whether there was ever any variety to the routine of Dr Komoti's life when suddenly things changed. It was a Friday afternoon, and Mma Ramotswe was ready to follow Dr Komoti back from work. The doctor was slightly late in leaving the hospital, but eventually he came out of the casualty entrance, a stethoscope tucked into the pocket of his white coat, and climbed into his car.

Mma Ramotswe followed him out of the hospital grounds, satisfied that he was not aware of her presence. She suspected that he might go to the Book Centre for his newspaper, but this time instead of turning into town, he turned the other way. Mma Ramotswe was pleased that something at last might be happening, and she concentrated carefully on not losing him as they made their way through the traffic. The roads were busier than usual, as it was a Friday afternoon at the end of the month, and this meant payday. That evening there would be more road accidents than normal, and whoever was taking Dr Komoti's place in casualty would be kept more than occupied stitching up the drunks and picking the shattered windscreen glass out of the road accident cases.

Mma Ramotswe was surprised to find that Dr Komoti was heading for the Lobatse Road. This was interesting. If he was dealing in drugs, then to use Lobatse as a base would be a good idea. It was close enough to the border, and he might be passing things into South Africa, or picking things up there. Whatever it was, it made him a much more interesting man to follow.

They drove down, the tiny white van straining to keep Dr Komoti's more powerful car in sight. Mma Ramotswe was not worried about being spotted; the road was busy and there was no reason why Dr Komoti should single out the tiny white van. Once they got to Lobatse of course, she would have to be more circumspect, as he could notice her in the thinner traffic there.

When they did not stop in Lobatse, Mma Ramotswe began to worry. If he was going to drive straight through Lobatse it was possible that he was visiting some village on the other side of the town. But this was rather unlikely, as there was not much on the other side of Lobatse—or not much to interest somebody like Dr Komoti. The only other thing, then, was the border, some miles down the road. Yes! Dr Komoti was going over the border, she was sure of it. He was going to Mafikeng.

As the realisation dawned that Dr Komori's destination was out of the country, Mma Ramotswe felt an intense irritation with her own stupidity. She did not have her passport with her; Dr Komoti would go through, and she would have to remain in Botswana. And once he was on the other side, then he could do whatever he liked—and no doubt would—and she would know nothing about it.

She watched him stop at the border post, and then she turned back, like a hunter who has chased his prey to the end of his preserve and must now give up. He would be away for the weekend now, and she knew as little about what he did with his time as she did about the future. Next week, she would have to get back to the tedious task of watching his house by night, in the frustrating knowledge that the real mischief had taken place over the weekend. And while she was doing all this, she would have to postpone other cases—cases which carried fees and paid garage bills.

When she arrived back in Gaborone, Mma Ramotswe was in a thoroughly bad mood. She had an early night, but the bad mood was still with her the following morning when she went into the Mall. As she often did on a Saturday morning, she had a cup of coffee on the verandah of the President Hotel and enjoyed a chat with her friend Grace Gakatsla. Grace, who had a dress shop in Broadhurst, always cheered her up with her stories of the vagaries of her customers. One, a Government Minister's wife, had recently bought a dress on a Friday and brought it back the following Monday, saying that it did not really fit. Yet Grace had been at the wedding on Saturday where the dress had been worn, and it had looked perfect.

"Of course I couldn't tell her to her face she was a liar and that I wasn't a dress-hire shop," said Grace. "So I asked her if she had enjoyed the wedding. She smiled and said that she had. So I said I enjoyed it too. She obviously hadn't seen me there. She stopped smiling and she said that maybe she'd give the dress another chance."

"She's just a porcupine, that woman," said Mma Ramotswe. "A hyena," said Grace. "An anteater, with her long nose."

The laughter had died away, and Grace had gone off, allowing Mma Ramotswe's bad mood to settle back in place. It seemed to her that she might continue to feel like this for the rest of the weekend; in fact, she was worried that it could last until the Komoti case was finished—if she ever finished it.

Mma Ramotswe paid her bill and left, and it was then, as she was walking down the front steps of the hotel, that she saw Dr Komoti in the Mall.

FOR A moment Mma Ramotswe stood quite still. Dr Komoti had crossed the border last night just before seven in the evening. The border closed at eight, which meant that he could not possibly have had time to get down to Mafikeng, which was a further forty minutes' drive, and back in time to cross again before the border closed. So he had only spent one evening there and had come back first thing that morning.

She recovered from her surprise at seeing him and realised that she should make good use of the opportunity to follow him and see what he did. He was now in the hardware store, and Mma Ramotswe lingered outside, looking idly at the contents of the window until he came out again. Then he walked purposefully back to the car park and she watched him getting into his car.

Dr Komoti stayed in for the rest of the day. At six in the evening he went off to the Sun Hotel where he had a drink with two other men, whom Mma Ramotswe recognised as fellow Nigerians. She knew that one of them worked for a firm of accountants, and the other, she believed, was a primary school-teacher somewhere. There was nothing about their meeting which seemed suspicious; there would be many such groups of people meeting right at this moment throughout the town—people thrown together in the artificial closeness of the expatriate life, talking about home.

He stayed an hour and then left, and that was the extent of Dr Komoti's social life for the weekend. By Sunday evening, Mma Ramotswe had decided that she would report to Dr Maketsi the following week and tell him that there was unfortunately no evidence of his moving in drug-abusing circles and that he seemed, by contrast, to be the model of sobriety and respectability. There was not even a sign of women, unless they were hiding in the house and never came out. Nobody had arrived at the house while she was watching, and nobody had left, apart from Dr Komoti himself. He was, quite simply, rather a boring man to watch.

But there was still the question of Mafikeng and the Friday evening dash there and back. If he had been going shopping down there in the OK Bazaars—as many people did—then he would surely have stayed for at least part of Saturday morning, which he clearly did not. He must have done, then, whatever it was he wanted to do on Friday evening. Was there a woman down there—one of those flashy South African women whom men, so unaccountably, seemed to like? That would be the simple explanation, and the most likely one too. But why the hurry back on Saturday morning? Why not stay for Saturday and take her to lunch at the Mmbabatho Hotel? There was something which did not seem quite right, and Mma Ramotswe thought that she might follow him down to Mafikeng next weekend, if he went, and see what happened. If there was nothing to be seen, then she could do some shopping and return on Saturday afternoon. She had been meaning to make the trip anyway, and she might as well kill two birds with one stone.

DR KOMOTI proved obliging. The following Friday he left the hospital on time and drove off in the direction of Lobatse, followed at a distance by Mma Ramotswe in her van. Crossing the border proved tricky, as Mma Ramotswe had to make sure that she did not get too close to him at the border post, and that at the same time she did not lose him on the other side. For a few moments it looked as if she would be delayed, as a ponderous official paged closely through her passport, looking at the stamps which reflected her coming and going to Johannesburg and Mafikeng.

"It says here, under occupation, that you are a detective," he said in a surly tone. "How can a woman be a detective?"

Mma Ramotswe glared at him. If she prolonged the encounter, she could lose Dr Komoti, whose passport was now being stamped. In a few minutes he would be through the border controls, and the tiny white van would have no chance of catching up with him.

"Many women are detectives," said Mma Ramotswe, with dignity. "Have you not read Agatha Christie?"

The clerk looked up at her and bristled.

"Are you saying I am not an educated man?" he growled. "Is that what you are saying? That I have not read this Mr Christie?"

"I am not," said Mma Ramotswe. "You people are well educated, and efficient. Only yesterday, when I was in your Minister's house, I said to him that I thought his immigration people were very polite and efficient. We had a good talk about it over supper."

The official froze. For a moment he looked uncertain, but then he reached for his rubber stamp and stamped the passport.

"Thank you, Mma," he said. "You may go now."

Mma Ramotswe did not like lying, but sometimes it was necessary, particularly when faced with people who were promoted beyond their talents. An embroidering of the truth like that—she knew the Minister, even if only very distantly— sometimes gingered people up a bit, and it was often for their own good. Perhaps that particular official would think twice before he again decided to bully a woman for no good reason.

She climbed back into the van and was waved past the barrier. There was now no sight of Dr Komoti and she had to push the van to its utmost before she caught up with him. He was not going particularly fast, and so she dropped back slightly and followed him past the remnants of Mangope's capital and its fantouche Republic of Bophuthatswana. There was the stadium in which the president had been held by his own troops when they revolted; there were the government offices that administered the absurdly fragmented state on behalf of its masters in Pretoria. It was all such a waste, she thought, such an utter folly, and when the time had come it had just faded away like the illusion that it had always been. It was all part of the farce of apartheid and the monstrous dream of Verwoerd; such pain, such long-drawn-out suffering—to be added by history to all the pain of Africa.

Dr Komoti suddenly turned right. They had reached the outskirts of Mafikeng, in a suburb of neat, well-laid-out streets and houses with large, well-fenced gardens. It was into the driveway of one of these houses that he turned, requiring Mma Ramotswe to drive past to avoid causing suspicion. She counted the number of houses she passed, though—seven— and then parked the van under a tree.

There was what used to be called a sanitary lane which ran down the back of the houses. Mma Ramotswe left the van and walked to the end of the sanitary lane. The house that Dr Komoti entered would be eight houses up—seven, and the one she had had to walk past to get to the entrance to the lane.

She stood in the sanitary lane at the back of the eighth house and peered through the garden. Somebody had once cared for it, but that must have been years ago. Now it was a tangle of vegetation—mulberry trees, uncontrolled bougainvillaea bushes that had grown to giant proportions and sent great sprigs of purple flowers skywards, paw-paw trees with rotting fruit on the stems. It would be a paradise for snakes, she thought; there could be mambas lurking in the uncut grass and boomslangs draped over the branches of the trees, all of them lying in wait for somebody like her to be foolish enough to enter.

She pushed the gate open gingerly. It had clearly not been used for a long time, and the hinge squeaked badly. But this did not really matter, as little sound would penetrate the vegetation that shielded the back fence from the house, about a hundred yards away. In fact, it was virtually impossible to see the house through the greenery, which made Mma Ramotswe feel safe, from the eyes of those within the house at least, if not from snakes.

Mma Ramotswe moved forward gingerly, placing each foot carefully and expecting at any moment to hear a hiss from a protesting snake. But nothing moved, and she was soon crouching under a mulberry tree as close as she dared to get to the house. From the shade of the tree she had a good view of the back door and the open kitchen window; yet she could not see into the house itself, as it was of the old colonial style, with wide eaves, which made the interior cool and dark. It was far easier to spy on people who live in modern houses, because architects today had forgotten about the sun and put people in goldfish bowls where the whole world could peer in through large unprotected windows, should they so desire.

Now what should she do? She could stay where she was in the hope that somebody came out of the back door, but why should they bother to do that? And if they did, then what would she do?

Suddenly a window at the back of the house opened and a man leaned out. It was Dr Komoti.

"You! You over there! Yes, you, fat lady! What are you doing sitting under our mulberry tree?"

Mma Ramotswe experienced a sudden, absurd urge to look over her shoulder, as if to imply that there was somebody else under the tree. She felt like a schoolgirl caught stealing fruit, or doing some other forbidden act. There was nothing one could say; one just had to own up.

She stood up and stepped out from the shade.

"It is hot," she called out. "Can you give me a drink of water?"

The window closed and a moment or two later the kitchen door opened. Dr Komoti stood on the step wearing, she noticed, quite different clothes from those he had on when he left Gaborone. He had a mug of water in his hand, which he gave to her. Mma Ramotswe reached out and drank the water gratefully. She was, in fact, thirsty, and the water was welcome, although she noticed that the mug was dirty.

"What are you doing in our garden?" said Dr Komoti, not unkindly. "Are you a thief?"

Mma Ramotswe looked pained. "I am not," she said.

Dr Komoti looked at her coolly. "Well, then, if you are not a thief, then what do you want? Are you looking for work? If so, we already have a woman who comes to cook in this house. We do not need anybody."

Mma Ramotswe was about to utter her reply when somebody appeared behind Dr Komoti and looked out over his shoulder. It was Dr Komoti.

"What's going on?" said the second Dr Komoti. "What does this woman want?"

"I saw her in the garden," said the first Dr Komoti. "She tells me she isn't a thief."

"And I certainly am not," she said indignantly. "I was looking at this house."

The two men looked puzzled.

"Why?" one of them asked. "Why would you want to look at this house? There's nothing special about it, and it's not for sale anyway."

Mma Ramotswe tossed her head back and laughed. "Oh,

I'm not here to buy it," she said. "It's just that I used to live here when I was a little girl. There were Boers living in it then, a Mr van der Heever and his wife. My mother was their cook, you see, and we lived in the servants' quarters back there at the end of the garden. My father kept the garden tidy . . ."

She broke off, and looked at the two men in reproach.

"It was better in those days," she said. "The garden was well looked after."

"Oh, I'm sure it was," said one of the two. "We'd like to get it under control one day. It's just that we're busy men. We're both doctors, you see, and we have to spend all our time in the hospital."

"Ah!" said Mma Ramotswe, trying to sound reverential. "You are doctors here at the hospital?"

"No," said the first Dr Komoti. "I have a surgery down near the railway station. My brother . . ."

"I work up that way," said the other Dr Komoti, pointing vaguely to the north. "Anyway, you can look at the garden as much as you like, mother. You just go ahead. We can make you a mug of tea."

"Ow!" said Mma Ramotswe. "You are very kind. Thank you."

IT WAS a relief to get away from that garden, with its sinister undergrowth and its air of neglect. For a few minutes, Mma Ramotswe pretended to inspect the trees and the shrubs—or what could be seen of them—and then, thanking her hosts for the tea, she walked off down the road. Her mind busily turned over the curious information she had obtained. There were two Dr Komotis, which was nothing terribly unusual in itself; yet somehow she felt that this was the essence of the whole matter. There was no reason, of course, why there should not be twins who both went to medical school—twins often led mirrored lives, and sometimes even went so far as to marry the sister of the other's wife. But there was something particularly significant here, and Mma Ramotswe was sure that it was staring her in the face, if only she could begin to see it.

She got into the tiny white van and drove back down the road towards the centre of town. One Dr Komoti had said that he had a surgery in town, near the railway station, and she decided to take a look at this—not that a brass plate, if he had one, would reveal a great deal.

She knew the railway station slightly. It was a place that she enjoyed visiting, as it reminded her of the old Africa, the days of uncomfortable companionship on crowded trains, of slow journeys across great plains, of the sugarcane you used to eat to while away the time, and of the pith of the cane you used to spit out of the wide windows. Here you could still see it—or a part of it—here, where the trains that came up from the Cape pulled slowly past the platform on their journey up through Botswana to Bulawayo; here, where the Indian stores beside the railway buildings still sold cheap blankets and men's hats with a garish feather tucked into the band.

Mma Ramotswe did not want Africa to change. She did not want her people to become like everybody else, soulless, selfish, forgetful of what it means to be an African, or, worse still, ashamed of Africa. She would not be anything but an African, never, even if somebody came up to her and said "Here is a pill, the very latest thing. Take it and it will make you into an American." She would say no. Never. No thank you.

She stopped the white van outside the railway station and got out. There were a lot of people about; women selling roasted maize cobs and sweet drinks; men talking loudly to their friends; a family, travelling, with cardboard suitcases and possessions bundled up in a blanket. A child pushing a home-made toy car of twisted wire bumped into Mma Ramotswe and scurried off without an apology, frightened of rebuke.

She approached one of the woman traders and spoke to her in Setswana.

"Are you well today, Mma?" she said politely.

"I am well, and you are well too, Mma?"

"I am well, and I have slept very well."

"Good."

The greeting over, she said: "People tell me that there is a doctor here who is very good. They call him Dr Komoti. Do you know where his place is?"

The woman nodded. "There are many people who go to that doctor. His place is over there, do you see, where that white man has just parked his truck. That's where he is."

Mma Ramotswe thanked her informant and bought a cob of roasted maize. Then, tackling the cob as she walked, she walked across the dusty square to the rather dilapidated tin-roofed building where Dr Komoti's surgery was to be found.

Rather to her surprise, the door was not locked, and when she pushed it open she found a woman standing directly in front of her.

"I am sorry, the doctor isn't here, Mma," said the woman, slightly testily. "I am the nurse. You can see the doctor on Monday afternoon."

"Ah!" said Mma Ramotswe. "It is a sad thing to have to tidy up on a Friday evening, when everybody else is thinking of going out."

The nurse shrugged her shoulders. "My boyfriend is taking

me out later on. But I like to get everything ready for Monday before the weekend starts. It is better that way."

"Far better," Mma Ramotswe answered, thinking quickly. "I didn't actually want to see the doctor, or not as a patient. I used to work for him, you see, when he was up in Nairobi. I was a nurse on his ward. I wanted just to say hallo."

The nurse's manner became markedly more friendly.

"I'll make you some tea, Mma," she offered. "It is still quite hot outside."

Mma Ramotswe sat down and waited for the nurse to return with the pot of tea.

"Do you know the other Dr Komoti?" she said. "The brother?"

"Oh yes," said the nurse. "We see a lot of him. He comes in here to help, you see. Two or three times a week."

Mma Ramotswe lowered her cup, very slowly. Her heart thumped within her; she realised that she was at the heart of the matter now, the elusive solution within her grasp. But she would have to sound casual.

"Oh, they did that up in Nairobi too," she said, waving her hand airily, as if these things were of little consequence. "One helped the other. And usually the patients didn't know that they were seeing a different doctor."

The nurse laughed. "They do it here too," she said. "I'm not sure if it's quite fair on the patients, but nobody has realised that there are two of them. So everybody seems quite satisfied."

Mma Ramotswe picked up her cup again and passed it for refilling. "And what about you?" she said. "Can you tell them apart?"

The nurse handed the teacup back to Mma Ramotswe. "I

can tell by one thing," she said. "One of them is quite good—the other's hopeless. The hopeless one knows hardly anything about medicine. If you ask me, it's a miracle that he got through medical school."

Mma Ramotswe thought, but did not say: He didn't.

SHE STAYED in Mafikeng that night, at the Station Hotel, which was noisy and uncomfortable, but she slept well nonetheless, as she always did when she had just finished an enquiry. The next morning she shopped at the OK Bazaars and found, to her delight, that there was a rail of size 22 dresses on special offer. She bought three—two more than she really needed—but if you were the owner of the No. 1 Ladies' Detective Agency you had to keep up a certain style.

She was home by three o'clock that afternoon and she telephoned Dr Maketsi at his house and invited him to come immediately to her office to be informed of the results of her enquiry. He arrived within ten minutes and sat opposite her in the office, fiddling anxiously with the cuffs of his shirt.

"First of all," announced Mma Ramotswe, "no drugs."

Dr Maketsi breathed a sigh of relief. "Thank goodness for that," he said. "That's one thing I was really worried about."

"Well," said Mma Ramotswe doubtfully. "I'm not sure if you're going to like what I'm going to tell you."

"He's not qualified," gasped Dr Maketsi. "Is that it?"

"One of them is qualified," said Mma Ramotswe.

Dr Maketsi looked blank. "One of them?"

Mma Ramotswe settled back in her chair with the air of one about to reveal a mystery.

"There were once two twins," she began. "One went to medical school and became a doctor. The other did not. The one with the qualification got a job as a doctor, but was greedy and thought that two jobs as a doctor would pay better than one. So he took two jobs, and did both of them part-time. When he wasn't there, his brother, who was his identical twin, you'll recall, did the job for him. He used such medical knowledge as he had picked up from his qualified brother and no doubt also got advice from the brother as to what to do. And that's it. That's the story of Dr Komoti, and his twin brother in Mafikeng."

Dr Maketsi sat absolutely silent. As Mma Ramotswe spoke he had sunk his head in his hands and for a moment she thought that he was going to cry.

"So we've had both of them in the hospital," he said at last. "Sometimes we've had the qualified one, and sometimes we've had the twin brother."

"Yes," said Mma Ramotswe simply. "For three days a week, say, you've had the qualified twin while the unqualified twin practised as a general practitioner in a surgery near Mafikeng Railway Station. Then they'd change about, and I assume that the qualified one would pick up any pieces which the unqualified one had left lying around, so to speak."

"Two jobs for the price of one medical degree," mused Dr Maketsi. "It's the most cunning scheme I've come across for a long, long time."

"I have to admit I was amazed by it," said Mma Ramotswe. "I thought that I'd seen all the varieties of human dishonesty, but obviously one can still be surprised from time to time."

Dr Maketsi rubbed his chin.

"I'll have to go to the police about this," he said. "There's going to have to be a prosecution. We have to protect the public from people like this."

"Unless . . ." started Mma Ramotswe.

Dr Maketsi grabbed at the straw he suspected she might be offering him.

"Can you think of an alternative?" he asked. "Once this gets out, people will take fright. We'll have people encouraging others not to go to hospital. Our public health programmes rely on trust—you know how it is."

"Precisely," said Mma Ramotswe. "I suggest that we transfer the heat elsewhere. I agree with you: the public has to be protected and Dr Komoti is going to have to be struck off, or whatever you people do. But why not get this done in somebody else's patch?"

"Do you mean in Mafikeng?"

"Yes," said Mma Ramotswe. "After all, an offence is being committed down there and we can let the South Africans deal with it. The papers up here in Gaborone probably won't even pick up on it. All that people here will know is that Dr Komoti resigned suddenly, which people often do—for all sorts of reasons."

"Well," said Dr Maketsi. "I would rather like to keep the Minister's nose out of all this. I don't think it would help if he became . . . how shall we put it, upset?"

"Of course it wouldn't help," said Mma Ramotswe. "With your permission I shall telephone my friend Billy Pilani, who's a police captain down there. He'd love to be seen to expose a bogus doctor. Billy likes a good, sensational arrest."

"You do that," said Dr Maketsi, smiling. This was a tidy solution to a most extraordinary matter, and he was most impressed with the way in which Mma Ramotswe had handled it.

"You know," he said, "I don't think that even my aunt in Mochudi could have dealt with this any better than you have."

Mma Ramotswe smiled at her old friend. You can go through life and make new friends every year—every month practically—but there was never any substitute for those friendships of childhood that survive into adult years. Those are the ones in which we are bound to one another with hoops of steel.

She reached out and touched Dr Maketsi on the arm, gently, as old friends will sometimes do when they have nothing more to say.

THE WITCH DOCTOR'S WIFE

A DUSTY track, hardly in use, enough to break the springs; a hill, a tumble of boulders, just as the sketch map drawn by Mr Charlie Gotso had predicted; and above, stretching from horizon to horizon, the empty sky, singing in the heat of noon.

Mma Ramotswe steered the tiny white van cautiously, avoiding the rocks that could tear the sump from the car, wondering why nobody came this way. This was dead country; no cattle, no goats; only the bush and the stunted thorn trees. That anybody should want to live here, away from a village, away from human contact, seemed inexplicable. Dead country.

Suddenly she saw the house, tucked away behind the trees, almost in the shadow of the hill. It was a bare earth house in the traditional style; brown mud walls, a few glassless windows, with a knee-height wall around the yard. A previous owner, a long time ago, had painted designs on the wall, but neglect and the years had scaled them off and only their ghosts remained.

She parked the van and drew in her breath. She had faced down fraudsters; she had coped with jealous wives; she had even stood up to Mr Gotso; but this meeting would be different. This was evil incarnate, the heart of darkness, the root of shame. This man, for all his mumbo-jumbo and his spells, was a murderer.

She opened the door and eased herself out of the van. The sun was riding high and its light prickled at her skin. They were too far west here, too close to the Kalahari, and her unease increased. This was not the comforting land she had grown up with; this was the merciless Africa, the waterless land.

She made her way towards the house, and as she did so she felt that she was being watched. There was no movement, but eyes were upon her, eyes from within the house. At the wall, in accordance with custom, she stopped and called out, announcing herself.

"I am very hot," she said. "I need water."

There was no reply from within the house, but a rustle to her left, amongst the bushes. She turned round, almost guiltily, and stared. It was a large black beetle, a setotojane, with its horny neck, pushing at a minute trophy, some insect that had died of thirst perhaps. Little disasters, little victories; like ours, she thought; when viewed from above we are no more than setotojane.

"Mma?"

She turned round sharply. A woman was standing in the doorway, wiping her hands on a cloth.

Mma Ramotswe stepped through the gateless break in the wall.

"Dumela Mma," she said. "I am Mma Ramotswe."

The woman nodded. "Eee. I am Mma Notshi."

Mma Ramotswe studied her. She was a woman in her late fifties, or thereabouts, wearing a long skirt of the sort which the Herero women wore; but she was not Herero—she could tell.

"I have come to see your husband," she said. "I have to ask him for something."

The woman came out from the shadows and stood before Mma Ramotswe, peering at her face in a disconcerting way.

"You have come for something? You want to buy something from him?"

Mma Ramotswe nodded. "I have heard that he is a very good doctor. I have trouble with another woman. She is taking my husband from me and I want something that will stop her."

The older woman smiled. "He can help you. Maybe he has something. But he is away. He is in Lobatse until Saturday. You will have to come back some time after that."

Mma Ramotswe sighed. "This has been a long trip, and I am thirsty. Do you have water, my sister?"

"Yes, I have water. You can come and sit in the house while you drink it."

IT WAS a small room, furnished with a rickety table and two chairs. There was a grain bin in the corner, of the traditional sort, and a battered tin trunk. Mma Ramotswe sat on one of the chairs while the woman fetched a white enamel mug of water, which she gave to her visitor. The water was slightly rancid, but Mma Ramotswe drank it gratefully.

Then she put the mug down and looked at the woman.

"I have come for something, as you know. But I have also come to warn you of something."

The woman lowered herself onto the other chair.

"To warn me?"

"Yes," said Mma Ramotswe. "I am a typist. Do you know what that is?"

The woman nodded.

"I work for the police," went on Mma Ramotswe. "And I have typed out something about your husband. They know that he killed that boy, the one from Katsana. They know that he is the man who took him and killed him for muti. They are going to arrest your husband soon and then they will hang him. I came to warn you that they will hang you also, because they say that you are involved in it too. They say that you did it too. I do not think they should hang women. So I came to tell you that you could stop all this quickly if you came with me to the police and told them what happened. They will believe you and you will be saved. Otherwise, you will die very soon. Next month, I think."

She stopped. The other woman had dropped the cloth she had been carrying and was staring at her, wide-eyed. Mma Ramotswe knew the odour of fear—that sharp, acrid smell that people emit through the pores of their skin when they are frightened; now the torpid air was heavy with that smell.

"Do you understand what I have said to you?" she asked.

The witch doctor's wife closed her eyes. "I did not kill that boy."

"I know," said Mma Ramotswe. "It is never the women who do it. But that doesn't make any difference to the police. They have evidence against you and the Government wants to hang you too. Your husband first; you later. They do not like witchcraft, you know. They are ashamed. They think it's not modern."

"But the boy is not dead," blurted out the woman. "He is at the cattle post where my husband took him. He is working there. He is still alive."

MMA RAMOTSWE opened the door for the woman and slammed it shut behind her. Then she went round to the driver's door, opened it, and eased herself into the seat. The sun had made it burning hot—hot enough to scorch through the cloth of her dress—but pain did not matter now. All that mattered was to make the journey, which the woman said would take four hours. It was now one o'clock. They would be there just before sunset and they could start the journey back immediately. If they had to stop overnight because the track was too bad, well, they could sleep in the back of the van. The important thing was to get to the boy.

The journey was made in silence. The other woman tried to talk, but Mma Ramotswe ignored her. There was nothing she could say to this woman; nothing she wanted to say to her.

"You are not a kind woman," said the witch doctor's wife finally. "You are not talking to me. I am trying to talk to you, but you ignore me. You think that you are better than me, don't you."

Mma Ramotswe half-turned to her. "The only reason why you are showing me where this boy is is because you are afraid.

You are not doing it because you want him to go back to his parents. You don't care about that, do you? You are a wicked woman and I am warning you that if the police hear that you and your husband practise any more witchcraft, they will come and take you to prison. And if they don't, I have friends in Gaborone who will come and do it for them. Do you understand what I am saying?"

The hours passed. It was a difficult journey, out across open veld, on the barest of tracks, until there, in the distance, they saw cattle stockades and the cluster of trees around a couple of huts.

"This is the cattle post," said the woman. "There are two Basarwa there—a man and a woman—and the boy who has been working for them."

"How did you keep him?" asked Mma Ramotswe. "How did you know that he would not run away?"

"Look around you," said the woman. "You see how lonely this place is. The Basarwa would catch him before he could get far."

Something else occurred to Mma Ramotswe. The bone—if the boy was still alive, then where did the bone come from?

"There is a man in Gaborone who bought a bone from your husband," she said. "Where did you get that?"

The woman looked at her scornfully "You can buy bones in Johannesburg. Did you not know that? They are not expensive."

THE BASARWA were eating a rough porridge, seated on two stones outside one of the huts. They were tiny, wizened people, with the wide eyes of the hunter, and they stared at the intruders. Then the man rose to his feet and saluted the witch doctor's wife.

"Are the cattle all right?" she asked sharply.

The man made a strange, clicking noise with his tongue. "All right. They are not dead. That cow there is making much milk."

The words were Setswana words, but one had to strain to understand them. This was a man who spoke in the clicks and whistles of the Kalahari.

"Where is the boy?" snapped the woman.

"That side," replied the man. "Look."

And then they saw the boy, standing beside a bush, watching them uncertainly. A dusty little boy, in torn pants, with a stick in his hand.

"Come here," called the witch doctor's wife. "Come here."

The boy walked over to them, his eyes fixed on the ground in front of him. He had a scar on his forearm, a thick weal, and Mma Ramotswe knew immediately what had caused it. That was the cut of a whip, a sjambok.

She reached forward and laid a hand on his shoulder.

"What is your name?" she asked gently. "Are you the teacher's son from Katsana Village?"

The boy shivered, but he saw the concern in her eyes and he spoke.

"I am that boy. I am working here now. These people are making me look after the cattle."

"And did this man strike you?" whispered Mma Ramotswe. "Did he?"

"All the time," said the boy. "He said that if I ran away he would find me in the bush and put a sharpened stick through me."

"You are safe now," said Mma Ramotswe. "You are coming with me. Right now. Just walk in front of me. I will look after you."

The boy glanced at the Basarwa and began to move towards the van.

"Go on," said Mma Ramotswe. "I am coming too."

She put him in the passenger seat and closed the door. The witch doctor's wife called out.

"Wait a few minutes. I want to talk to these people about the cattle. Then we can go."

Mma Ramotswe moved round to the driver's door and let herself in.

"Wait," called the woman. "I am not going to be long."

Mma Ramotswe leaned forward and started the engine. Then, slipping the van into gear, she spun the wheel and pressed her foot on the accelerator. The woman shouted out and began to run after the van, but the dust cloud soon obscured her and she tripped and fell.

Mma Ramotswe turned to the boy, who was looking frightened and confused beside her.

"I am taking you home now," she said. "It will be a long journey and I think we shall have to stop for the night quite soon. But we will set off again in the morning and then it should not be too long."

She stopped the van an hour later, beside a dry riverbed. They were completely alone, with not even a fire from a remote cattle post to break the darkness of the night. Only the starlight fell on them, an attenuated, silver light, falling on the sleeping figure of the boy, wrapped in a sack which she had in the back of the van, his head upon her arm, his breathing regular, his hand resting gently in hers, and Mma Ramotswe herself, whose eyes were open, looking up into the night sky until the sheer immensity of it tipped her gently into sleep.

AT KATSANA Village the next day, the schoolmaster looked out of the window of his house and saw a small white van draw up outside. He saw the woman get out and look at his door, and the child—what about the child—was she a parent who was bringing her child to him for some reason?

He went outside and found her at the low wall of his yard.

"You are the teacher, Rra?"

"I am the teacher, Mma. Can I do anything for you?"

She turned to the van and signalled to the child within. The door opened and his son came out. And the teacher cried out, and ran forward, and stopped and looked at Mma Ramotswe as if for confirmation. She nodded, and he ran forward again, almost stumbling, an unlaced shoe coming off, to seize his son, and hold him, while he shouted wildly, incoherently, for the village and the world to hear his joy.

Mma Ramotswe walked back towards her van, not wanting to intrude upon the intimate moments of reunion. She was crying; for her own child, too—remembering the minute hand that had grasped her own, so briefly, while it tried to hold on to a strange world that was slipping away so quickly. There was so much suffering in Africa that it was tempting just to shrug your shoulders and walk away. But you can't do that, she thought. You just can't.

MR J.L.B. MATEKONI

EVEN A vehicle as reliable as the little white van, which did mile after mile without complaint, could find the dust too much. The tiny white van had been uncomplaining on the trip out to the cattle post, but now, back in town, it was beginning to stutter. It was the dust, she was sure of it.

She telephoned Tlokweng Road Speedy Motors, not intending to bother Mr J.L.B. Matekoni, but the receptionist was out to lunch and he answered. She need not worry, he said. He would come round to look at the little white van the following day, a Saturday, and he might be able to fix it there on the spot, in Zebra Drive.

"I doubt it," said Mma Ramotswe. "It is an old van. It is like an old cow, and I will have to sell it, I suppose."

"You won't," said Mr J.L.B. Matekoni. "Anything can be fixed. Anything."

Even a heart that is broken in two pieces? he thought. Can

they fix that? Could Professor Barnard down in Cape Town cure a man whose heart was bleeding, bleeding from loneliness?

MMA RAMOTSWE went shopping that morning. Her Saturday mornings had always been important to her; she went to the supermarket in the Mall and bought her groceries and her vegetables from the women on the pavement outside the chemist's. After that, she went to the President Hotel and drank coffee with her friends; then home, and half a glass of Lion Beer, taken sitting out on the verandah and reading the newspaper. As a private detective, it was important to scour the newspaper and to put the facts away in one's mind. All of it was useful, down to the last line of the politicians' predictable speeches and the church notices. You never knew when some snippet of local knowledge would be useful.

If you asked Mma Ramotswe to give, for instance, the names of convicted diamond smugglers, she could give them to you: Archie Mofobe, Piks Ngube, Molso Mobole, and George Excellence Tambe. She had read the reports of the trials of them all, and knew their sentences. Six years, six years, ten years, and eight months. It had all been reported and filed away.

And who owned the Wait No More Butchery in Old Naledi? Why, Godfrey Potowani, of course. She remembered the photograph in the newspaper of Godfrey standing in front of his new butchery with the Minister of Agriculture. And why was the Minister there? Because his wife, Modela, was the cousin of one of the Potowani women who had made that dreadful fuss at the wedding of Stokes Lofinale. That's why. Mma

Ramotswe could not understand people who took no interest in all this. How could one live in a town like this and not want to know everybody's business, even if one had no professional reason for doing so?

HE ARRIVED shortly after four, driving up in his blue garage bakkie with TLOKWENG ROAD SPEEDY MOTORS painted on the side. He was wearing his mechanic's overalls, which were spotlessly clean, and ironed neatly down the creases. She showed him the tiny white van, parked beside the house, and he wheeled out a large jack from the back of his truck.

"I'll make you a cup of tea," she said. "You can drink it while you look at the van."

From the window she watched him. She saw him open the engine compartment and tap at bits and pieces. She saw him climb into the driver's cab and start the motor, which coughed and spluttered and eventually died out. She watched as he removed something from the engine—a large part, from which wires and hoses protruded. That was the heart of the van perhaps; its loyal heart which had beaten so regularly and reliably, but which, ripped out, now looked so vulnerable.

Mr J.L.B. Matekoni moved backwards and forwards between his truck and the van. Two cups of tea were taken out, and then a third, as it was a hot afternoon. Then Mma Ramotswe went into her kitchen and put vegetables into a pot and watered the plants that stood on the back windowsill. Dusk was approaching, and the sky was streaked with gold. This was her favourite time of the day, when the birds went dipping and swooping through the air and the insects of the night started to shriek. In this gentle light, the cattle would be walking home and the fires outside the huts would be crackling and glowing for the evening's cooking.

She went out to see whether Mr J.L.B. Matekoni needed more light. He was standing beside the little white van, wiping his hands on lint.

"That should be fine now," he said. "I've tuned it up and the engine runs sweetly. Like a bee."

She clapped her hands in pleasure.

"I thought that you would have to scrap it," she said.

He laughed. "I told you anything could be fixed. Even an old van."

He followed her inside. She poured him a beer and they went together to her favourite place to sit, on the verandah, near the bougainvillaea. Not far away, in a neighbouring house, music was being played, the insistent traditional rhythms of township music.

The sun went, and it was dark. He sat beside her in the comfortable darkness and they listened, contentedly, to the sounds of Africa settling down for the night. A dog barked somewhere; a car engine raced and then died away; there was a touch of wind, warm dusty wind, redolent of thorn trees.

He looked at her in the darkness, at this woman who was everything to him—mother, Africa, wisdom, understanding, good things to cat, pumpkins, chicken, the smell of sweet cattle breath, the white sky across the endless, endless bush, and the giraffe that cried, giving its tears for women to daub on their baskets; O Botswana, my country, my place.

Those were his thoughts. But how could be say any of that to her? Any time he tried to tell her what was in his heart, the words which came to him seemed so inadequate. A mechanic cannot be a poet, he thought, that is not how things are. So he simply said:

"I am very happy that I fixed your van for you. I would have been sorry if somebody else had lied to you and said it was not worth fixing. There are people like that in the motor trade."

"I know," said Mma Ramotswe. "But you are not like that."

He said nothing. There were times when you simply had to speak, or you would have your lifetime ahead to regret not speaking. But every time he had tried to speak to her of what was in his heart, he had failed. He had already asked her to marry him and that had not been a great success. He did not have a great deal of confidence, at least with people; cars were different, of course.

"I am very happy sitting here with you . . ."

She turned to him. "What did you say?"

"I said, please marry me, Mma Ramotswe. I am just Mr J.L.B. Matekoni, that's all, but please marry me and make me happy."

"Of course I will," said Mma Ramotswe.

THE STORM

"What just happened?" Carter shouted.

"Did we hit some rocks?" Buzz asked.

"Dad!" Vanessa shouted. "Dad? Can you hear me?" She started scrambling through the pile of debris on the floor, but she couldn't find the phone anywhere.

Instead, her hand landed in cold water. It was soaking the carpet, Vanessa realized. When she looked to her right, she saw it was also pouring in from under the small engine-compartment door.

At the same moment, Joe came barreling down the galley steps.

"What are you doing?" Vanessa asked. "Joe, where's Dex? There's water coming in!"

But Joe wasn't listening. He was holding the sideband radio transmitter with one hand and adjusting a dial on the console with the other.

"SOS, SOS, this is the *Lucky Star*," Joe said into the handset. "SOS, SOS, this is the *Lucky Star*, do you copy?"

Whatever was said next, Vanessa didn't hear. It was swallowed up by a brilliant flash of lightning and a crash of thunder too overwhelming to be anywhere but right on top of them.

In the next moment, the entire cabin was thrown into darkness.

The STRANDED Series

JEFF PROBST

and CHRIS TEBBETTS

SCHOLASTIC INC.

ISBN 978-0-545-58063-2

12 11 10 9 8 7 6 5 4   13 14 15 16 17 18/0

Printed in the U.S.A.   40

First Scholastic printing, January 2013

Design by Tony Sahara
Set in Century Schoolbook

Dedicated to Michael & Ava

It was my wife, Lisa, who had the original idea for
this series. It came from a desire to share stories
of blended families living out amazing adventures.
Whatever type of family you have, we hope it
inspires you!

—JP

CHAPTER 1

It was day four at sea, and as far as eleven-year-old Carter Benson was concerned, life didn't get any better than this.

From where he hung, suspended fifty feet over the deck of the *Lucky Star*, all he could see was a planet's worth of blue water. The boat's huge white mainsail ballooned in front of him, filled with a stiff southerly wind that sent them scudding through the South Pacific faster than they'd sailed all week.

This was the best part of the best thing Carter had ever done, no question. It was like sailing and flying at the same time. The harness around his middle held him in place while his arms and legs hung free. The air itself seemed to carry him along, at speed with the boat.

"How you doin' up there, Carter?" Uncle Dexter shouted from the cockpit.

Carter flashed a thumbs-up and pumped his fist. "Faster!" he shouted back. Even with the wind whipping in his ears, Dex's huge belly laugh came back, loud and clear.

Meanwhile, Carter had a job to do. He wound the safety line from his harness in a figure eight around the cleat on the mast to secure himself. Then he reached over and unscrewed the navigation lamp he'd come up here to replace.

As soon as he'd pocketed the old lamp in his rain slicker, he pulled out the new one and fitted it into the fixture, making sure not to let go before he'd tightened it down. Carter had changed plenty of lightbulbs before, but never like this. If anything, it was all too easy and over too fast.

When he was done, he unwound his safety line and gave a hand signal to Dex's first mate, Joe

Kahali, down below. Joe put both hands on the winch at the base of the mast and started cranking Carter back down to the deck.

"Good job, Carter," Joe said, slapping him on the back as he got there. Carter swelled with pride and adrenaline. Normally, replacing the bulb would have been Joe's job, but Dex trusted him to take care of it.

Now Joe jerked a thumb over his shoulder. "Your uncle wants to talk to you," he said.

Carter stepped out of the harness and stowed it in its locker, just like Dex and Joe had trained him to do. Once that was done, he clipped the D-ring on his life jacket to the safety cable that ran the length of the deck and headed toward the back.

It wasn't easy to keep his footing as the *Lucky Star* pitched and rolled over the waves, but even that was part of the fun. If he did fall, the safety cable—also called a jackline—would keep him from going overboard. Everyone was required to stay clipped in when they were on deck, whether they were up there to work . . . or to puke, like Buzz was doing right now.

"Gross! Watch out, Buzz!" Carter said, pushing past him.

"*Uhhhhhnnnnh*," was all Buzz said in return. He was leaning against the rail and looked both green and gray at the same time.

Carter kind of felt sorry for him. They were both eleven years old, but they didn't really have anything else in common. It was like they were having two different vacations out here.

"Gotta keep moving," he said, and continued on toward the back, where Dex was waiting.

"Hey, buddy, it's getting a little choppier than I'd like," Dex said as Carter stepped down into the cockpit. "I need you guys to get below."

"I don't want to go below," Carter said. "Dex, I can help. Let me steer!"

"No way," Dex said. "Not in this wind. You've been great, Carter, but I promised your mom before we set sail—no kids on deck if these swells got over six feet. You see that?" He pointed to the front of the boat, where a cloud of sea spray had just broken over the bow. "*That's* what a six-foot swell looks like. We've got a storm on the way—maybe a big one. It's time for you to take a break."

"Come on, please?" Carter said. "I thought we came out here to sail!"

Dex took him by the shoulders and looked him square in the eye.

"Remember what we talked about before we set out? My boat. My rules. Got it?"

Carter got it, all right. Arguing with Dex was like wrestling a bear. You could try, but you were never going to win.

"Now, grab your brother and get down there," Dex told him.

"Okay, fine," Carter said. "But he's not my brother, by the way. Just because my mom married his dad doesn't mean—"

"Ask me tomorrow if I care," Dexter said, and gave him a friendly but insistent shove. "Now go!"

Benjamin "Buzz" Diaz lifted his head from the rail

and looked out into the distance. All he could see from here was an endless stretch of gray clouds over an endless stretch of choppy waves.

Keeping an eye on the horizon was supposed to help with the seasickness, but so far, all it had done was remind him that he was in the middle of the biggest stretch of nowhere he'd ever seen. His stomach felt like it had been turned upside down and inside out. His legs were like rubber bands, and his head swam with a thick, fuzzy feeling, while the boat rocked and rocked and rocked.

It didn't look like this weather was going to be changing anytime soon, either. At least, not for the better.

Buzz tried to think about something else— anything else—to take his mind off how miserable he felt. He thought about his room back home. He thought about how much he couldn't wait to get there, where he could just close his door and hang out all day if he wanted, playing City of Doom and eating pepperoni pizz—

Wait, Buzz thought. *No. Not that.*

He tried to unthink anything to do with food, but it was too late. Already, he was leaning over the rail again and hurling the last of his breakfast into the ocean.

"Still feeding the fish, huh?" Suddenly, Carter was back. He put a hand on Buzz's arm. "Come on," he said. "Dex told me we have to get below."

Buzz clutched his belly. "Are you kidding?" he said. "Can't it wait?"

"No. Come on."

All week long, Carter had been running around the deck of the *Lucky Star* like he owned it or something. Still, Carter was the least of Buzz's worries right now.

It was only day four at sea, and if things kept going like this, he was going to be lucky to make it to day five.

Vanessa Diaz sat at the *Lucky Star*'s navigation station belowdecks and stared at the laptop screen in front of her. She'd only just started to learn about this stuff a few days earlier, but as far as she could tell, all that orange and red on the weather radar was a bad sign. Not to mention the scroll across the bottom of the screen, saying something about "gale-force winds and deteriorating conditions."

The first three days of their trip had been nothing but clear blue skies and warm breezes. Now, nine hundred miles off the coast of Hawaii, all of that had changed. Dexter kept saying they had to adjust their course to outrun the weather, but so far, it seemed like the weather was outrunning them. They'd changed direction at least three times, and things only seemed to be getting worse.

The question was—how *much* worse?

A chill ran down Vanessa's spine as the hatch over the galley stairs opened, and Buzz and Carter came clattering down the steps.

"How are you feeling, Buzzy?" she asked, but he didn't stop to talk. Instead, he went straight for the little bathroom—the "head," Dexter called it—and slammed the door behind him.

Her little brother was getting the worst of these bad seas, by far. Carter, on the other hand, seemed unfazed.

Sometimes Vanessa called them "the twins," as a joke, because they were both eleven but nothing alike. Carter kept his sandy hair cut short and was even kind of muscley for a kid his age. Buzz, on the other hand, had shaggy jet-black curls like their father's and was what adults liked to call husky. The kids at school just called him fat.

Vanessa didn't think her brother was fat—not exactly—but you could definitely tell he spent a lot of time in front of the TV.

"It's starting to rain," Carter said, looking up at the sky.

"Then close the hatch," Vanessa said.

"Don't tell me what to do."

Vanessa rolled her eyes. "Okay, fine. Get wet. See if I care."

He would, too, she thought. He'd just stand there and get rained on, only because she told him not to. Carter was one part bulldog and one part mule.

Jane was there now, too. She'd just come out of the tiny sleeping cabin the two girls shared.

Jane was like the opposite of Carter. She could slip in and out of a room without anyone ever noticing. With Carter, you always knew he was there.

"What are you looking at, Nessa?" Jane asked.

"Nothing." Vanessa flipped the laptop closed. "I was just checking the weather," she said.

There was no reason to scare Jane about all that. She was only nine, and tiny for her age. Vanessa was the oldest, at thirteen, and even though nobody told her to look out for Jane on this trip, she did anyway.

"Dex said there's a storm coming," Carter blurted out. "He said it's going to be major."

"Carter!" Vanessa looked over at him and rolled her eyes in Jane's direction.

But he just shrugged. "What?" he said. "You think she's not going to find out?"

"You don't have to worry about me," Jane said.

She crawled up onto Vanessa's lap and opened the computer to have a look. "Show me."

"See?" Carter said. "I know my sister."

Vanessa took a deep breath. If the idea of this trip was to make them one big happy family, it wasn't exactly working.

Technically, the whole sailing adventure was a wedding gift from her new uncle, Dexter. It had been two months since Vanessa and Buzz's father had married Carter and Jane's mother, but they'd waited until the end of the school year to take a honeymoon. Now, while their parents were hiking Volcanoes National Park and enjoying the beaches on Hawaii's Big Island, the four kids were spending the week at sea and supposedly getting to know one another better.

So far, the sailing had been amazing, but the sister-brother bonding thing? Not so much, Vanessa thought. The weather wasn't helping, either. It looked like they were going to be cooped up together for the rest of the day.

"Is that the storm?" Jane said. She pointed at the large red mass on the laptop screen.

"That's it," Vanessa answered. On the computer, it seemed as if the oncoming front had gotten even bigger in the last few minutes. She started braiding Jane's long blond hair to distract her.

"It's just rain, right?" Jane said. "If this was something really bad, we'd already know about it. Wouldn't we, Nessa?"

Vanessa tried to smile. "Sure," she said. But the truth was, she had no idea how bad it was going to get.

None of them did.

Jane sat on her bunk, with her back pressed against the wall to steady herself. The boat was rocking too hard to prop her camera on a shelf like she usually did. Instead, she held it out at arm's length and pressed Record.

"Hi, everyone. It's Jane B. again, reporting for Evanston Elementary."

It took more concentration to hold the camera steady than it did to say the words. "Today is June twenty-eighth, and it's the fourth day of our sailing trip. I don't know if you can tell, but the weather's not nearly as nice today. Here, I'll show you."

She held the camera up to the cabin's porthole to show the tossing waves outside. On the view screen, it looked as if the whole world were tilting back and forth.

She didn't need her whole class to know how scared she actually was. Not Vanessa and the boys, either. They all treated her like a baby to begin with. So she talked about other things instead.

"I read in one of Uncle Dexter's books that the Pacific Ocean is ten thousand miles across and has some of the strongest wind currents in the world," Jane narrated. "Less than one percent of the whole ocean is covered in land, so I guess there isn't much to stop the wind from blowing out here."

She'd done plenty of research for her report. She always did. Carter called her a brainiac for doing extra-credit work over summer vacation, but then again, Carter's best subject was gym.

Besides, it was something to do while this storm set in around them.

"Uncle Dexter says the weather can change really fast around here," Jane went on, as casually as she could. "In the meantime, there's not that much to tell. We're all just staying put and holding on tight. Dex calls it hunkering down, so I guess that's what we're going to do. Until later, this is Jane Benson, reporting from somewhere in the South Pacific."

By the time it started to get dark, Buzz was starting to feel normal again. Maybe the seasickness was finally behind him. Or maybe there just wasn't anything left to throw up, Buzz thought.

In any case, he still wasn't hungry. Nobody was. The weather had only gotten worse, and it seemed to have taken away everyone's appetite. The kids all spent the evening sitting around the galley table, holding on to the edges of things for balance as the boat rolled over the waves. Each time another one hit, it was like a jolt to the body.

While they waited for the storm to pass, Jane watched and rewatched all of the videos she'd made for her report so far. Vanessa sat and played the same game on her phone, over and over. She'd given up trying to text her friends days ago, when it became clear that there was no cell reception out here on the open ocean. Carter listened to music with his headphones on and practiced nautical knots with an old piece of rope.

Buzz just sat, listening to the wind whistling through the masts and the rain pelting the boat from all sides. He'd already run down the batteries on the handheld game he'd brought, along with his spare batteries. On top of that, without any sun all day, the boat's solar panel hadn't been able to generate any electricity at all for the *Lucky Star*. The only other source of power was the boat's engine, but Dexter wasn't keen to use that in the storm. Dexter had told everyone to conserve electricity until further notice. That meant no laptop, no DVDs, and as few lights as possible belowdecks.

Just after eight o'clock, when the cabin windows had gone completely dark, the hatch opened and Dexter came down the stairs. All week long, he'd been upbeat and smiley, like some kind of friendly giant who laughed at just about anything. But not now. His expression was grim as he ran a hand over his dripping-wet face.

"I hate to say it, guys, but it looks like this is going to get worse before it gets better. There's a crazy cold front playing heck with the forecasts. It's pushing some of this storm at us faster than we expected."

He stopped and held tight to the upright pole in the middle of the salon as the boat dipped and rose, and dipped again. Coffee mugs clattered against one another in the cabinet. Jane's camera slid across the table.

"This kind of thing's always a possibility, but not to worry," Dexter went on. "The only thing to do now is sit tight while we skirt around this squall a little farther."

"Does that mean we're changing course again?" Vanessa asked.

"Yep," Dex said. He went to the nav station, unrolled a chart, and looked at it. "But just temporarily. Today's Boomerang Day, and I'll have us right back on track by tomorrow."

Boomerang Day was Dex's name for the trip's midpoint, when they came around and headed back toward Hawaii. Maybe that was a good thing, Buzz thought. It meant they'd gotten half of this trip over with. Then again, it also meant that they were as far from home as they'd ever been.

When Dex looked up from his chart, he seemed to sense something in their faces. He turned toward the group again with his hands clasped in front of him.

"Guys, I think your parents would be proud to see how brave you're all being. I know it's scary, but you've got me and Joe up top, handling everything. I just need you to be down here, for one another. Make sense?"

"Yeah," Vanessa said quietly. Carter shrugged.

"Carter?" Dex said, leaning down to catch his eyes. "You got a problem with that?"

"No," Carter said. "I just wish I could help."

"You can help," he said. "Down here. Right now,

your job is to hang tough, and hang together, so you're ready to go when we need you on deck again."

Buzz looked down at the table, trying not to show his face. He didn't feel very tough right now.

"You know what?" Dex said. "I'm almost glad this storm came up."

That seemed to get everyone's attention.

"Why?" Jane asked.

"I've sailed with some rough-and-tumble crews before—even rougher than you four," he said with a wink. "I remember this one time, we were out fishing, a couple hundred miles north of Oahu. We got hit with the biggest, fastest-moving squall I've ever seen. It was like sailing sideways, with enough wind to blow you right off the deck. That storm made this one look like a little spring shower, and I don't think any of us thought we were going to see the morning."

"Um . . . Dex?" Buzz said. "I thought you said you were glad this storm came up."

"Right," he said. "My point is, we all pulled together that night and made it through. Not only that, but those guys are still some of my best buddies. A hard turn like this just brings you closer together. And let's face it, isn't that exactly what your parents wanted you kids to get out of this trip?"

Just then, the small companionway door at the back of the rear sleeping cabin opened up, and Joe shouted down from the cockpit.

"Dex? Can you get up here? *Now?*"

"What is it?" Vanessa asked, the worry plain in her voice. "What's going on?"

"Probably just a loose line. I'll go find out," Dex said.

"You sure you don't want some help?" Carter said. "I can hold the wheel."

Dexter turned and put out one of his big hands to stop Carter.

"There's nothing that needs doing right now," he said. "But I do want you guys to strap on your PFDs."

"What?" Buzz blurted out. PFD stood for

"personal flotation device"—also known as a life jacket. Dex already had his on, but he'd been working up top. "Why do we need those?"

"It's just standard operating procedure for a storm like this," Dexter said. "You never take chances on a boat." He pulled the four vests off the hooks where they hung by the stairs and dropped them on the galley table. Then he stopped, just long enough to show his old familiar smile. "There's nothing to worry about, guys."

Buzz glanced around at the others, to see if anyone was buying it. From the somber expressions all around, it didn't seem like anyone was. But Dex had already gone back up top and closed the hatch behind him.

"Watch out." Vanessa scooted Buzz out of the way as she got up from the table.

"What are you doing?" he asked.

"I'm calling Dad." She stepped over to the navigation station and pulled the black plastic satellite phone out of its wall-mounted charger.

They'd all been shown where it was and how to use it.

"But . . . we're only supposed to use that for emergencies," Jane said. Just then, another powerful gust of wind screeched from outside, tossing the boat into a hard tilt. Vanessa barely caught herself on the countertop to keep from stumbling, while the others struggled to put on their life jackets.

"Yeah, close enough," she said, and started to dial.

———

Vanessa held on to the nav station desk and sat herself down as the boat continued to tilt and roll. She didn't care if Dexter wanted them using the satellite phone or not. Maybe he'd been through worse, but she sure never had.

The phone wasn't complicated, either. They'd been shown all of the emergency equipment on the first day, when Dex and Joe had taken them through hours of "boat school" before they set sail. Vanessa hadn't paid attention to all of it, but this was something she remembered. She dialed zero-zero-one and then her father's cell number.

As soon as it started to ring on the other end, she felt tears begin to sting the corners of her eyes.

"Hello?" her father's voice came suddenly in her ear.

"Dad?" Vanessa shouted. "Dad!"

"Vanessa, what's going on?" Eric Diaz asked. "I can barely hear you."

"We're in a storm, Daddy. It's bad. Like, really bad."

Jane was there suddenly, reaching for the phone.

"Can I talk to Mom? Please? Pretty please?"

Then Carter was there, too. Only Buzz stayed where he was, but he watched just as intently as the other two.

"Where's Dex?" her father asked.

"He and Joe are up top," Vanessa told him.

"Everyone's okay. I'm just . . . I just wanted to hear your voice."

"Listen, sweetie, you're going to be fine. Dex and Joe know what they're doing. Just try to hold on and be brave, okay?"

Vanessa took a deep breath. "Okay," she said, mostly because there wasn't any choice. "Is Beth there, Dad? Jane wants to talk to her."

"All right. Hang on a second. I'll get her."

But before Vanessa could even hand over the phone, an enormous scraping sound screeched up from under the boat. Everything seemed to stop short with a sudden, violent jerk, as if someone had jammed on the brakes. Vanessa felt herself thrown toward the back of the boat. The others tumbled around, too, and the phone flew out of her hand. A cascade of books, dishes, storage baskets, and swiftly unrolling charts came down on top of her where she landed hard against the aft cabin door.

"What just happened?" Carter shouted.

"Did we hit some rocks?" Buzz asked.

"Dad!" Vanessa shouted. "Dad? Can you hear

me?" She started scrambling through the pile of debris on the floor, but she couldn't find the phone anywhere.

Instead, her hand landed in cold water. It was soaking the carpet, Vanessa realized. When she looked to her right, she saw it was also pouring in from under the small engine-compartment door.

At the same moment, Joe came barreling down the galley steps.

"Joe? What's going on?" Vanessa said.

He clambered over the mess as if none of them were even there, and fell onto the wooden stool bolted in front of the nav station.

"What are you doing?" Vanessa asked. "Joe, where's Dex? There's water coming in!"

But Joe wasn't listening. He was holding the sideband radio transmitter with one hand and adjusting a dial on the console with the other.

"SOS, SOS, this is the *Lucky Star*," Joe said into the handset. "SOS, SOS, this is the *Lucky Star*, do you copy?"

Whatever was said next, Vanessa didn't hear. It

was swallowed up by a brilliant flash of lightning and a crash of thunder too overwhelming to be anywhere but right on top of them.

In the next moment, the entire cabin was thrown into darkness.

CHAPTER 3

Buzz's mind was a jumble of panic, fear, and blind confusion. He heard everyone talking at once in the dark, but not what any of them were saying. Jane screamed. Joe was saying something about SOS. Vanessa and Carter were yelling, maybe at each other. The only light in the shifting galley came through the hatchway, from several more flashes of lightning, one after the other.

He was on the ground, somewhere near the back of the boat. That much Buzz knew. It felt like they had crashed, but if that was the case, why were they still moving?

The first thing that made any kind of sense was the stinging chill of water, rising fast around his feet and hands. The shock of it sent him into action, moving faster now than he had in a long time.

He felt his way through the dark, into the rear cabin. It was a small space, so it wasn't hard to find the two tall steps at the back. Struggling to keep his balance, Buzz reached for the place where he knew the companionway door to be. As soon as his fingers landed on the latch, he threw it open and leaned out into the cockpit, where Dexter was holding on to the captain's wheel, trying to steer the boat against the storm.

"What are you doing?" Dex screamed over the wind. "Get below!"

"We can't!" Buzz shouted back. "It's flooding. Water's coming in fast!"

He pointed back the way he'd come. Dexter crouched down to see past him, his headlamp shining inside. When Buzz turned to look for himself, he saw Joe herding the others up the stairs on the opposite side. The water had continued to pour in. It was past Joe's knees already and nearly up to Jane's waist.

Dexter pulled Buzz up onto his feet in the cockpit and slammed the companionway door closed.

"Take the wheel!" he shouted in his ear. There was no question of yes or no. "Hold on as tight as you can. I'll be right back."

"I don't know how to do this!" Buzz shouted. Carter was always the one begging to steer the boat, not him. And now he was supposed to learn in the middle of the world's biggest storm?

"You can do it!" Dex said. "Just hang on!"

"Wait!" Buzz's heart was racing as fast as the wind that whipped past him. There wasn't even time to think. "Where are you going?"

"To open the life raft!" Dex shouted, just before he left. "We're getting off the boat!"

Carter stood at the top of the galley stairs in the

downpour; Jane hovered just behind him, grasping his waist with both hands.

Vanessa was there, too, holding on to the small banister for balance. "Where's Joe going?" she asked.

"I don't know!" Carter said, and leaned farther out to see.

Joe had turned a one-eighty from the stairs and was working his way back toward the middle of the boat where Dex was waiting for him. They quickly started wrestling with the straps that kept the big life-raft capsule lashed to the deck.

Carter felt a cold sense of dread run through him. They were going to have to abandon ship, weren't they? This was even worse than he'd thought.

"Wait here!" Carter shouted at Vanessa and Jane. He clipped himself to the jackline on that side and started to follow back the way Joe had gone. He'd barely taken a few steps before the boat pitched hard again and sent him stumbling to his knees, then flat out on the deck. Even from where he was, though, he could hear the two men shouting at each other over the storm.

"I don't think we can launch in these conditions!" Joe yelled.

"We don't have a choice!" Dex bellowed back.

"But how are we—"

"One of us has to go in with it!"

That was it. There was no more conversation. Within a minute, they'd freed up the capsule. Each of them took a side and heaved the whole thing into the water, where it opened automatically, unfolding and inflating at the same time. Suddenly, there was a bright orange, canopied disc bobbing on the waves—but it was also drifting quickly away from the boat.

"GET IT!" Carter heard Dexter shout. "I'll throw you a line!"

Carter watched from the edge of the deck as Joe dove without any hesitation. He disappeared into the churning water and then resurfaced several yards away. With some effort, he managed to swim over to the raft and scramble up into it.

Working quickly, Dexter had already unspooled an orange floater on a line of rope and tossed it straight out to where Joe was. He wrapped the other end of the line around his own waist, wedged his foot against one of the cleats on the deck, and then motioned for Carter to bring the others over.

When Carter looked back, Vanessa was out on the deck, but she'd clipped herself in on the other side, away from the life raft. And Jane was still peeking around from the stairwell. He couldn't see Buzz at all.

"Come on!" Dex shouted. He held on to the line with one hand and motioned for them to stay low as they came. The boat heeled again to the side, and he stumbled to keep on his feet. "Let's go, let's go!"

"Are we getting off the boat?" Jane yelled when Carter reached her. It was easier to nod than to try and answer right now, and he still needed to get Vanessa and Buzz.

"Hurry!" Dex yelled again. Carter turned to look and caught sight of Buzz somewhere over near the cockpit.

That's when the next crash of lightning hit. Even with the storm raging, it was deafeningly loud.

Carter saw a bright flash from somewhere near the top of the mast, like an explosion of light and force. The sailboat itself twisted nearly all the way around with a violent turn. The life raft veered off in the opposite direction, and Dexter, still holding on to the line, lost his footing altogether. Before Carter could try to get to him, Dex slammed into the railing, flipped over it, and was dragged all the way overboard by the force.

Jane screamed.

"No!" Vanessa shouted.

In a matter of seconds, the boat was driven in one direction and the life raft in another. It was too dark to see clearly, but Carter could just make out the flashing orange light rigged to the raft and the vague glow of Uncle Dexter's headlamp in the water as Joe used the rope line to haul him in. Dex was shouting something back their way, but it was impossible to make out a single word.

Carter stepped onto the rail. He thought about diving in after them, but that seemed like suicide. And he couldn't leave the others. Instead, he looked around desperately for another length of rope or anything he might use to pull Dex back in.

But it was already too late. By the time he looked out toward the water again, Dex, Joe, and the life raft had all disappeared completely into the storm.

CHAPTER 4

Buzz couldn't believe what he'd just seen. It all happened in a matter of seconds. One moment, Dexter was motioning him over to get into the life raft, and the next, he was just . . . gone.

Now the four kids were alone on the sinking boat, left to fend for themselves against the storm.

Buzz stayed low in the cockpit, his arms threaded around the spokes of the captain's wheel. There was no trying to steer anymore. It was only a matter of holding on and trying not to get swept overboard himself.

Heavy sea spray and driving rain smacked

against his face as they crested another enormous swell. The entire boat seemed to stand on end for a moment, its bow pointed at the sky, and Buzz's stomach lurched wildly, just before the hull slammed down hard on the other side.

Keeping to a crouch, he looked around trying to spot the others. Carter and Vanessa were at the front now, hanging on to the rails on either side. Hopefully, they were both still clipped to their safety lines.

But Jane . . . where was Jane? Had she gone over, like Dexter? Buzz scanned the dark ocean all around him—what he could see of it, anyway. Even if he did spot her, he realized, he'd never be able to save her now.

Suddenly, another loud, cracking sound split the air. Not lightning this time. Something even closer. It wasn't until he looked straight up that he realized what it was. The fifty-foot mast towering over his head had begun to sway like a tree about to come down in the storm. And if it did, it was going to fall right toward the two at the front.

"Vanessa! Carter!" he screamed, but the wind seemed to whip the words right out of his mouth before they could do any good.

Next came the sound of popping bolts. Then the groan of metal buckling under its own weight as the mast started to fall.

"LOOK OUT!" Buzz yelled as loudly as he could.

But the storm was louder.

Carter never even heard the mast coming until it crashed onto the deck, just barely to his left. The impact sent him sprawling on his back again. Fiberglass tore like paper around him. Teakwood splintered and broke off at crazy angles. The mast itself dipped, top first, into the water, and then slid right off the boat like a giant goalpost, taking the entire side railing with it.

Before he could even try to move away from the edge of the deck, another wall of water slammed into the *Lucky Star*. It came from the left—port—

this time, sending the boat heeling sharply onto its right side.

Carter grabbed on to the only thing he had left—his safety line. As the boat tipped, gravity took hold, and his body pivoted toward the water. The mesh of the jackline dug hard into his palms, but it held him where he was.

At the same moment, a scream came from across the deck. He looked over—up, really—and saw Vanessa tumbling free of her own line, straight toward him. With the railing gone, there was nothing to keep her from dropping right off the edge and into the water.

Nothing but me, Carter thought, and strained to reach his hand out as far as he could.

Vanessa felt a sharp snap when her safety line gave way. She pinwheeled her arms to try and stop herself, but it was no good. Already, she was falling sideways with the tilt of the boat. Her shoulder pounded hard against . . . something . . . as the world turned upside down and over again in the dark.

The only thing left to grab was Carter's hand. Vanessa reached for it as she went past, and for a moment, they connected. But then her fingers slipped out of his. Her body flew across the last of the rain-slick deck and out over the water.

"Nooo!"

Just as quickly, she snapped back hard. The hood of her raincoat had caught on something, even as the waves below tried to swallow her up to the waist.

"I've got you!" Carter yelled from behind. "Give me your hand!"

Vanessa reached toward his voice, grasping blindly. She found his arm first and started to climb it like a rope, one hand over the other, until she could swing a leg back up onto the deck. She pulled herself the rest of the way on board and collapsed there, catching her breath while Carter clipped her onto his own line.

"Don't move!" he shouted.

Lying flat against the rocking deck of the boat, Vanessa caught sight of Jane huddled on the galley stairs. She was only a shadow in the dark from here, but the tiny size of her was unmistakable.

"Jane!" she yelled. *"Jane!"*

Jane barely moved at all. Her only response was to point back the other way, toward the front of the boat. When Vanessa turned to look, all she saw was a dark blur. But then, with the next flash of lightning, it became clear. The unmistakable, jagged mounds of a rocky shoreline loomed straight ahead of them.

"We're going to crash!" she screamed.

Jane wedged her foot against the opposite wall of the stairwell and squeezed her eyes shut, unable to move or even to yell out. It was like the voice inside her head was trapped there, even as her mouth opened and closed.

Wake up, wake up, wake up!

But this was no dream, and the crash came all too soon.

With one last surge, a huge swell of water rose up under the boat, even as it sent the whole craft hurtling forward. Another unbearable sound of rock tearing at the hull came from below. Jane heard breaking, splintering sounds—and then nothing at all, as the force of the crash sent her tumbling back down into the galley.

She felt herself turning over, and over again, as the water continued to flood into the boat. Then she slammed into something hard as everything came to a fast standstill.

For several bewildering seconds, Jane swung her hands around, trying to find something to grab on to. She couldn't even tell which way was up, and a wave of panic threatened to overwhelm her.

Finally, her feet found solid ground. She stood up quickly, gasping—the water in the cabin was now up to her chest.

But where were the others?

The boat had stopped moving—a bizarre feeling after the roller coaster of the storm—but the wind and rain and lightning were still raging outside as much as ever.

She heard Carter first, shouting her name in the dark.

"Jane? Jane!"

"I'm here!" she screamed back, and stumbled through the water until she hit the galley steps, just as Carter came down to get her.

Vanessa and Buzz were right behind, just shadows in the dark now.

"Are you hurt?" Carter asked.

Jane had banged both her knees, and her head, but nothing felt broken. When she tried to answer, all that came out was a choked sob. Carter pulled her closer and held on tight.

"Hang on, Janie. Don't be afraid," he said. "I've got you."

"What do we do now?" Buzz shouted.

But there was no answer for that, either. The boat seemed to be lodged against whatever rocks they'd landed on, at least for the time being. Everything beyond the edges of the deck was invisible in the dark, and the whole cabin down below was flooded. They were already doing the only thing they could, huddling together on the stairs for warmth, keeping as much out of the storm as possible and just waiting for it to be over.

CHAPTER 5

Carter blinked awake.

At first, nothing made sense. The clean white deck. The bright sunlight. The soft sound of the ocean.

He blinked again, several times, and then remembered where he was. Jane, Buzz, and Vanessa were all right there, still asleep on the stairs. The galley down below was a total wreck, but outside, it was a clear, blue-sky day. Even that seemed strange.

Carter eased his arm from around Jane to crawl up onto the deck and look around. His whole ribcage sent up a sharp wave of pain as he did—from the crash, he remembered. It was all coming back in pieces. When he lifted up his still-damp T-shirt, the bruises on his chest and midsection made him look like he'd gone a couple of rounds with a heavyweight champion.

But he was alive, anyway. They all were. The whole crash seemed like some kind of bad dream now.

Up on the deck, the first thing he saw was the high cliff wall they'd crashed into in the dark. The bow of the boat looked as if it had been chewed right off, leaving the rest of the *Lucky Star* wedged in among the rocks at a shallow angle. It was tricky keeping his footing, but not impossible.

Off to the right, Carter saw where the craggy shoreline continued on for a hundred yards or more before it curved away and out of sight.

To the left, down a short drop from the rocky shelf where they'd landed, was a long stretch of sandy beach. There were palm trees everywhere, and small crabs skittered around the water's edge.

It looked to Carter like somewhere he might want to go on vacation, if he were sitting at home and seeing all this on TV.

But I'm not, he thought. *I am so not.*

Then with a sudden flash of memory, Dexter and Joe came to mind. Carter whipped around to look out at the ocean, instinctively scanning for a flash of orange life raft. He checked the beach again, too, and even looked toward the woods that grew beyond the line of palms higher up on the shoreline.

There was no sign of them anywhere.

"Hello?" he shouted. "Dex? Joe? *Anyone?*"

The only answer that came back was from the other three as they started to stir on the galley stairs.

"Carter?" Vanessa called out.

"What . . .?" Buzz croaked. "Where are we?"

Jane looked up from where she was, wide-eyed and silent.

Slowly, the three of them came up onto the deck. They stayed low at first, as if the boat might start moving again without warning. But in fact, at least thirty yards of rock separated them from the ocean now. The storm's tide had turned around sometime in the night, leaving the *Lucky Star* high and dry.

Nobody said anything at first. Jane came and stuck closer to Carter. Buzz sat down cross-legged on the deck, looking stunned.

"Where are we?" he said.

"Good question," Carter answered.

After another long silence, Jane spoke up next.

"Do you think anyone got that SOS?" she asked, looking at Vanessa.

"I don't know. Probably," Vanessa said. "Maybe."

"Can we try and send another?" Jane asked.

Major duh, Carter thought. That should have been the first thing they thought of. Leave it to Jane. She was the smartest nine-year-old he knew.

Vanessa seemed to agree. Without a word, she'd already turned and run down the galley steps. Everyone else followed closely behind.

Down below, the boat's main cabin looked to Buzz like a disaster area. All the water had drained out by now, but the floor was covered with bloated books, sea charts, cushions, clothing, pots and pans, utensils, and even a few framed maps from the wall, with shattered or missing glass. It reminded him of one of those TV shows where the bad guys come in and trash the good guy's apartment while they're looking for something.

Already, Vanessa had picked her way over to the navigation station, where she was fiddling with several knobs and dials. She was good with computers at home and had spent more time on the boat with all this stuff than the rest of them had. If anyone could figure out how to use the radio, it would be her.

While they all watched silently, she picked up a handheld transmitter that dangled off the console. It was the same one that Joe used to send an SOS the night before.

"Hello?" Vanessa said into the transmitter. "Can anyone hear me? Hello?"

Buzz's heart thudded in his chest, waiting for something—a voice, or even just static. Vanessa flipped several more switches, but it was no good. The radio was clearly dead.

"There's no power," she said. "Buzz, check the engine. Carter, do you know how to try and start it?"

"For sure," Carter said, ducking into the aft cabin and up through the companionway door to the cockpit.

Buzz went to the engine compartment and opened it up. He'd looked in here only once before, and it had been mostly dark. Now, light flooded in where a long, jagged hole had been torn through the hull from the outside. It didn't take an expert to see how badly smashed the engine was. For all he knew, half of it had fallen out through that hole.

"Is anything happening?" Carter yelled down.

"Nothing," Vanessa called back up. "Are you sure you know how to start it up?"

"Yes, I'm sure," Carter snapped.

"Uh, guys? It's not going to happen," Buzz said,

pointing into the compartment. Vanessa came over to look, and then Carter, too, as he climbed back down to join them.

The only thing that seemed to be intact was the electrical bank. It looked like six car batteries, lined up on a shelf at the side of the compartment. Whether they were still hooked up to the rest of the boat, it was hard to say. Even if they were, Dexter had explained on the very first day that there were only two ways to charge those batteries. One was by running the engine. The other was through the boat's solar panel, which was now facedown on the deck, where it had ripped free of its mount during the crash.

"What about the laptop?" Jane asked, picking it up from the mess on the floor. As she did, water drizzled out from several of the ports and even through the keyboard. She tried the On-Off switch anyway, but nothing happened.

"We wouldn't be able to get online even if it was working," Vanessa said. "Not without the modem, and that takes electricity. My cell's around here somewhere, too, but I haven't gotten a signal since we left Hawaii. What we really need is. . . ."

She stopped then, and her hand went up to her mouth. For the first time, Vanessa looked excited.

"What is it?" Buzz asked.

"The sat phone!" she said.

"The what?"

"The satellite phone! I can't believe I didn't think of it before. If it's still charged, we could . . . omigosh! You guys, we could make a call!"

"Well, where is it now?" Carter said.

"I don't know!" Vanessa said. "But it's got to be here somewhere. Everyone . . . start looking!"

———

Vanessa racked her mind, trying to remember where, exactly, she'd been when she last had the phone. Not that it even mattered. After the crash, it could have wound up anywhere.

"Go through everything!" she told the others.

"Watch out for the glass, though. It's got to be here somewhere."

Soon, they were all picking through the mess and piling it, piece by piece, on the table, the galley counter, and anywhere else they could. It was agonizingly slow going, with so much to sort through. But then—

"Here it is!" Jane shouted. She poked her head out from under the galley table, and held up the chunky black plastic phone. The antenna was up, Vanessa saw, and the small screen above the keypad was lit.

"It's still on!" she said, pressing it to her ear. "Hello? Hello?"

Nobody was there, which wasn't a surprise. It had been at least ten hours since the crash. The question was—how long did these things hold their charge? When she looked at the display again, the green-and-black battery indicator was down to a single bar. But that could be enough.

"Who should we call?" Jane said. Vanessa didn't

have to think about it. She turned the unit off, then on again, and hit the Redial button, just like using a regular phone at home. A few seconds later, it started to ring.

"Please answer, please answer, please answer, please answer. . . ."

"Wait!" Buzz said suddenly. "Shouldn't we try to figure out where we are first so we can tell them?"

The truth of it hit Vanessa like cold water in the face. Of course that made more sense. But then all at once, Beth Benson was there on the phone.

"Hello?" she said frantically. "Dexter, is that you?"

"Beth! It's Vanessa!" she said. All three of the others crowded around, pressing their ears as close as they could get.

"Vanessa! Thank goodness! Is everyone okay?"

"No," Vanessa said. "We're not okay. We crashed, Beth. Is my dad with you?"

"Mom?" Jane called out.

"Jane? Is that you?"

"We're all here," Vanessa told her. "The four of us, anyway."

Beth's voice went up a step. "Where's Dexter?" she said. "Where's Joe?"

"We don't know," Vanessa told her. She heard her own voice crack as she said it, and took a deep breath. It wasn't going to help anyone if she lost it right now. "They were trying to help us into the life raft and it got pulled away before we could get in. Now we aren't sure where they are."

"Vanessa, you're going to be okay," Beth said. "Your dad and I are at the Coast Guard station in Kona. They've been trying to reach the boat all night. I'm going to put you on with one of the people who are going to come help you. Just hold on."

A moment later, an unfamiliar man's voice came on the line.

"Hi, Vanessa, my name's Commander Carl Blakey. I want you to listen carefully, okay?"

There were other voices in the background, too. They were on speakerphone now, and people were listening in. Vanessa imagined a whole room full of them standing there. Somehow, that only made her more nervous.

"Okay," she said. "But, I don't know how long this phone is going to stay charged. There's only one bar left."

"Then let's get right to it," the man said. Vanessa had already forgotten his name. "Where are you on the boat right now?"

"At the nav station," Vanessa told him.

"There should be a GPS unit, either up in the cockpit or right there at the navigation station," the commander said. "It might look like a small TV mounted on the wall, or it could be a handheld unit. Do you know what I'm talking about?"

"I think so," Vanessa said. She remembered Joe saying something about the Global Positioning System on the boat, but right now, she couldn't come up with a picture of it in her mind, and she didn't see anything that looked like a little TV as she scanned the console.

"I'm looking," Vanessa said. "But I'm not sure. Could they have taken it in the life raft with them?"

"That's possible," the commander said. "We never

received any SOS or distress call, so it's been hard to track your location."

Softly, the phone beeped twice in Vanessa's ear. When she pulled it away to look, the battery charge indicator was starting to flash.

"I think the phone's about to run out!" she said.

The commander's voice stayed calm, but he spoke more quickly now. "How about this, Vanessa. Can you tell me anything about where you are? Even just approximately?"

"Find the charts!" Vanessa whispered to the others. All three of them started rooting through the piles they'd just made, pulling out whatever they could find and spreading them on the table.

"Is there anything you remember about your location before the storm?" the commander asked her again.

"Not really . . . I'm sorry," Vanessa said. There were three different charts in front of her by now, but they all looked alike, with their circles, grids, and tiny numbers. "I'm looking, but I can't tell where we are."

Then Jane spoke up. "Boomerang Day!" she said, as if it had just come to her.

"That's right!" Vanessa said. "Right, right! We were just about to come around and head back to Hawaii. That means we were. . . ." She squeezed her eyes shut, trying to remember. "Nine hundred miles from Kona. That's how far we were going. Except then, he started changing course when the weather got bad."

"Your uncle did?" the commander asked her.

"Yes," Vanessa said. "Three times, I think. Or maybe four. We were supposed to—"

Again, the phone beeped twice.

"It's going to run out!" Vanessa said.

"Keep going," the commander told her. "You were supposed to what, Vanessa?"

"We were supposed to get back on course this morning. I know that."

"Which direction? Which way did Dexter alter his course, can you tell me?"

"I don't know!" Vanessa said. The tears were starting to come. She couldn't help it.

"Okay," the commander said. "Okay. Just hold on one second."

"I don't know if I have a second!" Vanessa told him.

And then sure enough, she didn't. There was no last beep, no click, no anything. The line just went dead.

"Hello?" she said. "Hello? Please? Are you there?"

But it was no good. The display on the phone had gone blank, and the people at the other end of the line—including their parents—were gone. All Vanessa could hear now was the wind outside, and the sound of waves breaking softly in the distance.

CHAPTER 6

Vanessa stared at the dead phone in her hand for a long time. She knew there was no way to get the commander back on the line, but that seemed unacceptable. There had to be a way, somehow.

But, of course, there wasn't.

"So, what now?" Carter was the first to say.

"I think we should stay put," Buzz spoke up. "That's what they always say you should do when you're lost, right?"

"We're not at the mall, Buzz," Carter said. "And *they* don't even know where we are."

"We have to find Dexter and Joe," Vanessa interrupted.

Everyone stopped to look at her.

"What do you mean?" Carter said. "How do you even know they're here?"

"They've got to be," Vanessa said.

If they weren't, that meant she was the oldest one here. And *that* meant she was supposed to know what to do. It was one thing to be in charge of the house for a few hours on a Friday night or to watch over Jane while their parents went to a movie. This was something else entirely—as in, life and death.

"They're probably a hundred miles from here by now," Carter insisted. "You didn't see what I saw. That storm blew them away faster than—"

Vanessa cut him off with a glare. "We'll find them," she said.

She knew he wasn't *trying* to scare Jane, but Carter did this kind of thing all the time—talking first and thinking later. Or not thinking at all. She looked him in the eye, then over at Jane, and back again.

"Yeah, okay," he said. "You're right. Let's start looking."

"Um . . ." Jane held up her hand as if they were at school. "I'm thirsty," she said. "Like, super thirsty."

"Actually, me too," Carter said.

"Me three," Buzz said. He was closest to the galley sink and tried the faucet. Nobody was too surprised when nothing came out. The crash had done a lot of damage to the boat.

"There's got to be water somewhere," Vanessa said. "A tank or something."

"There is," Carter said. He was already at the galley table, moving more junk out of the way. "Give me a hand here."

Carter knew exactly what to do next. Uncle Dex had shown them practically everything there was to know about the boat on the first day.

"The water's right there," he said. He went to the U-shaped bench around the table and lifted the long center seat straight off. A large, heavy-duty plastic tank took up most of the space underneath.

"My brother's a genius!" Jane crowed.

"I don't know about that," Carter said, but he liked hearing it all the same. It wasn't that often that someone called him *smart*.

"Okay, genius, how do we get in there?" Vanessa asked.

"It can't be that hard," he said. The tank was meant to be lightweight, for sailing. "We just need something to cut through that plastic. Like a big knife, or—"

"Or an axe," Buzz said. Already, he was unclipping the small axe that hung on the wall next to the fire extinguisher.

"That'll do." Carter grinned as he took it in his hands. This was the kind of thing you'd get yelled at for even thinking about at home. Now there was no choice.

"Be careful," Vanessa said.

"I'll be okay," he told her.

"I meant, be careful with the tank. That's our only water."

Carter nodded. He hadn't thought about that. But if there was one thing he had, it was good aim. He wasn't a two-time Little League all-star pitcher for nothing.

He pointed the tip of the axe blade at the top middle of the big plastic container so he wouldn't miss. Everyone seemed to hold their breath as he raised the axe halfway to his shoulder and brought it down—hard, but not too hard. The corner of the blade punctured the tank on the first swing.

It didn't take long after that. With half a dozen more chops, Carter opened up a triangle-shaped hole big enough to reach through. Soon, they were all dipping cups inside and drinking their fill. Buzz found a dry box of granola bars, too, and they all gobbled those down.

As soon as they had, it was as if everyone's thoughts turned back to Dex and Joe at the same time.

"The sooner we can find them, the sooner we can get out of here," Vanessa said. "Let's get moving."

There were no arguments there. The four of them moved back up the galley steps as a group, ready to step off the deck of the *Lucky Star* for the first time in five days.

CHAPTER 7

The rocky shoreline where they'd crashed looked to Jane like something from an alien planet. As they climbed off the ruined front of the *Lucky Star*, she saw that all the rocks around them were rough, black, and covered with tiny holes. They looked like giant petrified sponges that someone had charred to a crisp.

"I think this is lava," she said. She'd read about this before, how a lot of South Pacific islands had grown out of the ocean from volcanic explosions, over millions of years.

Nobody else seemed interested, though. The idea

right now was to find Dex and Joe. As soon as they'd all jumped from the rocks down to the soft sand below, everyone shed their rain gear and started up the beach, shouting at the tops of their lungs.

"HELLO?"

"DEX?"

"JOE?"

"ANYONE HERE?"

Without talking about it, they spread out as they went. Buzz moved down toward the water's edge. Vanessa stuck closer to the tree line, peering up into the jungle. And Carter and Jane walked straight up the middle of the wide beach.

"Do you think those Coast Guard people will know where we are?" she asked Carter.

"No doubt," he said, sounding sure of himself. "There's probably, like, a hundred people out looking for us right now."

"That's good," Jane said. She hoped it was true, but she'd also seen the way Carter and Vanessa had looked at each other on the boat. Everyone was always trying to protect her, whether she needed it or not.

As the beach started to curve around a bend, Jane stopped and looked back. She was surprised to see how far they'd come already. From here, the *Lucky Star* looked like a broken toy sitting on a stone shelf. The sight of it brought memories of the crash flooding back into her mind, and she couldn't help the tears that started down her cheeks.

As Vanessa and Buzz wandered over, Jane could see Buzz was crying, too. It only made her feel worse.

"What if something terrible happened?" she said with a sob. "What if Dex and Joe aren't . . . coming back?"

Vanessa took Jane by one hand and Buzz by the other. "Everyone sit down," she said. "Right here."

Her dark brown eyes were red around the edges, maybe from the salt air, but maybe from trying not to cry herself. Only Carter looked the same. His jaw was set hard, and his eyes were even harder.

"We're going to find them," Vanessa said. "They'll know what to do. And then they'll do it. I'll bet we'll be on a helicopter before lunchtime." She squeezed Jane's hand. "Okay, Jane?"

Jane nodded. She was glad Vanessa was here right now. She'd been like the big sister Jane had always wanted, even before their parents got married.

"Okay, Buzz?"

"Yeah," he said, and scrubbed his eyes with the backs of his hands.

"Okay, Carter?" Vanessa said.

Carter didn't answer. He was looking back toward the rocky shelf but higher up, above the boat.

"That's totally where we should go," he said.

Jane turned to see. "Where?" she said.

He pointed at a flat rocky outcropping at the top of the cliffs where they'd crashed. From here, it looked like the very ceiling of the island. "I'll bet the view is crazy from up there. That's the place to look for them."

"What do you mean?" Buzz asked. "Like, walk up there, through the jungle?"

"How do you even know you can get there?" Vanessa said.

Carter shrugged. "One way to find out. Who's in?"

Instead of waiting for an answer, he got up and started walking back the way they'd come.

Jane looked at Vanessa to see what she'd do. After a moment's hesitation, Vanessa shrugged, too.

"He's kind of right," she said, and then yelled at Carter's back, "Thanks for waiting!"

Carter didn't even slow down. Their mother always said he was part beagle, the way he liked to be at the front of the pack, no matter what he was doing. In any case, it was better than sitting around crying, Jane thought.

She got up, brushed the sand off her legs, and started following him up the beach. "Come on, you guys," she called back to the other two. "Let's go!"

———

Carter liked being in the lead. As soon as he'd gotten nearly all the way back to the boat, he looked toward the cliffs to get his bearings, then headed straight up into the jungle.

It was a strange feeling, leaving the beach behind, like moving from one world into another. The trees grew thickly here, in layer after layer of vegetation. Some of them towered over his head, others lay in a random crisscross on the ground, turning the whole forest into one giant obstacle course.

And then there were the mosquitoes—zillions of them, like a tiny army just waiting to attack as soon as someone entered their territory. Carter could hear Vanessa, Jane, and Buzz behind him, slapping at their arms and legs as he led the way.

Not far up the hill, the ground flattened out a bit. As Carter came around a large stone formation, he saw the black hole of a cave, straight ahead.

"Wow," Vanessa said quietly.

"Yeah," Carter agreed. "You could drive a semi truck through there."

The cave's opening was huge and extended farther back than any of them could see.

"Hello?" Carter's voice bounced off the rock walls. "Anyone home?"

"Do you think there are any wild animals around here? Like . . . predators?" Buzz asked tentatively.

"Probably," Jane said. "But not like bears or cougars or anything. More like wild boars."

It was kind of amazing, the way Jane could remember almost everything she ever read. And Jane read a lot. Sometimes Carter called her Chip, because her brain was like one big microchip.

"What's a wild boar?" Buzz said.

"Like a pig," Jane said. "With tusks."

"Oh, like the Minotaurs in Lost Temple 3?"

"I guess."

"Let's keep moving," Vanessa said, slapping another mosquito. "I'm going to run out of blood in a second."

There wasn't anything to see, anyway, so Carter pushed on. Soon, the ground sloped up again, into more woods. Before long, though, several patches of blue sky started to show through the trees overhead.

"I think we're getting there," he said. Straight ahead, he could see a steep, gravelly slope leading up to what looked like another patch of open ground.

"Are you sure this is the right way?" Vanessa asked.

"Totally," Carter said. He wasn't, exactly, but he knew if he admitted it, Vanessa would just try to take over.

He made a running start to get as high up the slope as he could, the shale and gravel sliding away under his feet. Fortunately, there were enough tree roots and larger rocks to give him a few handholds on the way up.

The others came behind. He saw Buzz slide all the way back on his first try, but Vanessa put out a hand to help him up. Jane's small size seemed to work for her, and she made steady progress, keeping low to the ground. She could be a little monkey when she wanted to. At home, she was practically as fast on the climbing wall at their mom's gym as Carter was.

But there was no way Carter was going to let Jane or anyone beat him to the top. He dug his toes into the ground and made it the rest of the way in one last, ragged sprint.

"This way!" he shouted back. "We're almost—AUGH!"

Carter stopped short, pinwheeling his arms to keep from falling over the edge of a sheer drop-off. It had only just shown itself as he reached the summit. His stomach flip-flopped, and he took a quick step back, kneeling down to steady himself on the ground.

"What is it?" Vanessa called up.

"Be careful," he shouted. "There's, like, a gorge or something up here."

What was in front of him now was a deep ravine that seemed to split the island's cliffs right in half. All he saw way down at the bottom was a jumble of brush and more rocks.

And straight across, Carter could see the rocky outcropping he'd spotted from the beach—so close now but completely beyond their reach.

CHAPTER 8

By the time Buzz got to the top of the gravel slope, Carter, Jane, and Vanessa already had a plan for what to do next. So much for taking a break and catching his breath.

"We're going to head over there," Carter said, pointing along the edge of the ravine.

Maybe fifty feet to the right, there was a stand of tall trees clumped together. One of them had come down—recently, from the look of it. Now it stretched across the gap like a natural bridge.

Buzz looked down into the ravine. It was like looking off the roof of a ten-story building, and it gave him a hollow feeling in the pit of his stomach.

"You want to cross that thing?" Buzz said.

"Do you see a better way?" Carter asked. Already, they were on the move, hiking laterally along the edge of the chasm.

It didn't take long to reach the base of the tree. Dirt clods hung off the exposed roots, and the leaves on the branches at the far side were still green.

"I bet it came down in that storm last night," Jane said. She looked nervous but ready to go.

Buzz took a deep breath. "Shouldn't we vote on this or something?" he said.

"What is it with you guys and voting?" Carter asked.

"That's what we always used to do at home," Vanessa told him. She meant before their parents had married each other. "Like when we'd rent a movie and couldn't decide what to watch."

"Yeah, well, we'd just rent both movies. That way, everyone gets what they want," Carter said. "I'm not turning around now."

"I think I'm going, too," Vanessa said, and put a

hand on Buzz's shoulder. "You don't have to come if you don't want. You can keep watch."

Buzz was already dripping with sweat, but he felt his face go a little warmer still. *Keep watch?* that was what the popular kids always told the fat kid when they didn't want him around. And he wasn't even that fat.

"I'm coming," he said before he could think about it too much. "Just . . . go."

Carter went first and climbed right up through the roots to stand at the very base of the trunk. The whole tree was huge, at least three feet thick.

"Feels solid to me," he said. Then he dropped onto his belly, straddled the trunk with his legs, and started pulling himself across.

Buzz watched what he did, trying to memorize every move. The only time he'd done anything even close to this, it had been with a game controller, an avatar, and a couple of spare lives.

He couldn't help feeling a little jealous of Carter. This kind of stuff was always so easy for him. In about three seconds, it seemed, Carter had made it across and was dropping to the ground on the far side.

"No sweat!" he shouted back. "Come on!"

Jane scrambled up next and started right across. Once she was out of earshot, Vanessa turned to Buzz.

"You really don't have to," she said.

"I know," he answered. But he was still going to do it. There were probably worse ways to die—not that he could think of any right now.

As soon as Jane had made it across, Buzz gritted his teeth and climbed up onto the base of the trunk.

"Stay low," Vanessa said softly. "And don't look down."

"Stay low. Don't look down," he repeated.

"And keep moving."

Buzz nodded, took one more deep breath, and then inched his way out over the edge of the ravine. This was like a platform game, only real. There was nothing to be afraid of, right?

"Nothing to be afraid of," he muttered to himself. "Nothing to be afraid of. Nothing to be—"

That's when he looked down. The only thing between him and the rocky bottom was ten stories of empty air. His stomach swooped, and his heart started thumping even faster. One false move, he knew, and he was boulder meat.

That's why you don't look down, Buzz thought.

"Keep going!" Vanessa yelled somewhere behind him. Always the cheerleader, his sister.

"Okay," he mumbled again. "Okay, okay, okay. I can do this."

He reached out, got a grip on the trunk in front of him, and pulled himself a little farther along. Then he did it again. And then again.

By the time he'd found a rhythm, Buzz realized he was more than halfway across. The far side of the ravine had somehow become the near side.

"You got it!" Vanessa shouted.

A few more pulls and he found himself climbing down through the fallen tree's branches to where Carter and Jane were waiting for him. In a weird way, the whole thing had gone by quickly, like a fast nightmare.

"See?" Jane said. "It wasn't that bad, was it?"

"Nah," Buzz said, playing it off. The truth was, he felt incredible—and incredibly relieved.

"Right here!" Carter reached out and gave him a rare high five. "You did it."

"Yeah," Buzz said.

"That was the hard part. Going back will be cake."

"Yeah . . . wait, what?"

Buzz realized he hadn't even thought about that. This was not a one-way trip. He was going to have to crawl back across that tree if he wanted to get back to the *Lucky Star*.

Still, there was nothing to do about it now. He was going to enjoy some solid ground for a while and worry about everything else later.

Either that, or the rescue plane could just pick him up here when it came.

⎯⎯⎯

As soon as Vanessa reached the others on the far side of the tree bridge, they all continued on together, up toward the rocky point Carter had spotted from the beach down below.

Coming out onto the open ground of the summit, the view was almost exactly what she'd expected—like a whole world of water spread out around them.

Straight down, she could see the *Lucky Star* where it sat, ruined on the rocks. And behind them, as Vanessa turned all the way around, the shape of the island itself came clear for the first time.

The whole thing was a giant ring of land, encircling an enormous lagoon of the most brilliant aqua-blue water Vanessa had ever seen.

"It's just a big circle," Buzz said.

"It's called an atoll," Jane told them. "That circle used to be the top of a volcano. Now it's sinking back into the ocean."

"How fast?" Buzz asked cautiously.

"Not that fast," Jane said.

The ridge where they were standing seemed to be the tallest and widest part of the island. As the land arced around, it thinned out into a green and sandy-brown strip on the opposite side, divided in several places by bright blue stripes of water. From here, that part of the island looked like giant stepping-stones.

The other thing that had become painfully clear was just how empty the ocean was, all around them. There was no sign of any other land. No sign of civilization, for that matter.

And worst of all—no sign of Dex and Joe.

"Anyone see them?" Vanessa asked. When nobody answered, it was like something breaking into a million pieces. She hadn't realized how much she'd been counting on finding them until it became clear that it wasn't going to happen. Now it seemed like she'd been fooling herself all along.

"Maybe they're in the woods or something," Jane said. "And we just can't see them."

"Maybe," Vanessa said, but she didn't believe it. She'd heard what Carter said earlier. That life raft had been blown clear away from the boat in seconds, and it hadn't been traveling toward the island. Besides, if Dex and Joe were here, they would have found the *Lucky Star* by now, wouldn't they? The island wasn't *that* big.

"Sorry, guys," Carter said. "I guess we came all the way up here for nothing."

"It's not your fault," Vanessa said.

"I didn't say it was my fault," he started up.

"Relax," she said. She'd already had enough of Carter for one day. "I was just saying—"

But then it was Buzz who interrupted them.

"Actually," he said, "there is one other thing we could do."

Suddenly, Buzz had everyone looking at him. He even almost forgot what he was going to say for a second.

"We need to build a signal fire," he told the others.

"A what?" Vanessa said.

"I've seen it on TV. You know, those shows where they drop some guy off in the middle of nowhere and he has to survive by himself?"

Carter looked over at him. "You watch survival shows?"

"I watch a lot of stuff," he said.

That's where his nickname had come from.

His father was the first to use it, because he said that Benjamin was always watching something or playing some game that went *crash*, *bang*, or *buzz*.

Buzz didn't mind. It was better than being called Benjamin, for that matter. Jane and Carter had only ever known him as Buzz, and that was just fine with him.

"The first thing those TV guys always do is build a fire, somewhere up high," he went on.

"Like right here," Jane said.

"Yeah. That way, if a plane or a boat comes around—"

"*When* a plane or a boat comes around," Vanessa interrupted.

"Okay. *When* that happens, we're going to be way too small to see. But a fire with a bunch of smoke can get their attention."

Carter was nodding the whole time and even seemed kind of impressed. "Boy, you do watch a lot of TV, don't you?"

Everyone seemed to be into the idea, so Buzz kept on talking.

"We're going to need some stuff from the boat," he said. "Like one of those signal flares in the cockpit and some rope."

Dexter had made them all go through hours of safety drills before they left Hawaii, and the coolest part of that training was, by far, the emergency flares. When you pulled the cap off the top of a flare, it self-ignited into a super-intense mini-torch. On the ocean, they were for visual signaling, but you could also use them to set almost anything on fire.

"I'll go," Carter said right away. "I'm the fastest."

"Of course you are," Vanessa said.

That sounded good to Buzz. "And get that axe, too," he said. "We're going to need to chop up some big branches."

Carter took off like he was in some kind of race, while Jane, Vanessa, and Buzz started collecting materials. It felt good, but also kind of weird, to see everyone doing exactly what he told them to do. Buzz wasn't usually the boss of anything in their family, especially not with Vanessa and Carter around.

"We need a bunch of really dry grass," he told the girls. "And then some little twigs, and then dry branches on top of that."

The fire was going to have to be tall, he knew, with room at the bottom for air to circulate. The bigger the stack, the bigger their signal would be when they set it on fire, and the better their chances of being spotted from far away.

Jane ran around and found an amazing amount of stuff to put at the base—dry grass, sticks, and even some papery tree bark. Buzz had seen the TV guys use coconut husks before, but the only coconut trees they'd seen so far were all down at the beach.

Carter was right about being fast, too. He got back with everything they needed just in time to start using the axe. He and Vanessa were also the strongest, so they took turns with it while the others carried twigs and dead branches over to where Buzz was putting it all together in a pile.

It was slow going. A few times, the whole structure collapsed in on itself and Buzz had to start over. At home, with a pitcher of lemonade or even just some shade, it might not have been so hard. But out here in the open sun, it felt like he'd sweated about eight gallons by the time it was done.

Just as the sun was heading down toward the horizon, the group put on some finishing touches. First, they wrapped the stack in the biggest, darkest palm fronds they could find. That was something else Buzz had remembered—that green leaves made bright white smoke when they burned, the kind that was easy to see from a distance.

After that, Carter cut up some pieces of rope with the axe, and they tied the whole thing up so the wind wouldn't take it apart while they were gone. Last, Buzz stuck the emergency flare all the way inside, at the base of the structure, for safekeeping. He hoped he could be the one to set it ablaze when the time came.

"There," he said, and stood back to look at what they'd done. "We're all set."

Now all they needed was a boat. Or a plane. Or a helicopter. Or anything at all to get them off this stupid island.

By the time they were all back down at the beach and climbing up onto the deck of the boat, Carter had exactly two things on his mind: food and water.

"I'm staaaarving!" he said. "What do we have to eat?"

They all moved straight down the stairs into the galley to start looking for whatever they could find. It was getting dark now, but Vanessa found a flashlight in the nav station, and that helped.

"Hey, look—marshmallows!" Buzz said.

"We've got some cans of beef stew," Vanessa said. "Chili. Ravioli. Fruit cocktail."

"I'll fill some cups," Carter told them, and went straight for the water. He pulled away the bench seat covering the tank, picked up a coffee mug from the table, and dipped it down in through the hole he'd cut that morning.

But instead of water, all Carter found inside was air.

"Hey!" he shouted. "Where'd it go?"

"Where'd what go?" Vanessa said.

"The water!" he said. "It's

"It can't be," she said, leaning over with a flashlight. She shone it inside the tank, then didn't say anything for a long time.

"What do you see?" Jane finally asked.

Vanessa sat down slowly. "He's right. There's a big crack all along the bottom. And one of these pipes is hanging off."

The news settled silently over the group.

"Maybe it broke when we cut it open with that axe," Buzz said.

"Don't blame it on me!" Carter told him.

"I'm not," he said. "I'm just saying what might have happened."

Vanessa slammed her fist against the table. "We shouldn't have been gone so long!" she said. "If we'd been here, we would have noticed, and we might have been able to do something about it."

Still, it felt a whole lot like blame to Carter. He also felt like he was suddenly three times thirstier than he'd been even a minute ago.

else is there to drink?" he said.

and Buzz were already on it. They
ere opening cabinets and looking in the little
refrigerator, but so far, they didn't have anything.

"One gallon of nasty-smelling milk," Buzz said,
taking it out. "And . . . not much else. Some carrots
and a bunch of D batteries."

"What about outside? It's not like we aren't
surrounded by water," Carter said.

"You can't drink seawater," Jane said. "It's so
salty, it just makes you thirstier. Or sick. I forget
which. Maybe both."

"There were a bunch of juice boxes before. And
some soda," Vanessa said. "I'm positive."

"We finished the soda on the second day," Buzz
said.

It was true. Dex had made a big deal about
bringing soda at all, since it was so heavy and
took up a lot of room. The juice boxes at least were
lighter and you could crush them up when they
were empty. But that also meant they could have

easily been washed away in the crash and the flood.

Carter looked around. A lot of provisions had been lost. He felt ready to start tearing the boat apart, piece by piece. He'd never cared about stupid juice boxes before, but he would have traded his BMX bike for just one of them right now.

This was unbelievable. The longer the day went on, the worse it got. The whole thing was starting to seem like the world's stupidest problem. Who got *shipwrecked* anymore? Dex was supposed to watch out for them. And where was he now?

"How could they just leave us on our own like that?" he blurted out.

"Who?" Vanessa said. "Dex and Joe?"

"Yes, Dex and Joe!"

"They didn't do it on purpose," Buzz said. "It was just an accident."

But Carter didn't want to hear it, especially not from Buzz, sitting there with his bag of marsh-mallows like this was some kind of camping trip.

"You're not much help, either," he said. "Where were you when the boat crashed last night?"

"I was trying to steer!" Buzz yelled back at him.

"Yeah. 'Trying.' Exactly," he said. "And when you were crashing the boat, I was saving your sister from going overboard!"

He was starting to say stuff he knew he shouldn't. But sometimes it was hard to stop once he got going.

"Vanessa's your sister now, too," Jane told Carter.

"Yeah," Buzz said. "And it wasn't me who crashed the stupid boat!"

"Have another *marshmallow*, Buzz." Carter felt ready to hit something, or explode, or both. It seemed like everyone was ganging up on him, even Jane.

"Don't talk to him like that," Vanessa said. "And stop acting like a little kid. You want to have a temper tantrum? Go do it somewhere else."

He glared over at her. She wanted him to go somewhere else? Fine with him. His mother was always telling him to count to ten when he got mad. So he counted his steps—right out of the galley and up onto the deck. When he got to the bow of the boat, he just kept going, onto the rocks, then down to the beach.

That's when he started running. Vanessa and the others were calling after him, but he didn't care. He just needed to get away, as fast and as far as he could.

He was crying now, too. Like a baby. He hadn't cried all day, not even once. But he couldn't hold back anymore. The tears just kept coming, streaking across his cheeks as he sprinted farther and farther up the beach. At least there wasn't anyone to see it.

Finally, he couldn't run anymore. His knees buckled as he rolled to a stop right there in the sand, panting and catching his breath. And thinking about the others.

Sometimes, he wasn't sure why he got so mad. He just did. One thing piled on top of the next, and then he lashed out. Usually at Buzz—he was too easy a target. But this wasn't Buzz's fault, he knew. It wasn't anyone's fault. It was just bad luck, the same as he'd been having all year long.

A week ago, it seemed like his biggest problem

was moving away from his old house, changing schools, and dealing with Vanessa's know-it-all attitude 24/7. Now all of that seemed like a joke in comparison to being stranded in the middle of nowhere.

There were no adults here to help, and someone had to take charge. There was so much they needed to do. They needed to find water if they were going to last. They needed to start keeping watch for rescue planes. They needed—

A sudden, loud rustling noise from the woods pulled Carter right out of his thoughts.

His heart jumped back up to full speed as he listened. Something was there. Something big, from the sound of it. He heard twigs breaking and underbrush being pushed aside.

In fact, it wasn't just one thing, he realized. It was a group of them. A group of . . . *something*. And they were right there, maybe twenty feet away, in the woods.

Carter stayed low in the sand and as still as possible. What was it Jane had said about wild animals? He couldn't remember. He hadn't really been listening, but now he wished he had.

The next sound he heard was a soft snorting—or a sniffing, like maybe one of them had just picked up his scent. Almost right away, the others joined in.

Without a weapon, or even a flashlight, Carter started to feel like a giant target, sitting there in the dark. Who knew how many of them there were? How outnumbered he might be? Maybe this place was full of predators—or whatever they were— roaming the island at night.

As the rustling in the woods grew louder, and then closer, one clear thought rose above the rest: *Time to go.*

The words went off in his mind like a starter pistol. Carter sprang to his feet, ducked his chin, and ran. He didn't look over his shoulder once. He just sprinted all the way back to the boat like his life depended on it. Which maybe it did, and maybe it didn't.

But this was no place to take chances.

CHAPTER 10

"**H**i, everyone, it's Jane B. again, reporting for Evanston Elementary."

Jane stood on the rocks next to the *Lucky Star*, holding her camera out in front of her. The sun was just coming up, and the others were all still asleep. But she'd been awake for hours, scratching her bug bites and trying not to think about how thirsty she was.

It was a surprise when she'd found the camera in one piece after the crash. Jane knew it was waterproof, but apparently, this one was shipwreck-proof, too. The battery still had most of its charge, so there was plenty of time to work on her report, if she wanted.

"Today is June thirtieth, and it was supposed to be the sixth day of our trip," she continued. "I kind of skipped a day yesterday, but let me show you why."

She moved the camera sideways now, to take in the huge hole in the side of the boat. It looked like a giant had taken a bite right out of it.

"That's the boat we were sailing on, until we crashed here," she said. "We don't even know where we are, exactly. I'm just calling it Nowhere Island for now. These rocks where I'm standing are Dead Man's Shelf. And up there . . ."

She leaned way back to show the place at the top of the cliffs where they'd built the signal fire.

"That's Lookout Point. Oh, and over here is Benson-Diaz Beach. See?"

The names were just something she'd thought up lying in her bunk, wide awake most of the night. Later, if she could find some dry paper and a pen, she'd start making a real map, too.

"Jane? What are you doing down there?" Vanessa

called out from the deck. She'd just come outside, still looking sleepy, but her dark hair was pulled neatly off her face in a short ponytail, and she'd put on clean shorts and a T-shirt. She looked ready for business.

For some reason, Jane felt embarrassed. "I was just working on my report," she said.

Vanessa gave her a look, the same one adults did sometimes. It was a confused sort of smile, like maybe Jane was too smart for her own good.

"You can work on that later," she said. "Come on up. I want to have a family meeting."

"About what?" Jane asked.

Vanessa shrugged, like it should be obvious.

"Everything," she said.

In the cockpit of the *Lucky Star*, Vanessa set out the last can of fruit cocktail, half a bag of marshmallows, and four spoons. There was still a full jar of peanut butter and some canned chili and beef stew they could eat, but for now it seemed like a good idea to stay away from anything that might make them even thirstier.

"Why do we have to have a family meeting?" Carter wanted to know right away.

"Because we have to figure out what to do today, and who's going to do it," Vanessa said.

"We don't need a meeting for that. We can talk while we're looking for water. That's, like, the world's biggest *duh* to me."

You're a big duh, Vanessa thought. But she held her tongue. There had been enough fighting the night before. Carter hadn't said a word when he came back to the boat, but he'd obviously been crying.

Now she couldn't help thinking about what her dad would say about all this. *Work it out.* Every time there was a disagreement in the new house—about computer time or who got which bedroom or whether someone had taken something that wasn't theirs—it was always the same: *You don't have to love everything about one another, but you do have to figure out how to get along. We're one family now, not two.*

So work it out.

"We definitely need water," Vanessa agreed. "But I've been thinking about that solar panel, too." She pointed over to where the broken panel was sitting facedown on the deck. "If we can get the satellite phone charged up again, we could make another call."

Carter looked at her like she was speaking Russian. "Are you serious? When was the last time you hooked up a solar panel?"

"Never," she told him. "But I'm good with stuff like that."

"It's true," Buzz said. "She is."

It wasn't like she knew for a fact that she could do it, but it was worth a shot. The back of the panel had only a few wires sticking out of it. Maybe it wouldn't be that hard.

"Uh, hello? Is anyone besides me really thirsty?" Carter asked.

"We don't need four people to look for water,"

Vanessa pointed out. "We can get more done if we split up."

"I think we should stick together," Jane said.

"I think we should stop talking about everything and start doing it," Carter said.

"Hey, and where are we supposed to go number two, anyway?" Buzz asked. Vanessa felt like she was ready to scream. This meeting was going downhill fast.

"Come on, you guys," she said. "We have to make some decisions. Let's just take a vote, okay?"

But Carter was already on his feet. "I vote I'm going to look for water so we don't all die of dehydration. Jane, you can come with me if you want."

Jane looked at Vanessa.

"Fine," Vanessa said. In fact, she realized, they both wanted the same things, anyway: water, rescue, and a little time apart from one another.

So much for their family meeting.

"Let's just get to work," she said.

Carter pulled the straps of his backpack a little tighter. Jane had one, too. Both of them were filled with as many jars and bottles as they'd been able to find on the boat. With any luck, all those containers would be full by the time they got back.

"Remember, stick to the beach," Vanessa called after them. "That way, you can't get lost."

She was just trying to help, Carter knew, but sometimes Vanessa sounded more like a mom than his mom did.

In fact, it had been Jane's idea to walk around the outside of the ring-shaped island. If there was fresh water here, it would flow downhill toward the ocean. With any luck, they'd cross paths with it along the way.

They headed off in the same direction as the day before, away from the crash site.

For the first long stretch of beach, Jane seemed fine. She'd even brought her camera and made some of her little videos while they walked. But then the land started to curve off to the right, and they quickly lost sight of the *Lucky Star* behind them. That's when Jane started getting nervous.

"I still think we should have stuck together," she said, looking back.

"Don't worry about it," Carter said. "Vanessa's right. We don't need four people to do this. But don't tell her I said that."

It was supposed to be a joke, though Jane didn't even smile. Instead, she started asking questions. That's what his sister did when she was anxious— she gathered information.

"How big do you think the island is?" she said.

"I don't know. Maybe five miles around," Carter told her.

"How long does it take to go a mile?"

"It depends. The world record is under four minutes, but that's on a track."

"Carter? What if we don't find any water?"

"We will," he said.

"How do you know?" Jane said.

Carter stopped walking. "Look around," he told her. "Half this island is green. There has to be water somewhere."

That seemed to satisfy her. Carter even felt a little proud of himself for thinking of it so fast.

But then she asked, "How long do you think this is going to take?"

That one was trickier. There was no way of knowing, but that seemed like the wrong thing to say.

"Not too long," he told her as casually as he could, then continued on up the beach.

It would be several hours before either of them

realized just how wrong Carter had been. But by then, it was going to be too late to do anything about it.

Vanessa stood on the deck, looking at the solar panel like some kind of giant puzzle. The glass surface was in a million pieces, but the inside still looked intact.

Maybe Carter was right. Maybe she was crazy to think she could ever do this. But she had to try.

"Help me lift this," she told Buzz. The panel wasn't heavy, but it was big and awkward. They each took a side and slid it up onto the cabin roof. Then they climbed up next to it and propped the whole thing against the metal bracket where it had lived before the crash.

Hopefully, this first part wasn't going to be super complicated. The back of the panel had one white wire and one black wire sticking out of it. Likewise, the electrical box on the mounting bracket had one white wire and one black wire, all of them with exposed copper ends where they'd torn free.

Vanessa looked across at Buzz. "White to white and black to black, right? That makes sense."

"I guess," he said. "Like that lamp Dad fixed a few weeks ago."

"Right." She remembered now. Anytime she'd seen their father do anything like this, the colors always matched up.

As she bent down to take a closer look, Buzz spoke up again, quietly this time.

"What do you think Dad's doing right now?" he asked her.

Vanessa didn't have to think about that one. "Looking for us," she said. "I'll bet he and Beth are on some Coast Guard plane right now, flying around up there."

When she looked at the sky, the clouds had started to roll in overhead. That was bad news. Even if they did get this panel hooked up correctly, they'd have to wait for the sun to come back before they could test it.

"Vanessa?"

"Yeah?"

"What happens if they can't find us?"

"I don't know, Buzz," Vanessa told him honestly. "We've still got the boat. There's still a bunch of food. Hopefully, Jane and Carter are going to find water. We'll just—"

"Just *what*?" Buzz was looking her right in the eye now. He didn't just want to know, she could tell. He *needed* to know.

"We'll work it out," she said. "Okay?"

That actually made him smile. "That's what Dad would say." She smiled, too.

"Now come on, let's do this," she said, and knelt down next to the panel.

There wasn't any electricity running on the boat, so there didn't seem to be any danger of getting electrocuted. Still, Vanessa was careful. She used a pair of rubber-handled pliers from the cockpit to twist the two white wires together, nice and tight. After that, Buzz had to lift the panel up so she could slide underneath it, like a car mechanic, and do the same thing with the black wires.

As soon as it was done, they both ran down to the main cabin. The batteries in the engine compartment looked like they were hooked up, but there was no way of knowing for sure. The console at the nav station still looked just as dead and blank as ever.

That was no real surprise. Until the sun came back, they wouldn't know if they'd made any progress here. Even then, they were going to need the satellite phone charger to work. And even *then*, they'd have to try and figure out where in the world they were so they'd have something to say if they finally got to make another call.

That was a lot of ifs and a lot of maybes, Vanessa knew. A total long shot. But an hour ago, they'd had no chance of reaching the outside world at all. Now they did.

And a long shot was way better than no shot at all.

CHAPTER 12

"**Y**ES!"

Jane looked up from tying her sneaker. Carter was walking in a small circle now, and he spiked an imaginary football over his shoulder.

"What is it?" Jane said.

"Over there! See?"

They'd been hiking for hours, with no luck, and the land around them had started to thin out. As the wall of the jungle dropped away behind them, they'd gotten their first look at the island's huge inner lagoon from ground level. Jane had seen the lagoon from above, on Lookout Point, but not the cliffs that faced it on this side.

The cliff walls themselves were dotted all over with dozens of black holes—more caves, Jane realized. Some were just small openings, but others were at least as big as the one they'd found in the woods on the opposite side of the island.

"Do you see it?" Carter said.

"See what?" Jane said.

"Give me your camera."

He took it and zoomed in on the cliff wall, directly across the lagoon from where they were standing. As the image came clear, Jane swallowed hard—or, at least, she tried to. Her throat was sore and as dry as paper.

But right there on the camera's view screen was a small waterfall. It spilled out of one of the caves from a height of about ten feet. The water cascaded over a rock formation into a pool down below, then continued on toward the lagoon.

Carter grinned. "I told you we'd find it. Come on!"

Jane didn't need any coaxing. She was exhausted

from the hike, but the sight of the falls got her moving again. It was too far to swim all the way across the lagoon, so they continued around it, in the same clockwise direction they'd been going.

Soon, they were at the very narrowest part of the island. The ground was just sand and beach grass here, with several small streams cutting across their path as they went. It was like a chain of tiny, sandy islands, one after the other.

The first water crossings were easy. They barely slowed down as they splashed right through. But then they came to a much deeper channel.

"Keep going," Carter said. "Hold my hand."

As they started to cross, it only took a few steps before the water was up to Jane's chin. The current was stronger than she'd thought, and her feet left the ground a few times before Carter pulled her back close. By the time they'd reached the next patch of dry sand, both of them were soaked and out of breath. Jane's wet pack felt twice as heavy as before.

"I hope that was it," she said.

But it wasn't. They'd barely scaled the next dune before Jane realized their luck was running out. What stretched in front of them now was something like a fast-flowing river, from the ocean to the lagoon.

"I think we have to go back," Jane said.

"I don't think we can," Carter told her. For the first time, he looked truly worried.

When Jane turned around, she saw why. The last channel they'd managed to cross was now just as high as the one in front of them. The tide was rushing in and their tiny island was shrinking by the minute.

"We're going to have to swim across," Carter said.

"It's too fast!" she said.

Jane was a good swimmer; she'd been doing it all her life. But that was in pools and in Lake Michigan back home. Here, there was nothing to stop her from getting carried off like a piece of driftwood.

"I'll check it out first," Carter said. "Then I'll come back for you."

"No, don't!" Jane said.

The only thing worse than being stuck here together would be if they got separated. She grabbed for Carter's arm, but it was like trying to stop a bulldozer.

He walked straight into the channel up to his waist, then dove away.

Carter was shocked at how quickly the current took him. The moment his feet left the ground, he felt himself swept sideways, away from the direction he wanted to go.

"Carter!" he heard Jane yelling, but there was nothing he could do now.

Immediately, he knew he'd made a mistake. He turned over in the water, trying to stroke his way back to shore. But it was too late for that. Before he could take another gulp of air, he felt himself tumbled back underwater by the current.

His pack wasn't helping, either. The straps bound him up as he tried to swim. The more he struggled, the more he felt wrapped up like a mummy, unable to move his arms at all. He had to get free of it or he'd drown.

Carter bucked and jerked with everything he had, struggling to ditch the pack. His lungs burned, desperate for oxygen that wasn't there. What he got instead was a giant gulp of salt water.

Finally, with a last desperate twist, he pulled one arm loose, and then the other. There was no thought of trying to keep the pack anymore. All his mind could perceive was the need to breathe, and he kicked toward the light at the surface of the water.

Just when it seemed as if his lungs were going to pop in his chest, Carter broke through, hacking up water and sucking down air practically at the same time.

"Carter!" Jane yelled somewhere behind him.

He spun around in the water toward her voice. That's when he realized just how far from the sandbar he'd been carried. Jane was a good hundred yards away. She'd dropped her pack but was standing in the channel up to her knees now.

"Jane!" he croaked out. His throat burned from the salt water. "Stay right there!"

She seemed to hear his voice but not what he was saying. Instead of staying put, Jane took another cautious step forward—and that was all it took. Carter saw his sister go down as the water swept her right off her feet.

After that, he couldn't see her at all.

CHAPTER 13

Buzz stood on the deck of the *Lucky Star*, scanning the beach with a pair of cracked binoculars. Carter and Jane had been gone all morning and now a good part of the afternoon as well. So far, there was no sign of them.

No water, either. The inside of his mouth felt like paste on paste.

"Hey, Vanessa?" he called down. "Don't you think they should have been back by now?"

"I don't know," she said. "This is Carter we're talking about. He won't be able to show his face unless he finds water."

It was true, Buzz thought. Carter was stubborn that way.

Still, it was hard not to worry. Once you'd gotten shipwrecked in the middle of nowhere, it was pretty easy to imagine other bad things happening, too.

"Maybe we should go look," he said. "Just walk up the beach or something?"

"If they're not back in an hour, we'll start looking," Vanessa said as she came up the galley steps. "But come here. Check this out."

She was carrying a spiral-bound book of maps in her hand, and she laid it open on the deck to show him. Buzz crouched down to have a look.

The map in front of him was a two-page spread with the title "Islands of Oceania" across the top. It showed the west coast of the United States in one corner, Australia in the other, and a wide expanse of Pacific Ocean in between.

"So, we set sail from here, six days ago," she said, putting her finger down over the big island of Hawaii. On the map, it was about the size of a Skittle. "And when we left, I'm pretty sure we sailed south and west."

She drew a diagonal line with her finger, past something called Johnston Atoll, then out into the biggest empty space of ocean on the page.

"This is about nine hundred miles from Hawaii," she said. "That's how far we were supposed to come. I don't know how much farther that storm blew us, or which way Dexter changed course, but I think we're somewhere around here."

Buzz felt a quickening inside him. They knew where they were! This seemed like it could be big— except . . . He glanced at his sister and saw the furrow between her eyebrows. Why wasn't Vanessa more excited?

The nearest land to where she'd pointed was the Marshall Islands to the northwest, then something called U.S. Kiribati to the southeast.

"What's U.S. Kee-ree . . . batty?" Buzz asked.

"It doesn't matter," she answered impatiently. "What I'm saying is, this whole area is about fifteen hundred miles across. And we're *somewhere* in the middle of it."

He looked back at the map again. Fifteen hundred miles was Chicago to California. Half of the United States.

"So, even if the Coast Guard is looking for us . . ."

Vanessa nodded. "It's like the biggest, worst game of hide-and-seek, ever."

"And we aren't even trying to hide," Buzz said.

The reality of it settled over him like a dark cloud. All day long, he'd been thinking about rescue. Hoping for it. Relying on it. Now it was starting to look like they might be stuck here for a lot longer than he'd imagined.

Buzz stood up and re-scanned the empty beach. Even though Vanessa had said not to worry about Carter and Jane, that didn't really seem possible anymore.

"Vanessa?" he said.

"Yeah . . . okay," she said. She already knew what he was thinking. "We can start looking for them right now."

Carter's heart leaped when he finally spotted Jane in the water. The current had her in its grip, carrying her right toward him.

"Jane!" he yelled, but she didn't seem to hear. She was struggling to swim, her head just barely above the surface of the water.

Carter stroked against the tide with everything he had. The most he could try for was to keep from drifting farther away, as Jane washed in his direction. It was like swimming upstream, and his arms weren't going to cut it much longer.

The next glimpse he got of her, she was less than twenty yards away and closing in fast—but just off to the side.

On instinct, Carter stopped trying to swim. He stretched his arms and legs into a wide X-shape instead, as much like a net as he could make himself. Jane was there now, and she caught his eye.

"Carter!" she yelled again. "Help me!"

They collided in the water and Carter grabbed hold. He flipped onto his back now, keeping his grip on Jane. His arms were too weak to swim against the tide anymore, but he could still kick. So could she.

"Turn over!" he yelled. With a fast scramble, they were hooked arm to arm, like one unit. "Now kick!" he said. "As hard as you can!"

The water at their feet roiled as they started to flutter and kick and inch their way back toward the shore. It was slow going, but they generated enough power to keep moving in the right direction. Carter aimed them for the middle of the sandbar, where the current was weakest.

Finally, the water grew shallow enough that he could see the lagoon's sandy bottom. "We've got it!" he said. He reached down with one foot, then the other, and found he could stand.

Jane was even more exhausted than he was. He wrapped her arms around his neck and her legs around his middle. Then he trudged them both back up onto the tiny island's shore.

As soon as he had dry sand under his feet, Carter collapsed onto his knees. A bellyful of salt water came up and burned his throat all over again. His vision blurred and fuzzed.

Jane rolled off him and lay on her back, panting.

"Are you okay?" he said.

She just nodded. There were no words right now, for either of them. Carter knew that this could have turned out even worse than it did. In a way, they'd been lucky.

After several minutes, he stood up again and looked around. The water was still rushing in from the ocean. As long as that was the case, they weren't going anywhere.

"How long does it take for the tide to turn around?" Carter asked. It seemed like something Jane would know.

"Maybe six hours?" she said. "But . . . I think that might be too late."

She was looking at the sky now, as if there were some answer up there. All Carter could see overhead was a solid gray sheet of clouds.

"Too late for what?" he said. He almost didn't want to hear her answer.

"For us," she said. "The tide has to go down sometime, but so does the sun. And I've got a bad feeling about which is going to happen first."

CHAPTER 14

Vanessa nearly cried when the rain first started. It came after hours of walking the shore of Nowhere Island, looking for some sign of Carter and Jane. She and Buzz stopped long enough to stand on the beach with their mouths open, letting the drops moisten their dry tongues and throats. It wasn't much, but the relief was intense.

Soon, they were up in the woods, where rain had started to gather on the thick foliage. It was Buzz's idea, something he'd seen on one of his shows. If someone had told her a month earlier that she was going to be licking plants for water, Vanessa would have thought they were crazy. Now the only thing that was crazy was how good it felt to lap up a tiny bit of moisture from a waxy green leaf in the middle of the jungle.

Still, the good feelings didn't last long. As darkness set in, there was no choice but to head back to the boat. They'd missed their chance for Lookout Point, too. Even if they could get through the jungle at night, they wouldn't be able to see anything until morning.

"We'll go first thing," Vanessa said. "We'll find them, Buzz. I promise."

Buzz only nodded. This seemed to be weighing even more heavily on him than it was on her. And the hard truth was, they were still going to have to worry about water no matter what happened. That meant collecting as much of this rain as they could, right away.

As soon as they reached the *Lucky Star*, Vanessa went straight downstairs to grab whatever containers she could find. She pulled a cooking pot and a frying pan out of the galley, set them up on the deck, and then ran down for more.

"Buzz? Where are you? What are you doing?" she yelled. There was no knowing how long this rain would last.

When she came back up with a flashlight and an armful of cracked coffee mugs, Buzz was standing on the cabin roof. He was trying to free what was left of the torn mainsail from what was left of the broken boom.

"Help me get this off," he said. "We can tie it across the deck and catch water with it."

Vanessa looked at her baby brother. It was a brilliant idea. One she never would have thought of. She set down the mugs and jumped up next to him. They worked as quickly as they could, untying lengths of cord and cutting through knots with a steak knife from down below. By the time they'd freed up the sail, they had an enormous parachute-sized piece of material to work with.

"Over here," Buzz said. "Quick."

Following his lead, Vanessa helped stretch the sail across the back of the boat. They tied it to the rail on two sides and to the captain's wheel in the cockpit. When they were done, the whole thing hung loosely over the deck like a giant cloth bowl. A small pool had already started to collect in the center.

"Buzz, you're some kind of genius," Vanessa said, standing with him in the pouring rain. "Did you see that on TV, too?"

"No," Buzz said.

"Some video game?"

Buzz shook his head. "It was just something I thought of," he said.

It seemed like he didn't want to talk about it. Vanessa felt pretty sure that he was already back to thinking about Carter and Jane. Back to worrying, too.

Still, she couldn't help noticing that Buzz was adapting to all of this faster than anyone. Maybe he was going to surprise them all before it was over.

In fact, he already had.

Jane shivered in the dark as the rain poured down on their little sandbar.

It didn't matter if the tide had gone out now or not. Without any moonlight or even starlight to navigate by, there was no way to leave. The darkness was complete here, like the definition of pitch black.

At first, the rain was a good thing. They'd lain flat on their backs, catching what they could in their mouths and in some of the jars they'd brought. She still had her pack, but Carter's was gone. They only had half as many containers as when they started.

Now, hours later, the rain was just one more torment to deal with. If Jane had wondered how things could get worse since the crash, this was her answer.

"What time do you think it is?" she asked Carter.

"I dunno," Carter answered dully. It was the same voice he used whenever one of his teams lost a game.

"I think the sun comes up around six," she said.

"Whatever," he answered, and hunched his shoulders a little tighter.

Besides everything else—the hunger, the rain,

the darkness—Jane was also chilled to the bone. She and Carter huddled together on the sand for warmth, and she tried to use her empty pack as a blanket, but none of it did any good. Their one lucky break was that the water had stopped rising before it swallowed their tiny island completely.

"Carter?"

"What?"

"Do you think Vanessa and Buzz are out looking for us?"

"They'd be stupid if they were," he said. "They should just wait until we come back tomorrow."

Jane hugged herself and tried to stop shivering. "Do you think it's at least midnight by now?" she said.

"I don't want to talk about what time it is."

"Okay."

Instead, she shut her eyes and thought about that word, *tomorrow*. Hopefully, the sun would come up extra-extra early in the morning. She imagined it, rising over the cliffs and shining warmly down on her face.

Then slowly, the image faded and another one took its place. She saw her mother and Eric now. They were standing on the front porch of the house, waving at her to run up the sidewalk and come inside.

That part was the hardest of all—thinking about home. Their kitchen full of food. Her warm bed. Her friends. All of it was five thousand impossible miles away. Even getting a hug from her mother right now would have been like winning some kind of big prize.

But still, Jane was determined not to cry. Not in front of Carter. At least, not until she saw the sun again. Then she could do whatever she wanted, she told herself.

In the meantime, she just had to hang on.

Buzz took the first watch that night. He let Vanessa get some sleep and stood on the deck in his raincoat, watching the dark beach.

He kept the flashlight, too. He pointed it up the shore and clicked the button—on, off, on, off, on, off. Every minute or so, he repeated the pattern. The beam didn't reach far, but it was something Carter and Jane could follow if they were trying to get back this way.

It was also something Buzz could do. He had a terrible, helpless feeling in his gut, wondering where they'd gone. It kept reminding him of what Jane had said that morning.

I think we should stick together.

Now he wished more than anything that he'd listened. They all should have. Maybe Jane was the littlest, but she was probably the smartest one in the group. Because right now, letting those two go off by themselves felt like the stupidest mistake they could have possibly made.

CHAPTER 15

Carter woke up scratching.

Somewhere in the night, the rain had stopped and the bugs had moved in to take its place. Even as he sat up, he was waving away a cloud of them. When he looked at his arms and legs, they were lit up with dozens of small red welts. Maybe hundreds. And every single one of them was itchy.

It was the first night any of them had slept outside, Carter realized. Just one more reason why he couldn't wait to get back to the *Lucky Star*.

And that's where there was some good news. In the early-morning light, he could see that the water had finally gone down. Their sandbar had grown overnight, and had even reattached itself to the larger curve of the island. They were free to go.

"Jane, wake up," he said. He was already on his feet, still scratching as he put all the bottles and jars back into her pack.

"What happened? You look like you have the measles," she said. Her own arms and legs were nothing compared to his.

"I guess I taste better to mosquitoes," he said, shouldering the pack. "At least someone got to eat last night."

It had been over thirty-six hours since they'd had anything besides rainwater, he realized. The inside of his belly felt like it was grinding against itself. His steps weren't as sure-footed anymore, and his head swam a little as they set out. The hike back to the boat was going to be rough, but he tried not to think about it. If Jane could do this without complaining, then so could he.

Slowly and steadily, they came around the curve of the lagoon toward the falls. Neither of them had the energy to run, but they did pick up their pace as they came within striking distance.

The falls themselves spilled out of a cave opening, about ten feet off the ground. The water flowed over a jumble of rocks and into a small pool, which fed into the lagoon. With one last burst of adrenaline, Carter and Jane splashed right through the little pool to stand at the base of the falls. The water was ice cold, but Carter let it spill right over him. It felt amazing on his burning skin, and then even more amazing to finally drink his fill.

It wasn't exactly the chocolate-chip-pancake breakfast with bacon and sausage, scrambled eggs, and everything else he'd been dreaming about all night. But for right now, it would have to do.

As soon as Jane had enough to drink, her thoughts turned to the cave where this water was coming from. In fact, she'd been thinking about it all night. And she'd begun to wonder if maybe . . . just maybe . . .

"Carter? What do you think is up there?"

"What do you mean?" he said, wiping his mouth.

"Well, if we could drill a hole straight through this cliff, how close to our beach do you think we'd come out?"

Carter shrugged. He never had any patience for the little mind puzzles she liked so much.

"What are you talking about?" he said.

She pointed up at the cave again. "Where do you think that goes?"

Now Carter seemed to get her drift. "I don't know. Maybe nowhere," he said. "Where do *you* think it goes?"

"I'm not sure," Jane said. "But . . . maybe somewhere."

It was worth checking, anyway. They'd spent the whole previous day getting this far around the island. If they could find a way through, it would be the world's best shortcut.

She let Carter climb first, as they headed up the rocks along the side of the falls. It was harder to concentrate on an empty stomach, so she took her time and followed Carter's steps from one foothold to the next.

As she scrambled up over the lip of the cave, cool air rushed out to greet her. It felt air-conditioned inside, and her wet skin prickled with goose bumps.

Jane took a few steps farther in. It was hard to see very far before the darkness took over. The ground sloped up from here, and a fast-moving stream ran down the middle of the rock floor, on its way to the falls.

"Jane, I don't know about this." Carter sounded wary.

"No, this is perfect. We can follow the water," Jane said. "Then, if we think we're lost, we can just follow it right back here again."

"I wish we had the flashlight," Carter said. The ground underfoot was uneven and hard to see even near the mouth of the cave.

But that's when Jane remembered her waterproof camera.

"Maybe we do," she said. She turned Carter around and unzipped the front pocket on the pack.

Then she took out the camera and switched it on.

The battery charge was down to about half by now. Hopefully, that would be enough. She flipped it over to play mode and pressed the Start button.

> *"Hi, everyone, this is Jane B. again. Today is July first, and we're out here looking for water . . ."*

As her most recent journal entry played, the view screen lit up with a small glow. In the dark of the cave, it was just enough to show Jane the ground in front of her, if she held it low enough.

"Nice!" Carter said. She felt a high five whiff past her ear. "You want me to go first?"

"I'll do it," Jane told him. The idea of leading the way into this pitch-dark hole was scary, but she kind of liked it, too. She'd never led Carter *anywhere*.

"Come on," she said. "Stay close."

CHAPTER 16

Please, please, please . . . oh, please.

Vanessa stood on Lookout Point, silently begging for some sign of Carter and Jane to show itself. It had been almost twenty-four hours now. Wasn't that when you were supposed to call the police?

But, of course, that wasn't going to happen. They were on their own here.

"You see anything?" Buzz asked.

"Nothing," she said. The shore was empty, and the jungle was too thick to see into from up here. She kicked at the ground in frustration. "They could be anywhere in those woods. I told Carter to stick to the beach, but he's so stubborn, he probably went tromping around in there just because I said not to."

"We should keep moving," Buzz said. They'd been on the point for at least half an hour now. "If they're not back at the boat when we get there, I think we should start walking again. All the way around the island if we have to."

Vanessa nodded, but she was also torn. She hated to leave this spot. At the same time, she hated to think that Carter and Jane could be hurt and waiting for them to come help. Maybe she and Buzz should split up to cover more ground. Or maybe that was the worst idea in the world.

There were no perfect answers for this. Not even any good ones.

* * *

The cave led uphill into the dark and quickly banked to the right. Soon after that, Carter couldn't see any light behind them at all. The only thing they had to go by was the six inches or so that Jane's camera lit up in front of them.

"It couldn't have just been a straight shot, could it?" Carter grumbled. " 'Cause that would have been too easy, right?"

"What was that?" Jane said, stopping all at once. Carter brushed something away from his head as it flitted past. Or, at least, he could have sworn he felt something. Already, the dark was playing tricks on them.

"Any way we can go faster?" he said.

"Not really," Jane said. The stream was still on their right, and he could hear another waterfall up ahead. The sound had been muted at first, but it was getting louder with every step.

"Watch out for this," Jane said. They'd just come to a low wall of some kind. Carter kept one hand on her arm and felt his way along with the other as they climbed up to stand on a higher elevation.

They'd just come into a much bigger space, from the sound of it. Everything was more echoey here, including the falls, which were somewhere off to the side.

In front of them, in the camera's light, Carter could see the edge of a pond or a pool of some kind. It was impossible to know how big it was, but it was feeding the stream they'd followed inside. The falls he heard seemed to be flowing down into the same pool. That meant the water was coming from somewhere even higher up.

It was easy to imagine the whole cavern as some kind of crazy, multilevel maze—the kind you walked into and never came back out of. The thought of it put a shiver down his back.

And right now, they had a big decision to make.

"Which way?" Jane said. With the pool in front of them, there was no more stream to follow, or to lead them back if they got lost.

Just then, something else whizzed past Carter's ear. A bug or a bat or . . . something.

"Let's just keep moving," he said right away.

"Follow the edge of the water. We can always track it back to the stream, right?"

"Yeah . . ." Jane said tentatively. "Unless there's a whole bunch of streams. How will we know which one to come back to?"

It was a good question. Getting lost would be a pretty stupid move, Carter thought. But then again, turning around might be, too, if they were getting close.

And standing still in the pitch dark was starting to drive him crazy.

"I say we go for it," he told her.

Buzz still didn't love crossing the tree bridge, but Carter had been right. The first time was the hardest. And Vanessa was right, too. It helped if he stayed low, kept moving, and most of all, didn't look down.

The rest of the way to the beach was familiar by now, and easy. They slid down the gravel slope on their butts, using their heels to brake as they got near the bottom. Then they continued on around the giant rock formation and started past the mouth of the cave in the woods, before the ground began another downward slope.

It was quiet as they walked. Neither of them seemed to have much to say. But then, as they passed the cave, Buzz thought he heard Vanessa mutter something under her breath.

"What?" he asked.

"Huh?" Vanessa said.

"What did you just say?" he asked her again.

"I didn't say anything. What did you hear?"

Buzz stopped to listen.

"Nothing, I guess," he said.

And then—there it was again. Some kind of mumble.

He and Vanessa stared at each other, wide-eyed. She'd heard it, too. It was coming from the cave. The hairs on the back of Buzz's neck stood up. Was it a wild animal? One of those boars Jane talked about?

"Hello?" Vanessa called out.

And then, a small voice came back. "Hey! Vanessa? Is that you?"

It was Carter . . . somehow. Buzz felt more shock than relief at first. None of it made any sense, almost as if they were hearing things.

Both of them rushed in through the mouth of the cave, as much as they could. The daylight from the woods behind them didn't reach very far. Soon, Buzz was facing a wall of blackness he didn't know how to navigate.

"Carter? Jane?" he yelled. "Are you in here?"

"Keep talking!" Carter called out. "Where are you?"

It was hard to know how to answer that one. "We're . . . here!" Buzz yelled. "Where are *you*?"

He could feel Vanessa's hand on his shoulder behind him. "Should we get the flashlight?" she said. "It's still on the boat."

"I don't know," Buzz answered.

Then he saw it for the first time—a faint, tiny glow just coming around some unseen corner in the dark. That's all it was at first, until Jane called out again.

"There they are!" she said. "Omigosh . . . it really is . . . Carter, we did it! We're back!"

Before Carter could stop Vanessa, she had her arms around him, in a big hug.

"I'm so glad to see you!" she said. He could barely breathe, she was squeezing so tight. "I never should have let you go off like that!"

Carter's first thought was, *What do you mean, let us?* But this was too happy a moment to worry about that right now.

"Okay, okay," he said, stepping back. He was glad to see them, too, but there didn't need to be a whole production about it.

It was hard to believe, but Jane's idea had actually worked. If it weren't for her, they would have spent the whole day hiking back to the boat on empty stomachs.

"Where did you come from?" Buzz asked, peering into the dark.

"From the other side," Jane said excitedly. "These cliffs are like Swiss cheese. There are caves everywhere."

"And we found water, too," Carter said. "There's a falls back there. At the lagoon."

"It's called Carter's Falls," Jane said with a grin. "You could get there in two minutes with a real flashlight."

For everything they'd been through, she seemed pretty pumped, Carter thought. And pretty tough, for a nine-year-old.

"But, I don't understand," Vanessa said. "Are you guys okay? Why didn't you come back last night? What happened?"

"We're okay," Carter said. Already, he was heading toward the mouth of the cave ahead of the others. "Let's talk about all that on the boat, because I'm staaaarving!"

CHAPTER 17

Lunch was a celebration—two cans of ravioli, one of beef stew, one of chili, and four spoons.

"Cheers!" Jane said, holding hers up. She'd never thought she'd be so glad to eat cold ravioli.

"Cheers!" everyone said, and they clinked cans right before they all dug in. It felt good to be back together, like a real family. And now, between Carter's Falls and the rainwater Vanessa and Buzz had collected, they could get as thirsty as they wanted. There was plenty to drink.

While they ate, Carter and Jane told the whole story of what had happened to them. Then Vanessa

155

and Buzz told about Buzz's sail rig for catching water and the solar panel they'd put in place.

"Maybe it's all hooked up, and maybe it isn't. I just don't know," Vanessa said. "We need some sun to find out for sure. This weather's driving me crazy."

It was just starting to rain again, and Jane could hear thunder rumbling in the distance. It looked like the weather was going to get worse before it got better, but she didn't even care. At least they were inside the boat this time.

And they were making progress, too. It was exciting to think that they might actually be able to use the satellite phone again. Maybe even in the next day or so. She couldn't wait to talk to Mom and Eric.

When they were done eating, it was time to get back to work. Vanessa and Carter spent most of the afternoon going over every inch of cable they could track, from the solar panel to the engine compartment and over to the nav station, trying to make sure everything was good to go.

Buzz worked on organizing all of their provisions and bottling up the rainwater he was collecting in the mainsail.

And Jane did some investigating of her own. Vanessa had already started to figure out their location on a map, but not in a way that was going to help them tell the Coast Guard where to look.

There were lots of navigation materials in the cabin down below. Most of them had been scattered around in the crash, then piled into one corner or another. Some of the sea charts were on the table, others were rolled up in the nav station. There was also a huge stack of books on the floor by the rear cabin door. Jane started digging through them, and that's where she found Uncle Dexter's captain's log.

It was a tan clothbound book with an image of a jumping swordfish on the cover. Whether Vanessa had been through this stack or not, Jane didn't know. But the log grabbed her attention right away.

Inside, Dex had filled page after page with his small, sloppy handwriting. There were dozens of sketches and diagrams, too. He'd dated every entry, going back for three years. It was kind of like looking at Dex's homework.

As Jane flipped through, she saw drawings of dolphins and whales; descriptions of places Dexter had been to, like Samoa and Fiji; and tons of notations about latitude, longitude, and other words she didn't even recognize.

At the back, on the very last written page, Jane found an entry marked for 10:00 a.m. on June 28— the day of the big storm.

Got a cold front coming in, faster and slipperier than I thought it was going to be. Heading into some tricky water to try and get around this storm. The kids seem kind of nervous, but they're troupers.

Jane stopped there and stared at the page. She wondered if Dex and Joe were still out on that life raft somewhere. It had been three whole days now. Did they have water? Food? Could they fish?

Had they been rescued? She hoped so, for everyone's sake. If there was anyone who could tell the Coast Guard where to look for Nowhere Island, it would be them.

She looked down at the journal again. She'd seen Dex scribbling in it before, a little bit every day, when he worked on navigation with Joe. Usually, they'd look at the charts in the morning, then he'd write in his log while Joe steered the boat. She'd even gotten a little of that on camera for her report.

And that's when it hit Jane. Maybe, just maybe, there was something she'd recorded that they could use.

She ran back to her bunk and got her camera off the shelf where she kept it. Then she sat right down on the cabin floor and started looking.

It didn't take long. Within a few minutes, she found the exact entry she'd been thinking about.

"Hi, everyone, it's Jane B., and today is June twenty-seventh. It's the third day of our sailing trip, and today, I'm going to show you how navigation works. . . ."

Jane's heart sped up right along with the video

as she pressed Fast Forward. When Dexter came onto the screen, she let it play again.

"So you see, this is the sea chart we're looking at today," Dex's voice said over the tiny speaker.

As he unrolled the chart, she pressed Pause. Looking as hard as she could, it was still impossible to pick out any real details on the view screen. It was too small. But then, when she hit Play again, Dexter picked up a pencil and circled something several times.

"This is a coral reef. That's something we want to make sure and work our way around. . . ."

Again, she froze the image. She jumped up and ran over to the galley table, starting to flip through every chart she could find.

Vanessa and Carter were peering into the engine compartment as she did, and they looked over now.

"Jane? What are you doing?" Vanessa asked.

"I think I may have figured something out," she said. "I was just looking at one of my videos—"

"You should really save the batteries on that thing," Vanessa said.

"Don't worry about that," Jane said, pulling out another chart.

And there it was—the ragged circle of pencil from before. She looked back at the camera's screen one more time to be sure.

Yes. It was the same circle. The same chart.

"This is where we were, just before the storm," she said, pointing.

"How do you know?" Carter asked. Buzz was just coming belowdecks now, too, and they all crowded around.

Slowly, Jane told them everything that she'd just figured out. Vanessa looked at the chart, then compared it to a map she'd found in a spiral-bound book.

"Okay . . ." she said excitedly. "Okay . . . we might be closer to . . . here." She put her finger down on the chart. "Five hundred miles northeast of the Marshall Islands. At least I think so."

"There's this, too," Jane said, holding up Dexter's

journal. "We might be able to find out more about which way we came."

The others were all looking at her now, smiling a little with their eyebrows raised. She'd seen that look before, in school. It happened every time she answered a problem one of her teachers thought nobody would ever get.

Nobody but Jane Benson, that is.

Vanessa couldn't sleep. She lay on her bunk across from Jane, staring at the dark ceiling of their cabin and listening to the rain pound down outside.

Instead of getting any sun before the end of the day, they'd only gotten more and more rain. More wind. More thunder and lightning. It was beyond frustrating, when the sun was the one thing they needed most at this point.

As she lay there with nothing to do but think, Vanessa realized she was also starting to hear a new sound from outside. Something that hadn't been part of the mix before.

It was almost like a washing machine, sloshing clothes around and around. The noise came, then stopped, then came again.

What is that? she thought.

The next time, it was twice as loud—not just a soft splashing, but more like a watery crash against the side of the boat. She'd heard that sound before, she realized, on the worst night of her life.

The flashlight was on a sill next to her bed, where she'd left it. She grabbed it now and stood up. The wind was kicking around outside, along with the rain beating against the cabin roof. Vanessa took her slicker off the hook by the galley hatch and zipped it up tight around her. With the bad weather, the temperature had dropped considerably.

A downpour hit her in the face as she slid back the hatch. It felt like sharp little droplets, stinging her cheeks and making it hard to look around.

Keeping as low as she could, she came off the galley stairs and shone the flashlight back toward the rear of the boat, past the cockpit. What she saw took her breath away.

It was almost as if they were at sea again. The ocean had advanced on their rocky shelf, and deep water was pooled all around them. Before Vanessa could even make sense of that fact, a heavy wave rolled in from out of the dark and broke hard against the back of the *Lucky Star* in a burst of sea spray. The sight of it shocked her into action.

She scrambled back down the stairs, not even bothering to close the hatch this time.

"You guys!" she shouted. "Wake up! Right now!"

She went to Jane first and pulled the blankets off her, shaking her awake. Then she went to the boys' bunks, where Carter was stirring and Buzz was already sitting up.

"What's going on?" Buzz asked.

"Get up! There's water all around us," Vanessa told them. "I think we have to get off the boat before it's too late."

"*What?*" Carter was wide awake now, too.

"Get whatever you can," Vanessa said. "But fast."

"Are you sure?" Jane said, standing close now, right behind her.

Before Vanessa could answer, there was another rushing, watery sound all up and down the side of the boat. For the first time since the crash, the *Lucky Star* moved. It rose out of the tilt where it had been for the last several days, listed up and over, and then came down hard on its other side with a resounding thud.

"Yeah," Vanessa said, starting to gather up whatever was closest to grab. "I'm sure. Now move!"

Carter's mind raced. His pack was long gone, somewhere in the middle of the lagoon, so he pulled the case off his pillow and started grabbing what he could. If they were getting off the boat, this might be his only chance to save a few things. And they were going to need all they could get.

"Vanessa! We need the flashlight!"

"Get out here!" she screamed from the galley. "We'll take what we can."

Buzz had balled up their two blankets and got

out the door ahead of Carter, though Carter was right behind.

Water was pouring in from both ends now, and it sloshed around their feet. It reminded Carter that he wanted his shoes, but when he looked back, the cabin was clearly too dark to try and find anything in there.

Vanessa was gathering something from the nav station. Jane had her own pack and was pulling what she could from the galley. With everything in shadow, it was hard to see or know what to do or what to grab. The first thing Carter recognized in the dark was the axe. He stuffed it head down inside his pillowcase pack.

Again, a wave broke outside the boat. Again, the *Lucky Star* lifted and floated free for just a moment before it slammed down hard against the rocks. Carter heard the hull cracking, as it had on the night of the crash. His heart pounded. There was no knowing how much time they had left—but it didn't seem like much.

"We have to go!" he said.

"I know!" Vanessa yelled. "Come on."

Buzz was throwing what he could up onto the deck, while Carter wrapped his arms around the pile of charts and books on the galley table. There was no seeing which was which in the dark. All of that was secondary right now. He stuffed what he had into the pillowcase and let the rest drop to the ground, forgotten.

Then he grabbed Jane by the arm and pushed her up the galley stairs.

Then Buzz, then Vanessa.

Carter was the last one out.

Jane stood on the deck, trying to take in what was all around them. Vanessa was up ahead with the flashlight, shining it off the bow of the boat. She motioned the rest of them over and pointed down toward the beach.

"We need to time this right!" she shouted. The waves were rushing in to hit the cliff wall in front of them, then pulling back, then rushing in again. It explained how the *Lucky Star* had gotten this far up Dead Man's Shelf to begin with. But Jane also realized that the boat wasn't going to stay there for much longer. Each wave sent it shuddering back and forth now, almost as if it were restless and ready to go.

Jane felt Carter's hand on her shoulder again, urging her up toward the bow. When the boat tipped suddenly to the side, both of them fell to the deck. They stayed down and crawled to where Vanessa was waiting for them.

"Buzz!" she shouted as they got there. Jane looked back, and he was bringing up the rear, his arms filled with whatever he had grabbed.

Carter left her there with Vanessa and went to help him up the slippery deck.

"Ready?" Vanessa shouted in her ear. "We're going to jump after the next wave comes."

"We have to wait for them!" Jane said, looking over her shoulder. They couldn't leave the boys alone on the ship.

"They're coming!" Vanessa shouted. "Let's go."

Jane was just as terrified of staying as she was of jumping. They'd done it in the daylight with no problem, but not like this. Never like this.

Still, there was no choice. She locked arms with Vanessa and shut her eyes as the next explosion of water hit the cliff wall in front of them, then pulled back.

"Now!" Vanessa said.

Blindly, she jumped and hit Dead Man's Shelf, just a few feet below. Her grip left Vanessa's, but only for a moment. They found each other again and scrabbled together, over the rocks and toward the beach. Jane could feel the sharp edges cutting into her hands, but it was hard to care about that right now. When they reached the drop-off, they jumped again, this time onto wet sand.

"Keep moving!" Vanessa said. She pulled Jane along, up toward the woods. Jane could hear the scraping sound of the boat over the rocks. And she could only hope that the boys were right behind her, too.

Buzz and Carter reached the edge of the deck at the same time. With the bundle in his arms, it was hard for Buzz to see ahead, but he was going to hold on tight to everything he had for as long as he could.

"Come on! We can do this!" Carter yelled. There was no time to think. "Ready? One, two, three!"

They jumped onto the rocks and continued in the same direction Vanessa and Jane had just gone. A few moments later, they were down on the sand, looking around for the girls.

"Up here!" Vanessa shouted from somewhere just inside the tree line. He saw them then, huddled under a low-hanging palm. Vanessa gestured them over, while the rain continued to beat down.

"Is everyone okay?" Carter asked as soon as they were all together again. Buzz nodded. He was as okay as he could be, considering.

The next thing they heard was the crash of another wave, and then a long, loud scraping sound, different from the ones before. He leaned out to see back toward the beach and the rocks. Vanessa shone the flashlight that way, just in time to show them the *Lucky Star* as it was washed away from its former resting place and back out toward the ocean. It was like watching a house get swept away. In fact, it *was* their house.

However far the boat got, Buzz couldn't see. It slipped beyond the edge of the flashlight beam with one last groaning, splintering sound, and disappeared.

When he looked around at the other three, each of them was just a shadow in the dark.

"What are we going to do now?" Buzz asked.

"The cave!" Jane shouted.

It was a good idea. The cave was farther uphill but not too far to reach. It would at least let them get out of the storm until they could make sense of everything that had just happened.

There was no need for any more conversation. All four of them turned at the same time, holding on to one another as they pressed up into the woods behind Vanessa's flashlight beam.

"Stick together!" Buzz shouted. He'd never meant anything more in his life. Everything they thought they had going for them had just been washed away, back into the ocean.

All they really had now was one another.

EPILOGUE

CASTAWAYS FOUND ADRIFT AT SEA—
FOUR STILL MISSING

KONA, HAWAII—A sea captain and his first mate were rescued early this morning, adrift in the life raft that was meant to save all six people on board their sinking boat.

Captain Dexter Kingson and First Mate Joe Kahali, both of Kona, Hawaii, spent the last four days with only emergency rations as the swiftly moving southerly Pacific currents swept their small raft farther and farther from the site where Captain Kingson's boat, the *Lucky Star*, ran aground of a rocky shoal on the night of June 29.

Also on board the *Lucky Star* were four young passengers—Vanessa Diaz, 13; Benjamin Diaz, 11; Carter Benson, 11; and Jane Benson, 9. Coast Guard representatives in Kona have confirmed hearing from the children, but communication was lost before a specific location could be determined.

Search and rescue operations are working with Captain Kingson and Mr. Kahali, trying to recreate the life raft's drift since it was separated from the *Lucky Star*, but recent weather conditions, combined with seasonal wind and water currents, have frustrated their efforts. The search continues daily.

ACKNOWLEDGMENTS

I'd like to thank anyone, anywhere, who had anything to do with making this project happen. And, because writers are supposed to be specific, I'll add a few names here:

Thank you to sailors extraordinaire Jill Kuramoto, P. Milo Frawley, and Sam Culver for sharing their knowledge and experience with us. This adventure never could have left port without them. The same goes for Tom Champlin and Carl Elwert at Alteris Renewables, who taught me a thing or two (or three) about solar power.

Thanks also to some of my favorite *Survivor* survivors—Kathy O'Brien, Cirie Fields, Rob Mariano, and Amber Brkich—as well as Dr. Liza Siegel, for their unique insight on what it means to be a castaway.

This story also benefited from some good ideas, careful reading, and friendly encouragement along the way—starting with Paul Lasher, Angela

Galyean, and their amazingly thoughtful students at Hinesburg Community School. It also included early-draft readers Jan Donley, Barbara Gregorich, Vicki Hayes, and Joe Nusbaum, who shone a light on the good, the bad, and the in-between. Kyle Jablonski could always be counted on for a great idea in a pinch. And Jonathan Radigan is—and always has been—the muse with the mostest.

Thanks also to George Nicholson and Caitlin McDonald at Sterling Lord Literistic, and to copy editor Sandy Smith and to Abigail Powers and Pat Shuldiner at Puffin for their eagle eyes.

And lastly, a big double down ditto on all of the above, with thanks to our editor at Puffin, Jennifer Bonnell, who is as patient and insightful as she is great to work with and good at what she does.

—CT

The adventure continues in

They thought it couldn't get any worse. They were wrong. Being shipwrecked on a jungle island was bad enough. But now that Carter, Vanessa, Buzz, and Jane have lost their boat to another storm, it's like starting over. Survival is no individual sport in a place like this, but there's only one way to learn that. The hard way.

Look for book three!

STRANDED 3
SURVIVORS

JEFF PROBST (www.jeffprobst.com) is the multi-Emmy Award–winning host and executive producer of the popular series *Survivor*. He is also the founder of The Serpentine Project, a nonprofit organization designed to help young adults transition out of the foster care system, and has worked with the larger nonprofit organization Alliance for Children's Rights, which has provided one hundred thousand kids in Los Angeles with free legal assistance and advocacy. Each season, *Survivor* memorabilia is auctioned off, and, to date, the auctions have raised hundreds of thousands of dollars for the organization.

A native of Wichita, Kansas, Probst is married and lives in Los Angeles with his wife and two children when not traveling the world.

He can be followed on Twitter @jeffprobst and online at www.jeffprobst.com.

CHRIS TEBBETTS is the *New York Times* bestselling coauthor of James Patterson's Middle School series. Originally from Yellow Springs, Ohio, Tebbetts is a graduate of Northwestern University. He lives and writes in Vermont.